Murder on the Air

by Ralph Warner and Toni Ihara

Edited by: Stephanie Harolde and Susan Doran
Cover Design & Graphics: Glenn Voloshin
Typography: Accent & Alphabet

ISBN: 0-917316-77-0

Nolo Press
950 Parker St.
Berkeley, CA 94710

Thank you:

Stephanie Harolde and Susan Doran made numerous helpful manuscript suggestions. We have been honored to have the help of such talented friends. We are also extremely grateful for the honest, loving criticism of Denis Clifford, Joyce Cole, Ann Dilworth, Barbara Hodovan, Babette Marks, Steve Murray, Verna Murray, and Carol Pladsen.

This is a make believe story

Because we borrowed bits and pieces of the background of this book from our home town, Berkeley, California, it's particularly important to tell you that we made the whole story up. None of our principal characters, whether police officers, reporters, environmentalists, or educators are based on any living person. What's more, we particularly want you to understand that our descriptions of both the University of California and the Berkeley Police Department are the product of our twisted little imaginations and are simply not true. This will be obvious to those readers who know and respect these institutions. We ask our other readers to understand that we needed a police department and a university and rather than fabricating institutions, we borrowed the names—but not the substance—of the ones on our doorstep. Finally, we have carefully checked to be sure none of the names or physical descriptions of our characters even inadvertantly came close to any real person, but just on the off-chance we missed someone we have had our phone disconnected and are planning to move to Daly City.

Toni Ihara
Ralph Warner

1

The evening was gray-black and soggy when Sara Tamura left the Rialto Theatre, an old warehouse in the Berkeley industrial district that had been converted to an off-beat film palace. As she made her way to the bus stop at San Pablo Avenue, she reflected on the odd pairing of movies she had seen — *The Thin Man*, 1930s Hollywood at its frothiest, and *Woman in the Dunes*, 1960s Japan at its most introspectively intense.

Despite her pure Japanese ancestry, Tamura felt closer to the Thin Man than the dune woman. Tamura was *sansei* — third-generation Japanese-American — and raised in Los Angeles, where the tea ceremony and the art of flower arranging had long since been pre-empted by baseball, bubble gum, and double features. Nick and Nora Charles, detectives extraordinaire, had always ranked high on her list of late-night heroes, at least on those nights when the noble Sandy Koufax and the incomparable Maury Wills weren't trouncing Mays, Marichal and the rest of the black-hearted Giants. When, at the onset of her teens, her child's imagination reluctantly came to terms with her budding body, she gave up the hope of becoming the first girl shortstop to dazzle them at Chavez Ravine and substituted the image of herself as a beautiful and witty private investigator. Indeed, looking back, it was Myrna Loy and William Powell who planted the seed which, after an odd turn or two, had resulted in her current job as —dum, da, dum, dum— Berkeley, California police officer, Badge #1642.

Tamura transferred once and finally alighted from the green and silver AC Transit bus at Sacramento Street, in the heart of a quasi-respectable Asian, black, and student ghetto. It was a neighborhood where everyone — even the graying hippies who looked as if they wanted nothing more than to find the lost path back to the sixties — worked hard to keep the kids in Nikes and ten-speed bikes, and a loaf of sourdough on the table next to the mountain red. The Flats, as it was called, wasn't a bad place; joggers, artists, left-wing politicos, and old black women pulling two-wheeled wire carts along side streets to the Co-op, coexisted in something surprisingly reminiscent of a neighborhood. People weren't afraid of the parks. They ate in good, cheap ethnic restaurants, rode bikes, and raised a couple of marijuana plants in the back yard. There were the usual urban problems, of course—crime, traffic, and a 7-11 store on University Avenue which sold little besides balloon bread and slurpees and attracted half the crazed teenagers within five miles. But in the final analysis, Tamura had concluded, the Flats had three of the important requisites to civilized living—plenty of trees, reasonable rents, and a good Chinese laundry.

Tamura walked a few blocks south along Sacramento Street, a grass-divided artery that cut through the traffic-barrier maze of Berkeley's streets like a cleaver through sashimi. Her home was one of several tiny cottages encircling a patch of lawn in the heart of the 2200 block. To reach it, Tamura turned right along a narrow path between a row of post–World War I bungalows crowding close to the big street like three-cent postage stamps trying to move an envelope in a twenty-three-cent world. Behind the truncated back yards of the bungalows, she reached a half-dozen stucco cottages which looked remarkably like the motor court in *It Happened One Night*. When she'd first moved in, Tamura had been tempted to hang a sign out by the parking lot saying "Tourist Cabins – Free Radios."

As she sloshed across the lawn towards the second cottage on the left, Tamura saw it was past time to dig out the stone pathways, which were again overgrown by Bermuda grass. In exchange for cheap rent, the owner had put her in charge of the grounds. He was an elderly Irishman who firmly believed that the Chinese should wash clothes, the Jews take care of money, and the Japanese tend gardens. She had explained to the good-natured old racist that she couldn't tell a daffodil from a daisy, preferred brown plants to green, and thought all grass better off dead, but she hadn't come close to convincing him. He just flashed his new dentures, mumbled something about not overdoing the fertilizer, and handed her the pruning shears.

Well, black thumb or not, she knew there was no place in Berkeley she could live as comfortably and cheaply, so the grass became the intimate albatross that kept her from being too pleased with her good fortune. And a greedy and impatient albatross it was — refusing absolutely to be confined to its designated area. Every day, every hour, every minute the evil stuff seemed to spread. If she overslept, it covered the central barbecue pit. If she turned her back for a day, it wolfed down a small flower bed. And of course, no matter what she did, it was always leaping across the brick pathways. Sometimes she turned her head quickly to see if she could catch it moving, but it was wily as well as quick and always froze in mid-swallow, denying her even the small pleasure of catching it in the act.

Tamura turned her key in the lock and glanced up at the leaden sky. Tomorrow was her day off. If it cleared, she could hack at the lawn for a bit in the morning and still make it up to Tilden Park in the early afternoon.

She side-stepped quickly as she crossed the kitchen threshold. Her otherwise only normally neurotic cat, Annie, had developed an alarming foot fetish which involved lying in wait for the first toe through the door. The pumpkin-colored cat executed her attack ritual with such demented regularity that Tamura was convinced the cat had studied karate in another lifetime. Tonight, undaunted by an initial miss brought about by Tamura's fast footwork, Annie skittered across the linoleum and managed two successful heel pounces and a glancing blow to the instep before Tamura reached the refrigerator and grabbed the small beast's favorite tranquilizer — red meat tuna.

As she dished out the oily fish, adding a dollop of soy sauce just in case the cat did have Asian ancestors, the phone rang. She placed Annie's dish on the floor, wiped her hands on a paper towel, and grabbed the receiver. It was Amanda Gonzales, called "Demanda" by the police brass ever since she had taken a women's assertiveness training seminar the previous spring. Amanda was a night dispatcher, and a friend.

"Business or pleasure, mi amiga?"

"Es trabajo por seguridad, Sara-san. We've got a double homicide down at the Marina. I haven't been able to raise 'His Arrogance' yet, so it will be your baby to start. Lorenzo and Mary are there, trying not to pee in their pants until someone from Violent Crimes shows up. It's at KILO — the radio station north of the pier. Saddle up and get down there pronto. And compadre," Amanda added, her voice softening, "buena suerte."

As Tamura cradled the receiver, she felt the adrenalin begin to flow. Here it was again, another beginning, the call to action — and at least for a short time she would be working solo, not as tag-along to her immediate superior, mighty James Rivers. Although she took a certain satisfaction in routine police work, she doubted that she would continue putting up with all the boy scout bullshit if it weren't for these occasional rushes.

Tamura moved quickly into her small bedroom, wriggled out of her skirt and pulled her sweater over her head. The real mystery of her job had nothing to do with police work, she thought, but centered on the Jekyll-and-Hyde effect that Lieutenant Rivers had upon her usually even temperament. It wasn't so much that he was nasty, but that he essentially ignored her. In spite of, or perhaps because of, her status as the first Asian woman to work in Violent Crimes, Rivers and his boss, Captain Rafferty, acted as if she didn't exist. It was as if the white male police brass, having learned that outright discrimination was counterproductive, had adopted a more subtle approach, one which substituted benign neglect for hostility.

As she stepped into a burgundy-colored leotard, Tamura's mind continued to bump along the same track. The fact that she and Lieutenant Rivers interacted so badly had been upsetting her for months. Along with Captain Rafferty, she and Rivers were the only Berkeley cops permanently assigned to Violent Crimes and they were together daily. Her impatience with Rivers not only clashed with her cultural heritage, which taught the wisdom of getting along with even the most difficult people, but she knew it made others at the station uncomfortable. And it was so unnecessary. All of her life she had been a friendly extrovert — the sort who uses quick wit and a smile to put people at ease. And dammit, she wasn't a phony. She was willing to back up a good first impression with diligent, competent work. But what was the use of trying hard when the one person she was trying to please had already written her off?

Rivers was simply unwilling to give her a chance, she thought, as she took a deep breath and buttoned her black corduroy pants. It galled her most to know that basically it was her gender and her race, not her inexperience, that fatally prejudiced her case. Sure she was new both to plainclothes and to Violent Crimes, but she wasn't stupid; she could learn. Why the hell couldn't he just suspend his disbelief and treat her like any other rookie detective?

When you came right down to it, Rivers' attitude toward women was all of a piece. He leaped into bed with one art teacher, actress, or half-octave voice coach after another. Above all, his women friends had to be paragons of traditional femininity. No athletes, carpenters, businesswomen, or—come to that—cops for Lieutenant Rivers. The only way she'd really get Rivers' attention, she thought, as she tied the tails of a black-and-white-checked flannel shirt around her waist, would be to walk into his office wearing nothing but her badge. Perhaps then he'd find time to train her. She chuckled as she reached for her tall leather boots and imagined trying to attach the large, heavy detective shield to her bare left breast. But somehow, taking it all off didn't seem a practical strategy. Until she thought of something better, she would continue to be feisty. Rivers couldn't ignore her forever.

Tamura was more or less dressed for action. Her eye shadow would have to last a few more hours. She grabbed her rain parka, dug her revolver out of the breadbox, and walked into the night. It had begun to drizzle again and she pushed her long hair into the parka. As she crossed the yard, she kicked absent-mindedly at a chunk of grass blanketing the main path and began humming the theme from *The Thin Man*.

2

Jeannie Walborsek pulled her yellow cotton-knit shirt over her head, dropped her drawstring pants and sat easily on the foot of her bed, legs crossed. Leaning against the wall, a pillow behind his shoulders, Rivers watched through half-open eyes, admiring her round, firm, almost plump body and the thick mane that tumbled over her shoulders to her waist. He wished Jeannie would move slightly so that her right nipple would peek through the veil of white-blonde hair. Instead, she sat with exaggerated stillness, holding her best Mona Lisa smile. Finally, Rivers reached for the decanter of brandy on the nightstand and poured a finger and a half into each of the tiny cut-crystal glasses. As he moved to replace the decanter, the quilt that had covered him to the navel slipped down, and his lean, almost skinny, body lay exposed. Jeannie's half smile broadened into a full-fledged grin as she tossed her hair over her shoulders and down her back.

Rivers chuckled.

Jeannie chuckled.

They leaned toward each other to touch glasses. The tiny chime of crystal was lost in the louder demand of the telephone.

"Damn," Jeannie said, taking a quick sip of brandy and fishing under the bed for the telephone. "It's for you, Sherlock—sounds like work. Are you here?"

He answered by leaning forward and taking the red receiver from her hand.

"This is Rivers."

"Sorry to call you on a Sunday evening, sir, but you left this number on your emergency list," Amanda Gonzalez said, her brisk tone belying the ritual politeness of her words.

"Sure, sure. What's happening?"

"It's happened—a double 187. The beat officers called it in and it sounds pretty gruesome."

"Where?"

"In one of the studios at radio station KILO. That's . . ."

"I know where it is, I'll be there in fifteen minutes. Get Tamura if you can find her. Have you called the coroner and the tech squad? Who are the patrol officers?"

"Lorenzo Jones and Mary Finnegan called it in. I got Tamura a while ago and she's already down there. The support troops are on their way. You were the last person I got hold of—there were so many numbers . . ."

"Make sure there are enough patrol people down there to close the place off," Rivers interrupted quickly. "Does the Chief know?"

"He's at his daughter's wedding in Palos Verdes, south of L.A. He won't be back until Tuesday."

"I think you'd better track him down, wedding or no wedding," Rivers added with finality.

"Wait. Sir, don't hang up. Finnegan's on the other line. Apparently the killings knocked KILO off the air and the station people insist some federal law says they have the right to start broadcasting again immediately."

"Bullshit. One less radio station for a few hours won't make a rat fuck's difference to the FCC or anyone else. Tell Mary to tell Tamura to keep things as undisturbed there as possible. Goodbye."

Rivers stood up quickly, slipped his long legs into a pair of faded jeans, stepped into battered Birkenstocks and retrieved a cotton pullover from under the rocking chair. He ran out the back door and took the steps two at a time to his own second-story flat. Jeannie yelled after him that coffee would be ready in a minute.

Rivers was back down in less than three, his bulky goosedown vest only partially hiding a snub-nosed 38 Smith and Wesson nesting under his left shoulder. Jeannie handed him an oversized mug of black coffee, as she stood on tiptoes and kissed him hard on the lips.

"I'll check on Julie and Mickey later and, if you end up doing an all-nighter, I'll get them off to school," she said.

"Thanks, pal. Sorry to trash a nice evening."

"Don't lie to me. You love this Dick Tracy stuff," she said with a laugh. "For your next birthday, I'm getting you an inflatable Fly-face to play with on slow days. But really, it's okay. Joe said something about maybe coming over after he closed the restaurant, and I was going to have to get rid of you soon anyway."

* * * *

As he turned Dartha, his not quite decrepit green Dodge Dart, into the KILO parking lot at the north end of the Berkeley Marina, Rivers was surprised to see more than a dozen vehicles scattered among the puddles on the poorly drained pavement. He looked at his watch, It was exactly 10:32—less than 17 minutes since he'd gotten the call. Even so, he was obviously late.

The searchlights from a police van lit up the psychedelic-painted facade of the two-story stucco building. It had probably looked good in 1969, but now, like an abandoned circus wagon, it looked silly and sad. A knot of people stood under a concrete carport by the front door. The rain had almost stopped and the air was heavy and mild.

Instead of parking in one of the lined-off spaces and threading his way between the lake-sized puddles, Rivers drove close to the front door, his brights making mirrors of the standing water. When you're late to a party, he thought, you may as well pretend you're the guest of honor.

A crowd of people gathered around before Dartha was fully stopped. Rivers recognized several, including some from the East Bay bureaus of the San Francisco papers and a remote reporter for a TV news show. It occurred to him that he was the only one who didn't know who had been murdered.

Rivers wished he had time to do some deep breathing to force his heart to slow down. A sense of calm would go a long way toward making the next few hours easier. Instead, he swallowed the last sips of lukewarm coffee, opened the door, and stepped onto the shiny asphalt.

One of the two officers guarding the KILO front entrance blocked his way. He looked barely old enough to be a hall monitor and Rivers couldn't remember having seen him before.

"Glad to see you, sir," the young man said. "Things are sure, well, uh . . ."

"Keep still," Rivers snapped, none too pleased at having to deal with an excited kid in front of a half dozen people with their notepads poised—especially when he had no idea himself what was going on. "Save the explanations for inside," he added in a fierce whisper.

Easing his way through the cluster of reporters, Rivers nodded, ignoring questions. He placed exaggerated attention on locating the few dry spots between car and porch. The reporters, suckers for a developing story, stopped asking questions and watched. Some even clapped when he jumped over the last puddle, took the steps in a bound, and despite open-toed sandals arrived dry-shod on the cement slab.

"Hello, James."

Rivers smiled in response to Officer Mary Finnegan's greeting as he faced the media people.

"Do me a favor—do yourselves a favor. Relax for an hour. Send someone out for coffee and rolls. There's a place that's still open at San Pablo and University and the coffee's drinkable, even if they do heat the rolls in a microwave." He glanced at his watch. "It's 10:30. In exactly an hour I'll make a statement. If I'm late, honk. In the meantime, don't bug every technician who comes in and out."

As he turned toward the door, Rivers bumped into a very tall, very wide, and very angry-looking black man.

Rivers moved to his right. The big man, wearing an exquisite dove-gray suit, moved with him. Rivers moved quickly back to the left, only to find the elegant suit once again blocking his way. Giving up on end runs, Rivers attempted to plunge straight ahead. He was stopped in his tracks by a Cyclopean hand gripping his right shoulder.

Rivers was puzzled as well as pissed. Who was this 6′6″, 250-pound Gucci-clad hunk, and why was he imitating the Great Wall of China? Rivers, who didn't have a lot of use for the "if you have it, put it on your back" approach to life, nevertheless felt small and shabby.

"Listen, Officer," boomed a voice as big as its owner, "I'm managing director of KILO and I have a legal right to enter. You people are committing a federal offense by keeping me out and if you don't stop this bullshit, I'll sue for every penny you've got and garnishee your wages for the next ten years. The FCC guarantees me the right to get KILO back on the air immediately and...."

Had the giant, who Rivers later learned was a retired football player of considerable note and part-owner of KILO, been as smooth as his clothes, he might well have parlayed Rivers' brief feeling of intimidation into an invitation to enter. After all, it was his radio station. But as the man's blustering rap continued, Rivers' mood changed from intimidation to anger. He had been trained as a lawyer, an experience which had left him singularly unimpressed when anyone threatened him with "the law."

If the man simply barged into the station, it would be a sticky job to toss him out—any toy-grabbing three-year-old knows possession is nine-tenths of the law. But the prospect of a court action was a joke. The American legal system had long since degenerated into a game of fear and greed, the first rule of which is *anything* can be delayed at least three years.

"Fuck off," Rivers said in his loudest voice as he knocked the man's arm off his shoulder with a quick up-thrust of his right hand. In a quiet voice that forced the cluster of reporters to lean forward to hear, Rivers added, "You couldn't care less about the FCC or 16 federal offenses. You just want to tell the world about the blood on your linoleum and scoop the rest of these folks. Now get out of my way or I'll handcuff you to a lamp post."

Several of the reporters at the bottom of the steps laughed.

One said, "Heavy." The station manager turned angrily toward his new tormentors.

Rivers stepped through the door, winking at Officer Mary Finnegan as he went. Finnegan was a large-boned, sandy-haired woman in her early thirties with the face of a well-fed angel. Some of the macho types on the force called her "two-ton Finnegan." Rivers liked her. More important, he knew no interlopers would pass a door she guarded.

"Well, Lieutenant, it's nice of you to drop by," a cool, slightly throaty female voice greeted him.

"Cut the crap, Tamura. I've had more than enough already."

"Oh my—the great detective is sensitive tonight. This humble assistant will tread lightly and speak in whispers."

"I made it all the way through the parking lot without slashing your tires—why the hell are you piling it on?"

"Maybe because none of us has ever handled a murder this big before and we don't like admitting we're a little scared."

Rivers made himself stop and face his assistant. For perhaps the thousandth time he damned the Tuesday four months before when Phil Orpac, his assistant and friend, had been transferred and Sara Tamura, riding a wave of affirmative action, had been assigned to replace him. He agreed in principle that discrimination against women should be corrected, but that didn't mean promoting everyone in the building who sat down to piss—even those with no experience, and no tact. Budget cuts had eliminated one person from Violent Crimes. Now affirmative action was in effect eliminating another.

Not only was Sara Tamura a bitchy feminist who could barely drive a car, but as little as he cared to admit it, Rivers couldn't ignore the obvious. She was, quite simply, the most beautiful woman he had ever set eyes on. Why couldn't she be as homely as she was nasty? Tamura lied about being 5'5" of course, but even at 5'2¾" she was closer to physical perfection than anyone had a right to be. If she had a clue as to what she was doing, she would certainly be the perfect plainclothes officer. Bad guys were always so busy staring at her perky tits, or admiring her impossibly wide cheekbones, that it never occurred to them she might have a gun in her waistband. Of course, since she was probably carrying it backwards and had forgotten to load it, it didn't make much difference. Just the same, it was a pity such a delicate, turned-up nose and full, heart-shaped lips were wasted on a shrew.

Rivers took a disgusted breath. As usual, if he were to get anyplace with Tamura, he couldn't give an inch. To deal with aggressive women you had to be tough.

"First, I want to know exactly who was killed—when and how. The dispatcher told me it was a double killing; that's all I know.

Then I want you to stuff that kid out front in a closet somewhere so he doesn't trip over his shoelaces in front of a camera. Finally, I need a hand coordinating details. If we're going to conduct an investigation with every reporter west of the Sierra on our doorstep, we better do it right. By the way, is there any coffee?"

"Shall we start with the coffee or the murders?" Tamura asked, her voice mock-sweet.

Rivers grunted. Why the hell did asking your assistant for coffee have to be interpreted as a put-down? Let her choke on her own bitchiness, he thought.

Tamura began reading from the top page of her clipboard. "One of the men who was shot and killed is Frank Rathman, Public Affairs Director of KILO, age 29, divorced, originally from Boston, where he worked in radio news and wrote a column for a weekly newspaper, which I gather is on the order of the *Bay Guardian*. For the past two years he's lived in Oakland, near Piedmont Avenue, a couple blocks from Fenton's Creamery. His guest on KILO's Sunday evening talk show—which incidentally is called "The Talkies"— was the other victim, Aldo Speldon, the numero uno environmentalist. Heard of him?"

No wonder, Rivers mumbled to himself.

Then, looking Tamura in the eyes for the first time, "Are you sure? It's hard to believe Speldon could be dead. He seemed so indestructible—like some great, snow-capped mountain. I . . ."

Tamura nodded. "I've never climbed higher than the fourth floor, and even I recognize him, not to mention his I.D."

"Jesus, I saw him at an anti-nuke benefit a couple of weeks ago," Rivers said, talking more to himself than to Tamura. Then, catching himself spacing out, he snapped, "Okay, give me the rest of what you've got before I check the blood and guts."

"Why not look at the bodies first," Tamura said innocently.

That bitch, Rivers thought. She knows damn well I turn green at the sight of blood. Then, seeing that Tamura expected a response, he said, "It's not likely the stiffs are going to walk out on me."

Looking suddenly serious, Tamura grimaced her agreement.

"Especially not those two. They're, well . . . they're pretty bad. Here's what we have," Tamura continued. "Speldon was on Rathman's 8:30 talk show to oppose the construction of several nuclear power installations in the Delta. At 9:02 p.m. the station went off the air. I got that from a KILO engineer who was listening at home. Radio stations aren't supposed to konk out, so she phoned to see if Rathman needed help. When she got no answer, she drove down as quickly as possible; it's less than a mile from her house. She found the two men in the main studio with their heads blown off. We received her call at 9:12. Finnegan and Lorenzo were down by Spenger's and got here less than five minutes later."

"Okay," Rivers cut in before she had a chance to remind him that it was now past 10:30, "you do something about the kid out front and I'll take a look. Which way?"

"Down the hall and then left. You'll see the others."

Rivers pushed off the desk top where he had been perched. At first glance people often thought him skinny. With not quite 170 pounds spread over a 6'2" frame, it was a natural mistake. But a second look would reveal powerfully muscled upper arms and a well-defined torso. His body was like a young panther's, full of strength and energy, more at home in strenuous physical activity than at rest. He had the look of an overgrown boy though he was almost 37. Rivers was all angles and colors. When his energy was high, he was better-looking than the average TV detective; when he was depressed or tired, he looked like Abe Lincoln agonizing over a Union defeat.

Rivers was pleased he had gotten rid of Officer Tamura so easily. If he was going to lose his supper, he preferred not to do it in front of his derisive assistant.

Half a dozen people were gathered outside the door to one of the studios. When they saw him, they stopped talking and drew themselves together. Rivers knew that many people thought he was an arrogant bastard, and secretly he enjoyed it. He didn't think his reputation was quite prickly enough to warrant such a collective intake of breath.

John Fritch, the whisper-thin Deputy Coroner, spoke first. "It's a bad one, James—I don't envy you and Sara."

Rivers relaxed. The situation had everyone uptight, not just him. But he was taken aback too. Fritch, who had been collecting bodies for the county since the year Rivers graduated from junior high, was normally as unflappable as a wet kite.

"Okay, let's take a look," Rivers said, with what he hoped sounded like a take-charge voice.

"Jesus, this looks more like a war than a killing," he exclaimed as he moved into the small studio.

The extent of the destruction made it difficult for Rivers to understand what had happened. A table and two—no, three—chairs were tipped over in a pile of microphones, wires, and other electronic gear. Broken glass was everywhere—some from smashed lights, but more from a decapitated glass-topped partition and a large window which had been replaced by a black hole to the damp night.

Rivers forced his reluctant eyes to focus. The bodies looked small and crumpled, their arms touching in macabre fraternity. One was face up, but had no face. The other, Speldon, lay belly down and had lost most of the back of his head. The similarity of the raw, gaping wounds made the men look curiously alike; twins playing in a pool of blood and broken glass.

For a moment, Rivers' conscious mind tried to reject the horror. He saw the fragments of flesh as the soft petals of red roses and the shards of bloodstained glass as a crystal and crimson mandala. They almost hypnotized him. Then as the congealed blood and twisted, broken flesh began to look all too real, his head, legs, and most of all his stomach, lost their equilibrium. As the room began to spin, Rivers pulled his gaze away, reaching for a handhold on the corner of the recording console.

As he steadied himself, he cursed his own stupidity. Staggering about leaving fingerprints on the furniture was a hell of a way to start an investigation.

"What happened, Carl?" Rivers asked, turning toward Carl Burnett, the well-padded technical sergeant standing to his right.

"It took us a few minutes to rig our lights, so we're still working out the details, but it probably went something like this: Rathman and Speldon were sitting at that small, round table near the window. Rathman faced the window, his back to the control panel. On a low-budget operation like this, he had to talk to Speldon and be able to swivel around and act as his own engineer. Speldon was sitting on the other side of the table, not directly across but a little to the right, with his back a few feet from the window. As you can see, the glass was thick and opaque, good for privacy and to deaden sound. Most of the lights were between Rathman and the door. From the outside, both men would have been outlined against the window. The gunman simply shot at the silhouettes."

"How would the killer know who was in the studio if he could only see shapes?" Rivers asked, keeping his eyes on Burnett and off the blood-spattered floor.

"Yep, that's the obvious question, isn't it?" Burnett replied. "The answer is, he couldn't have positively identified anyone through that glass."

"It wouldn't take a genius to know who was in the studio if you staked the place out," Tamura said from behind the two men. "Simpler still, you could switch on your radio."

Rivers turned. Tamura was standing just inside the door, her weight shifted mostly to her right leg, her skin-tight cords stuffed into the tops of her boots. He hadn't heard her come in.

"Aren't lots of interviews pre-taped?" Rivers said, doing his best not to sound hostile in front of the others. "How would someone listening know the program was live?"

"It was a call-in show," Tamura replied, not bothering to hide her impatience. "Interview programs are mostly taped, but call-in shows obviously can't be . . . although I suppose it's possible to re-play a tape of a live talk show," she conceded reluctantly.

Tamura, surprised to see that everyone, including Rivers, looked interested, continued. "Rathman's show was fairly popular and KILO has undoubtedly been running promo spots all week hyping the fact a big name in the anti-nuclear movement would be on. Speldon was sure to be a big draw. The point is, any listener who thought for a moment would realize, first, that Rathman and Speldon were doing the show live, and second, they were almost certainly doing it from the KILO studio."

"How did the killer know the heads behind the window belonged to Speldon and Rathman? Other people could have been in the building too," Rivers pointed out, wondering if Tamura would let her enthusiasm run ahead of her facts and end up looking silly.

"The killer might have known night deejays do their own engineering, or he or she could have gotten down here early," Tamura replied seriously, treating Rivers' plodding query as typical.

"Probably, the answer is easier," Carl Burnett remarked, as if talking to himself. "The killer blundered along after the program started, saw two cars in the lot, two heads silhouetted against the one lit window and went bang, bang."

Rivers smiled. As usual, the technical sergeant had come up with the simplest explanation.

Carl Burnett was unique, even on a force known widely as a haven for bizarre characters. At 45, he was graying, paunchy, almost fat; his soft brown eyes peered sadly through a web of red lines. Habitually dressed as if he shopped at a thrift store dumpster, Burnett curiously resembled a beagle on a bender. He had come to the Berkeley force after five years with the CIA where, it was said, he had learned to kill a man with his bare hands in less than a second. Most people on the force were a little afraid of him. But what unnerved everyone even more than his superspy background was Burnett's rare combination of personal traits. Burnett quite obviously didn't give a damn about money or possessions or status. He worked because he felt like it. In a world where the levers necessary to manipulate most people stuck out like porcupine quills from a spaniel's nose, Carl Burnett, ever polite in an exaggerated southern way, simply didn't seem to have any.

"Did the killer use a cannon, Carl?" Rivers asked.

"More likely a pump shotgun, James," Burnett answered in the soft North Carolina voice that invariably hooked everyone into leaning forward. "My guess is he stood about 15 feet from the window, squeezed off five or six loads, took a gander through the hole to see if anyone was moving, and left. It would have been about as hard as shooting deer at night with floodlights on and the sheriff at the other end of the county."

"You keep saying he; how do you know the killer was male?" Tamura asked in a tone that indicated long experience battling masculine pronouns.

"Sara, with all due respect to you and Lucy Stone, God rest her soul, I've never heard of a woman killing with a big shotgun. And if you don't think that this old southern chauvinist's opinion is worth much, take a look at the boot tracks in the mud. The killer wore size twelve or thirteen, with big cleats like you find on workboots or hiking boots."

"So what," Tamura muttered to herself.

"So, Berkeley may be the world capital for dinosaur-sized dykes, but I haven't seen many with paws that big," Burnett replied with a polite twang.

Tamura, starting to reply, reconsidered. What was the use? If she said what was on her mind, her reputation as a fruitcake feminist would only grow. She would keep an open mind just the same. The ritual male assumption that a woman would never kill with a shotgun was laughable. A few decades ago women didn't work outside the home, climb mountains, build nuclear weapons or, for that matter, investigate crimes. Any man who believed a 1980s woman couldn't stuff a sock in the toes of big boots and pull the trigger on a shotgun was going to have a hard time with the last decade of the twentieth century.

"What makes you sure the killer used a shotgun, Carl?" Rivers asked.

"We picked up some good-sized shot—maybe aught or double aught. The killer probably used a deer gun with a fairly wide choke and shot a pattern to be sure to get both men. The pellets would spread some, which is why the whole window is gone. Those poor bastards were hit with a wall of glass and lead."

"You can't figure anything out from this mess that would help you identify the gun?" Tamura half stated, half asked, moving her dark almond eyes around the room in a quick circle. She would restrict herself to asking questions and not let Rivers maneuver her into stating any grandiose theories that would make her seem foolish to the others.

"There are a bunch of mathematical equations that relate to shotguns," said Carl. "We know the size of the shot, the tracks tell us where the killer stood, and we can probably figure out how much the gun was choked from what hit the back wall. Once we put it together, we should be able to make a good guess as to the general type of gun." Carl spoke as if he were a teacher answering an attentive student.

"That's not going to help much," Rivers said impatiently. "We can't run a ballistics check on a shotgun even if we find the right one."

"Never said we could," Carl said as if sucking on a piece of grass. "Still, we'll figure out what we can, and if you catch a likely looking boy with a 12-gauge Remington under his woodpile, you'll more than likely listen to everything I can tell you."

"John, what have you got?" Rivers asked, turning to the deputy coroner.

"They look just as dead to me as they do to you. I doubt the docs will be able to tell you anything more interesting tomorrow morning. But I do know one thing—someone is making a hell of a noise out front."

"Reporters. I told them to honk if I didn't come out in an hour; they started 30 minutes early. Tamura, tell them if they don't start counting better, I'll put off the press briefing 'til a week from yesterday. Also, take care of notifying the families. Speldon lives in Kensington someplace and has a wife, I think."

"According to his wallet, Speldon lived on Highland. That's a few blocks above the Arlington," Tamura replied.

"Have Mary Finnegan go up. What about Rathman?"

"While we were waiting for you, I checked the KILO personnel files," Tamura replied promptly. "His parents live in Providence, Rhode Island. Rathman's address is on 15th Street, in that old section of Oakland beyond the Lake. There is no indication he's married."

"I'll call Providence. Have the Oakland people knock on the door. And could you please arrange to have someone pick up some coffee?" Rivers asked.

Tamura's head jerked back as if she had been slapped. "Sugar and cream?" she asked quietly.

Rivers stared her down, thinking in spite of himself how desirable she looked, legs apart, hands on hips, eyes flashing. He turned and walked into the hall.

Rivers found a phone in the station manager's office, charged the call to the department, and awakened two middle-aged people on the other side of the continent. It only took an instant to add anguish and despair to a cold Rhode Island night.

His least pleasant duty done, Rivers stood quietly for a moment. A babble of voices reached him from the studio where the technical people were involved in their gruesome routine. He couldn't cope with going back in. Instead he went along to the end of the hall and shouldered a door marked "emergency exit."

KILO sat on filled land barely 70 feet from San Francisco Bay. The weather was clearing. Looking west across the bay, Rivers could see the lights of Sausalito twinkling above the dark hulk of Angel Island like candles on a chocolate cake. Tomorrow would be a cool, windy, high-sky day and everything would seem less grim, Rivers thought as he tried unsuccessfully to squeeze his big hands into the front pockets of his jeans. He followed the lights of a ship, probably a tanker headed for the Contra Costa oil docks. The fresh wind coming through the Golden Gate smacked his face, and his eyes began to water. The tears felt good.

They were honking out front again. Rivers turned his back on the bay and began squishing toward the parking lot, his momentarily lightened mood sucked away by the mud pulling at his sandals. As he made his way along the north side of the studio, he almost bumped into the rookie officer he had snapped at earlier. The youngster was guarding a roped-off area outside the broken studio window. His earlier excitement had been replaced by the look of a scarecrow forgotten in a December field.

Rivers nodded in what he hoped was a friendly way and ducked under the rope. As he took his next step, cold muddy water oozed over the end of his sandals and crept between his toes. In an odd way, it was a relief, as if his effort to hold himself separate from the events of the evening was finally over.

Rivers turned back to face the scarecrow. "When the reporters leave, bring a car over by this side of the lot and watch from there. By the way, what's your name?"

"Lassiter, sir. I mean, Lassiter, Lieutenant Rivers."

"Okay, Lassiter. I'll have some work for you as this thing unwinds."

The young officer forgot to look forlorn. "Gee, that would be great," he said to Rivers' back as the latter tramped off, sloshing determinedly through the soupy spots.

For Rivers, the rest of the night was a blur.

He talked to the reporters, telling them little more than the identities of the dead men—information they'd known before he'd gotten out of Jeannie's bed.

He stood patiently in a puddle under the blaze of TV lights while an overdressed young woman from one network station, and an overdressed young man from a second, interrupted one another to ask if he didn't agree that the killings were a terrible thing.

He agreed.

When they both assured him that he had their complete support—and by implication, the support of everyone in TV-land—in bringing this "barbaric" (Channel 3), "deranged" (Channel 8) criminal to justice, he thanked them.

Tamura watched Rivers' performance with mixed feelings. On the whole, she thought it would have been less hypocritical if he had admitted they didn't have the vaguest idea who had done the killing or why. Still, given the media's obvious desire for reassurance, she had to admire his style. He was quick, authoritative and, best of all, he had everyone cheerfully packing up their cameras and pocketing their notebooks within five minutes. Just the same, there was something about the conspiratorial nature of press and police presenting a united front which disturbed her. It was as if they'd struck a deal in advance to make each other look good at all costs. And if that meant substituting a palatable fairy tale for a nasty truth, so what. TV seemed to dictate its own content, and to appear on "The News" meant you accepted an appointed role. It was all so transparent she wondered again why anyone watched anything on TV except old movies.

After the cameras were finally dark, Rivers announced all detailed questions would have to wait until one o'clock the next day at a press conference at the police station. When he finally got free, he arranged for the still-fuming KILO manager to broadcast from an undisturbed part of the building. Then he performed his easiest task of the night—taking a call from the sleepy deputy D.A. and convincing her to check things out first thing in the morning.

Next, Rivers got through to his slightly tipsy and none too pleased Chief at the La Venta Inn on the Palos Verdes Peninsula. It was no pleasure to step on the nub of his evening. But there was a positive element. He got Bacon to agree that with the head of Violent Crimes out of the country, Rivers would temporarily direct the investigation with full authority to muster the help he needed.

Finally, Rivers said goodnight to John Fritch. The deputy coroner was standing by a battered Econoline van smoking a last cigarette. The bodies dressed in their plastic bags were safely stretched out in back.

By the time Rivers dropped his soggy sandals on the front mat, it was after 2:30. He left a note on the refrigerator telling the kids to go down to Jeannie's for breakfast, drank the last two shots of the good French cognac he saved for special evenings, set the alarm for 8:45 and tumbled into bed.

What a night, he thought. And tomorrow I'll have to stagger about with six hours' sleep. If I ever write a book, I'll call it *The Sleeping Policeman*. The detective will solve crimes in wonderfully creative dreams, sleep 14 hours a night, and make all his arrests at 10:00 a.m., after waffles and eggs at The Homemade Cafe.

3

Rivers was stretched out, face down and naked, on a hot rock that rose phallus-like from a great blue lake, watching two women swim lazily in the clear water below. They were treading water, heads thrown back, staring up at him. Now and then their nipples touched the surface, rippling the mirror-like calm. One woman was blonde, the other velvet black. He felt himself grow hard against the hot granite of the rock.

The electric alarm buzz hit Rivers like a straight-arm to the head, knocking him out of the Guatemalan sunshine. Reality was less perfect. He was tangled in sweaty sheets and had a difficult time getting a hand free to muzzle the clock.

As Rivers struggled to his feet cotton-mouthed and clumsy, he wondered how the dream would have ended. Oddly, except for color, the two women were identical. He knew their shared face was one he should recognize. Too bad he didn't have time to write out the dream. Sometimes he was able to start with a few lingering images and end by pulling the whole wriggling thing from his unconscious.

Rivers reached for the phone. If he was going to remain in charge of the investigation, he had better save lecherous fantasies for a slower morning. A little hesitation today and he would be working for someone else.

When he got to the dispatch officer, Rivers rattled off a list of names and orders that they be asked to meet him in Captain Rafferty's office at ten o'clock. The patrol officers who had found the bodies, Lorenzo Jones and Mary Finnegan, along with young Lassiter, Tamura, and Carl Burnett would be no problem, but he was less sure about his authority to recruit his old partner Phil Orpac, and Ben Hall from Narcotics. True, the Chief had told him to grab the people he needed, but Bacon had been pretty far into the

Mumms at the time. This morning he might have second thoughts, especially when he realized that Rivers wanted eight officers, full time, just to start. Berkeley only had 170 officers to police an always complex and generally quirky city of 125,000, where to be bizarre was expected and to be sensible was to have moved to Walnut Creek. Rivers knew Chief Roger Bacon wasn't exaggerating when he told the City Council each year at budget time that the department was dangerously understaffed.

Rivers asked the switchboard to connect him with Captain Genn, in charge of sex crimes, and then Katzin in Narcotics. Just as he'd hoped, neither was in yet. He left brief messages to the effect that Bacon had asked him to take Hall and Orpac for the duration of the Speldon murder investigation. This was stretching the truth a little, but with luck he wouldn't be challenged. Aldo Speldon was a big name, and everyone would realize it wasn't going to be much fun being a Berkeley cop until the right tail was pinned on the right donkey.

By a few minutes after nine, Rivers was showered and dressed in brown cotton slacks, one of his two remaining Brooks Brothers lawyer shirts, a tan tweed jacket, and Roman-type leather sandals. The Chief didn't approve of sandals, but then he wasn't wildly enthusiastic about Nikes either, which, except for a variety of boots and the muddy Birkenstocks, were all Rivers had. He moved into his old, high-ceilinged kitchen where he squeezed and gulped down two glasses of orange juice. As he rinsed the glass, he spotted a note under the rubber chocolate chip cookie magnet on the refrigerator door.

James, Love—
Heard the early radio news. The KILO reporter acted like he was Edward R. Murrow at the Battle of Britain. Sounds like you'll have a big day (week? month?). Don't take any radioactive alibis (ha! ha!). Told the kids to report to me after school and for the next few days. Good luck.

Ciao!

P.S. Don't kid yourself, tough guy. I'm writing down every

27

child care hour. I expect to be far enough ahead of you by the end of this to have earned a week on the slopes.

P.P.S. The Walnut Street Shadow knows you wolfed down the rest of the "hot date" cognac. Phillip Marlowe would have at least tossed the evidence in the recycling box.

By 9:30 a.m., Rivers was sitting happily in the coffeemaker corner of the Dream Fluff donut shop on Ashby Avenue. As always when his sweet tooth got the best of his common sense, he was pleased with himself. No raisin bran and running five miles this morning; it was going to be a long day and needed to start with a treat. And perhaps things were about to look up. He had found a parking spot almost directly in front of the faded green shop. In the trendy College–Elmwood area, where the locksmith, five and dime, and barber had long since been driven out by an army of thirty-dollar hair salons, imported cheese emporiums, and boutiques full of Balinese skirts and Guatemalan shirts, it was a major victory to find a crack between the BMW's and Accords large enough to park a moped, to say nothing of a Dodge almost old enough to vote.

Good parking karma had been quickly followed by an even better omen—a penny, face up, on the pavement. In his lexicon of common superstitions, finding a penny wasn't quite as good as a first-star wish, but it beat seeing a Studebaker, or getting a postcard from Greece. Finding one before breakfast was a strong sign he would turn to the Sporting Green to find a favorite team had won.

Rivers sat on a stool facing a narrow shelf built out from the wall. Lined up before him as carefully as five Englishmen at a tram stop were a mug of steaming coffee, a French donut (all sugar and air), a chocolate old-fashioned donut (solid and filling), the *Chronicle* Sporting Green, and a yellow legal pad. The dim, almost grubby shop was crowded but peaceful, in keeping with the unwritten house rule that in exchange for the best donuts in town, silence was to be maintained until 10:30.

Rivers peeked at the sports section. His heart accelerated. Sure enough, the Warriors had pulled one out in overtime. It was sure to be a good day now, what with the parking, the penny, and a winning jump shot at the buzzer. He gulped down the coffee, swiveled his stool toward the Silex machine and poured more. He ate the donuts with the second cup, the French first.

By the time he headed for the 1920s-style police headquarters behind what used to be City Hall, Rivers had filled three legal-size pages with notes. Legal pads had been high on his hate list for the five years he'd practiced law, but by that sunny spring morning when he surprised himself by walking out of the public defender's office never to return, they had become a habit. Now he even wrote his erotic fantasies on these most hackneyed of lawyer props, telling himself that other paper ended too soon.

It was still on the morning side of 10:15 when Rivers arrived. Everyone was waiting for him in Captain Rafferty's large corner office on the second floor, drinking coffee and eating leaden donuts from the franchise place on University Avenue. He noted with pleasure that both Orpac and Hall were there.

Rivers wheeled Rafferty's chair from behind the plain old oak desk and joined the circle, turning slightly to look away from Tamura and out the schoolhouse-style window to the Berkeley Hills. The first hint of winter green showed against the sun-scorched brown grass that had covered the hills since June.

"James, the Chief lands at Oakland at 11:50 this morning," Phil Orpac said, handing Rivers a cup of black coffee.

"Someone who can run down what's been happening better get out there—not that we know much more than is in the papers. Tamura, I guess that's you. Remember, Bacon has to host the press conference at one o'clock."

"James, I've got more work to do at KILO, and the station people are hollering at us to get out of there. Do you really need me here?" Carl Burnett asked.

"I do. But we'll finish by eleven, so they won't yell for long," Rivers replied. "I have a few thoughts and then I'll open it up. Unless one of you has picked up on something I've missed, we have no idea who killed Speldon or why. The murder itself is vivid— everything else is in deep shadow. So let's start by trying to understand what the murder itself has to tell us. Carl, you know most about the technical side, which is why I want you in close touch. How about all of us getting together at 8:00 each morning until the

killer is found? Someone has said that the 80s are a time of commit-
tees talking to computers. I don't know where the computer will fit
in, but I think we can get farther, faster, if we brainstorm this thing
together."

"Lieutenant, sir," a thin, black, uniformed officer piped up in a
tone of slightly exaggerated respect. "Will you please disclose to us
poor ignorant cops the name of whatever detective guru provides
you with such brilliant insights?"

Appreciative snorts circled the room.

"Sorry, Lorenzo, I protect my sources," Rivers replied, as the
snorts turned to laughter.

"James, why am I here?" asked a stocky black man with a salt-
and-pepper goatee and enough gold in his mouth to start a pawn
shop. All eyes swung to the corner of the room, where the power-
ful-looking plainclothes officer sat balanced on a spindly wooden
chair tipped back against the window ledge.

"Last night the Chief gave me free reign to fill out the investigation team as I wished," Rivers replied. Then, swiveling slightly
toward the other corner of the room, he added, "Lorenzo and
Mary, you're here because KILO is your beat. I'll arrange for you to
be free of patrol duty until further notice. I want you on this full
time. Phil, I grabbed you because of your experience in homicide.
And to answer your question, Ben," Rivers added, rotating his
chair back in toward the big man, "I asked you for two reasons.
First, because you've worked here eighteen years and I respect your
ability, but also, frankly, because of your race. I'd be surprised if
you haven't already heard I had a run-in with the director of KILO,
Charles Dorsey, last night. If I try hard enough, chances are I can
convince him not to put arsenic in my soup. But even if I improve
my public relations, the truth is you can probably do a better job
finding out what's going on at a black-owned business than I can."

Hall sat very still. The clock clicked a minute closer to eleven.
Still he made no reply. Finally he said, "Send a nigger to catch a
nigger—is that it, James?"

This time it was Rivers who sat impassively, as if he couldn't
quite believe his ears. "You can't win for losing in this department," he finally responded. "Come on, Ben, I wasn't trying to be

obnoxious—just racially balanced."

"You know, James, it was probably karma, not color, that got you in trouble," Lorenzo Jones remarked in a friendlier tone. "Your highly refined diplomacy, brilliant public relations skill, and ingratiating social charm probably zapped your ass again."

"Could be, Lorenzo," Rivers replied with a chuckle, reaching out for the olive branch behind the sarcasm, "but I'm still convinced that when we're dealing with what the police manual refers to as a 'Multi-Ethnic Investigation,' it makes sense to set up your team in the same way."

"James, when you say it like that, I can hear you," Ben Hall said, shifting his chair so that all four legs rested on the floor. "If you don't mind my saying what I think now and then, I'm in. But I haven't worked outside Narcotics since I escaped the squad car, so I may need a little coaching. We get plenty of bodies, but most of them come on the end of a needle."

"Where do we start? Any theory at all?" Phil Orpac asked in a tone that left little doubt he was tired of the barbed preliminaries.

"Nope," Rivers replied, glancing around the circle in hopes of being contradicted. "We're just going to have to pull threads and see what we can come up with."

"Pull threads?" Mary Finnegan inquired pleasantly in her sweet voice.

"Not the yarn-ball theory again!" Tamura muttered under her breath.

Lorenzo Jones shot her a sympathetic wink.

Rivers caught it and gave them an annoyed glance. "When we get a homicide, unless we have some information that points another way, a robbery for instance, we start by assuming that the killer and the victim knew each other. They don't always, but somebody with a computer figured out that about 70 percent of the time they do. Figuring there is a connection, we pull and poke at the victim's life until we get some answers."

"I've taken criminology 101, James. Where do the threads come in?" Finnegan asked again, as sweetly as the first time.

"They probably don't when a public figure like Speldon is killed," Tamura responded. "Lieutenant Rivers likes to compare a murder case to a snarled ball of yarn. Before you try to untangle either, you first turn it this way and that, to locate the loose ends. Only then do you gently and slowly pull on an individual strand. If there is resistance, you stop and try another. Eventually, if you are patient, the whole mess will unravel easily."

Tamura stopped herself mid-gesture, an imaginary ball of yarn in one hand and a loose end in the other, realizing that she was making her semi-parody of Rivers' theory sound almost convincing. She was about to add that the yarn-ball theory sounded splendid when you were stoned, but meant little in the real world, when Mary Finnegan interrupted.

"A woman would never think of an image like that, James. We would have had the yarn properly rolled in the first place."

Rivers was interested in Tamura's crack about Speldon's public image. She was right. When a public figure was the homicide victim, it made sense to approach the investigation differently. Speldon hadn't been as famous as John Lennon or Bobby Kennedy, but the point was well taken. One thing was odd though. If this was a celebrity killing, where was the obliging killer yelling "mea culpa, mea culpa"?

While Rivers was daydreaming Mary Finnegan began recounting her brief interview with Mrs. Speldon the night before.

"The TV people had been calling since about ten, when they were pretty sure of what had happened, so my visit wasn't a surprise. She was upset, but handled it well. I'd say she's had plenty of experience with coping. It was the middle of the night by the time I got there and it seemed tasteless to question her in detail. When a friend came over, I left. She knows someone will contact her about identifying the body this morning and that we'll want to talk to her later on."

"That someone is you, Tamura," Rivers said. "We need background on Speldon—family history, heirs, girlfriends, problems with the kids, etc. Write it up quickly and get it to the rest of us. I'll talk to her later, but I'd be surprised if she's involved. A wife has easier ways to get rid of her husband than a shotgun in the night. Lorenzo, you and Mary check out the Marina area. Put yourselves in the killer's shoes. Figure out how he got in and how he got out. Go over the ground like you were looking for a contact lens. Talk to everyone you can find. Carl, I'd appreciate you helping to get the search set up. Don't forget to do some work this evening after the shifts change at the restaurants and the motel.

Ben, start with KILO, be casual, make friends, and focus on gossip—who's scratching who on the back with what. Phil, you coordinate here for now, while I spend some time trying to understand what's going on with this nuclear fight. Some hysterical environmentalists are sure to claim Speldon was offed as part of a conspiracy by the military-industrial complex."

"They might be right," Tamura interrupted.

"That did occur to me," Rivers responded impatiently."

"We already have a few dozen calls in on that subject," Orpac put in from where he relaxed in a black naugahyde swivel chair to the right of Tamura. Orpac worked out with weights several nights a week at the YMCA across from the post office and a good chunk of his 155-pound body was muscle. He had choirboy looks and love of the ridiculous. That combined with a quick intelligence and stubborn determination even when things looked hopeless, made him an excellent cop.

"A bunch of people want to know if we're going to call in the Feds on grounds of national security," Lorenzo Jones added with a chuckle.

"What did you tell them?" Carl Burnett asked.

"The Marines will land just this side of the Bay Bridge in time for high tea," Orpac responded, running his hand through his cowlick and rolling his baby blue eyes.

"When in doubt, try the truth." Tamura contributed, wondering again if Phil was gay.

Everyone burst out laughing. Tamura found herself pleased when Rivers laughed too, not that she gave a damn, of course.

"James, pardon an interruption by a mere collector of bootprints and fingernail dirt, but aren't you forgetting the fable about the king and the servant?" Carl Burnett asked as the chuckles faded.

Rivers grunted noncommittally and look pointedly at the clock.

The others broke into a chorus of groans.

"The plot is older than writing, but the odd thing is it cropped up in my own family not so long ago," Carl said, raising his hand

33

when Rivers looked about ready to cut him off. "I know we all have to get moving, so I'll be quick. And Ben," he added, nodding at the narcotics officer, "I know you don't like stories about the old South, but relax, I'm not going to burn a cross on your lawn.

"My great granddaddy was a county judge in rural South Carolina just before the War Between the States. He botched a case something like ours because he forgot the slave. It seems a Mr. Ambrose Early, the biggest landholder in the County, was shot dead from ambush. He was riding in a two-wheel carriage next to his driver and the shotgun blast killed the slave too. Anyway, to snip a pup's tail before it grows longer than the hound, Early, who was known to have a knack with the ladies, was coming home from diddling the wife of a young lawyer down at the county seat. Later that same night, they found the attorney, dirty and drunk, in a roadhouse fifteen miles along the pike. He righteously denied the killing even though he was packing the right sort of gun, and it had recently been fired. In addition, he refused to say where he had been. Great Granddaddy held a short trial before he hanged him.

"A few days after the hanging, the Methodist preacher's daughter in Greenville cut her wrists," Carl Burnett continued in his soft southern cadence. "She left a note saying she wished to join her everlasting love—a gentleman so noble he went to his grave rather than disgrace her. That fouled the water worse than a sidewheeler trying to get off a sandbar. No one really knew what to think— least of all Great Granddaddy, who was too busy organizing a regiment to march with Stonewall Jackson to Manassas Junction to care. After the war was lost, and half the boys in the county, along with it no one gave a damn about an old murder.

"It wasn't until almost forty years later that my granddaddy, who by then had been county judge himself for almost two generations, received a letter from Canada that cleared up the mystery. The writer was an elderly former slave named Walter Johnson, who said he wanted to clear his conscience before he passed over. It seemed he and Ambrose Early's driver had a yen for the same girl, a beautiful sixteen-year-old who was learning to cook up at the big house. When the driver seemed to be winning out, Johnson just went out of his head in a jealous rage and put a stop to him. He was real sorry he had hit Master Early too, but the confusion had made it a lot easier for him, and Mary, the girl, to get away North. In closing, he wanted granddaddy to know he had a successful dry goods business in Halifax, Nova Scotia and raised five kids to fear the Lord."

"You're right, Carl. We better pull some strings in Rathman's life too," Rivers said.

"Let me start on that. There's not much to coordinate right now anyway," Phil Orpac said.

"Great. If Ben checks Rathman out at KILO and you look at his personal life, the two of you may close in on something."

"Lieutenant, is there something I can do, er, to help, or..." Lassiter asked haltingly, his child-like moon of a face reddening.

Rivers, suffering a momentary caffeine and sugar withdrawal, felt like saying "Go chase yourself." He got the better of his anti-social urge.

"Sure, help Lieutenant Orpac with the administrative side of things. Sit by the phone and take messages. There will be lots of tips and probably a few confessions. Get the details — names, dates, times — and give them to Phil when you get a stack. Also, and this is important, keep track of where each of us is at all times."

Noting the young patrolman's slight slump of disappointment, Rivers relented further. "If you manage all that for a few days, maybe something more exciting will turn up."

As everyone started for the door, Rivers touched Mary Finnegan on the arm. He couldn't help but notice how pleasantly plump she was in her tan uniform and wondered, not for the first time, how it would be to spend a night nuzzling her large, relaxed breasts.

"Do you come down Ashby in the morning?"

"Yes, I turn on Grove," she replied seriously.

"Great, could you stop at Dream Fluff and get some decent donuts?"

"No problem, Lieutenant, I'm a sucker for your masterful tone of command," Mary replied with a giggle. "What's your favorite?"

"French and chocolate old-fashioned, and this police person will take a small step toward liberation and stop at Peets for some decent coffee. If we're going to play who-killed-cock-robin at the crack of dawn, we may as well have decent worms."

4

As Tamura hurriedly left the conference room, she caught her heel on a loose piece of carpet and stumbled, dropping a file folder. Kneeling to retrieve the scattered paper, she wanted to blame Rivers, not only for her own clumsiness, but for her lousy morning. And it had been particularly rotten. Semi-dazed after only five hours of sleep, her first move had been to pour rancid milk on her Wheatabix. Giving up on breakfast, she hunted for her raspberry-colored shirt, only to remember she hadn't picked up her laundry and had nothing to wear but her unlucky leotard. Now, she was to begin her biggest murder investigation as a gopher. She enjoyed the occasional mindless assignment, but playing friendly, knowledge-able chauffeur to the Chief of Police didn't qualify, combining as it did, meaningless work with an atmosphere of tension. Not that Roger Bacon was completely intolerable. He wasn't nearly as one-dimensional as most police brass, but in her limited contact with him, she had seen nothing to contradict the prevailing department view that he dealt with every difficult situation by calculating his personal advantage.

Tamura sighed as she stood up and grabbed her leather jacket from a hook behind the door, thinking that if she had to spend many more days-off like this, she might as well quit and finish her Masters in anthropology. As tedious as studying the exchange of cowry shells for pigs in pre-colonial Borneo had once seemed, it couldn't be more boring than fetching and carrying for James Rivers. The clock in the hall showed 11:06, forty minutes to get to the Oakland Airport. No need to hurry, but just the same she took the back stairway two steps at a time. Keeping Roger Bacon waiting would be a guaranteed way to finish off her morning. As Tamura walked quickly through the short hallway leading to the parking lot, Joey—equipment coordinator and psychic—leaned out of a doorway, the keys to an unmarked Chevy Nova dangling from his right forefinger.

"Welcome to the friendly skies," he chortled, flashing her a happy leer.

Tamura rolled her eyes by way of reply. She regretted that she had no time for their customary chat. Rapping with Joey always lifted a down day. It was like stepping back into the late sixties when, for one wild and wonderful moment, the fantasy that everything was going to be groovy forever appeared to be more than a hashish dream. Indeed, Tamura was still attached to Berkeley, because despite a decade's heavy evidence to the contrary, it was still home to a few people like Joey, who truly believed the age of Aquarius was just around the next daisy.

As she slipped behind the wheel of the Nova, Tamura once again gave silent thanks to the Arabs. If gas was still fifty cents a gallon, the Department would never have given up their hulking Dodges. Having resisted learning to drive until five years before, she deeply mistrusted all cars and used mass transit whenever possible. However, it didn't take a genius to guess that Roger Bacon wouldn't be enthusiastic about waiting at the Coliseum BART station for a Richmond bound train.

Tamura found a fifteen-minute meter just south of the concrete crescent of the Oakland terminal building. With ten minutes to spare, she tuned in KILO on the car radio.

" . . . says the spokesperson for the Berkeley Police Department. Next we'll be hearing from Sandy Van Owen on Sportsline with the latest details of the Warriors stirring come-from-behind victory. But first, a word from the Melody Motors people — remember, you can get a new car for a song at . . ."

Tamura punched the button off. Not even a killing in the main studio could slow the march of news, weather, and sports. She thought it sad. Sure, it made media sense. There were lots of Warriors' fans who had never heard of Aldo Speldon when he was alive and wouldn't suddenly take an interest now that he was stretched out on a slab. Just the same, to be so driven by the ongoingness of the trivial, not to be able to pause when one of your own reporters is killed, told her more about the ethics of the radio business than she wanted to know.

Tamura joined a half dozen people in the lounge just as the pink-and-red striped PSA jet, complete with idiotic grin, taxied to a stop. It occurred to her that the people who painted the plane could never have seriously intended to go up in it. Flying was in itself a presumptuous business, but to flaunt colors guaranteed to make the sky gods cringe took a degree of chutzpah that bordered on the nutty.

Roger Bacon was last off the plane. He struck a pose at the top of the portable stair. Too bad he's playing to an empty house, Tamura chuckled to herself, her sarcasm tinged with a degree of admiration. At fifty-one, Bacon not only kept his body as firm as a hickory stick, he clothed it like a prince. Indeed, there was something almost Machiavellian about his external perfection, as if the hard body, the elegant clothes, the hawklike face, and the courtly manner disguised some shortcoming. She hadn't deduced what it was yet. But even if the waters of Bacon's being did not run deep, they unquestionably bubbled gracefully on the surface.

Bacon strode through the terminal door and again paused, seeming to mentally straighten his tie. When he recognized Tamura, he strode towards her purposefully.

"Officer Tamura, so glad it's you who's come."

"The press will be waiting for your statement at headquarters," Tamura said, as she shook hands. "Lieutenant Rivers didn't know just how you would want to handle it, but he's tentatively scheduled a press conference for one o'clock. I can fill you in with what little . . ."

"Good, good . . . why don't you save it for the ride, my dear?"

Bacon's progress through the airport was both easy and authoritative. People moved out of his path as if he were a hearse with its lights on. Tamura, left in his wake, was bumped by a boy scout, blocked by an elderly woman with a walker, and importuned by a bald young person of indefinite sex who tried to sell her an incense stick. As she hurried to catch Bacon, she almost applauded. There was clearly something to be learned from this man who could so convincingly turn prosaic events into pregnant moments.

Bacon placed his tan Gucci travelling bag in the Nova's trunk and then extended his hand, palm up. When Tamura hesitated, he said in the silkiest of voices, "I hope you won't be offended, Sara, but I prefer to take the wheel."

Tamura was amazed. Bacon made Rivers look like a cheerleader for the ERA. Hardly missing a beat, she dropped the keys into his extended hand and replied, "No problem—very few men know how to be good passengers."

Before Bacon could respond, Tamura climbed into the passenger seat.

After a few minutes of noncommital silence, Tamura began recounting the events of the previous night. Occasionally, the Chief would interject an impassive grunt, but for the most part he seemed absorbed with maneuvering the car through the light midday traffic. It was true that he was a better driver, she conceded to herself. Tamura finished her chronology as they rounded the big freeway curve on the bay side of Oakland's seedy downtown area. As always, her admiring eye found the Oakland Tribune Tower, standing like an elderly queen over a court of derelicts and desperados.

Tamura continued to look out the window. She had been daydreaming about the bizarre scrap-wood sculptures that peppered the mudflats. It seemed peculiar to her that every time she passed, a giant chicken, dancing alligator, or some other creature had joined the menagerie, although she'd never seen anyone putting them together. It was as if they had pulled themselves up from the bay ooze, following their own path of oddball evolution.

Bacon made a vague gesture in the direction of the water. "It's a big one, Sara. What do you think?"

Tamura was surprised and pleased that Bacon seemed to enjoy the driftwood fantasyland, too. Then, just as she'd begun to point out her favorite, she experienced a moment of confusion. Was Bacon talking about the sculpture or the murder? Remembering her grandmother, Tamura nodded her head. Obachan, who had emigrated to the United States as a young woman in 1910, never learned much English but didn't like to admit it and when confronted by the incomprehensible questions of an inquiring "hakugin," she simply nodded.

Apparently the old family subterfuge was still effective in the third generation. At any rate, Bacon probed no further for the rest of the short drive to headquarters.

5

The voice asked, "What city please?"

"Berkeley, or maybe Oakland, for Environmental Advocates, or, if that doesn't work, try Lawyers for the Environment," Rivers said.

The operator finally found the number under "Defenders of the Environment," and seemed pleased when Rivers thanked him warmly. Rivers always did, sure that next time he punched 411, he would be told that the information service had been discontinued on the grounds that it was too reliable and efficient to be tolerated at the end of the twentieth century.

He pushed the proper buttons, asked for Charles Pierce, gave his name to a receptionist, and finally heard, "Howdy Classmate."

"Hello Charles. I guess you do remember me from school."

"Of course, Sherlock, you're famous. The only graduate of the West's best law school ever to become a cop. You must have missed that first year lecture when they explained cops go to night school to become lawyers, lawyers become judges, and judges become statues. Seriously, I've read about your big successes in the last couple of years. I almost called you this morning when I heard about Aldo."

"Why? Do you know something?"

"Easy on the cross-examination counselor. I don't know a thing, but I guessed you might be able to use some help separating the black hats from the white ones in the big nuclear brouhaha we have going. Then there's my personal interest. When I'm not saving trees, I read stacks of detective novels and I'm curious about how a real investigation resembles the paperback variety."

"Do you think there might be a connection between Speldon's death and nuclear politics?" Rivers persisted.

"Wouldn't bet on it, but how come I'm explaining why I thought of calling you, and you haven't told me why you called me?" Pierce responded with the knowing chuckle of a man with long experience in ducking one question by asking another.

"Okay, I'll admit it. I need help. I don't know how to approach the possibility that Speldon's death was politically motivated."

"I'll point you in the right direction if I can. As far as nuclear power plant construction is concerned, and increasingly on the defense issue too, public enemy number one on the environmental shit list is Roger Warren, the boss of Warren Construction. He's the guy behind those construction site signs that say 'We build it bigger and tougher—to serve you better.' Now, don't get me wrong, James. I'm not suggesting Warren or anyone else from the nuclear industry is involved, but if—and remember, I said if—Aldo's death is connected with the anti-nuclear fight, Warren would know how to find out. You could do worse than starting with him."

"Where does he hang out, Charles?"

"Company headquarters is in San Francisco. He's usually there if he's not paving jungles in Brazil or chairing a presidential commission advocating more and bigger nukes. You know, improving America's ability to deter totalitarianism."

"Don't tell me—the Warren building must be the biggest and toughest in the City."

"Bull's eye. It's that massive tower with the crossed black steel girders. I've always thought of it as the Black Knight's castle. Come to think of it, I'm pretty sure Warren is in town. I just saw him interviewed on a local TV show last Tuesday. He was blasting Speldon and his army of D.L.D.'s."

"His what?"

" 'Daisy Loving Dopes.' Among other things, he described Aldo's political tactics as akin to slipping a bird's nest in the path of an earth mover just before screaming that helpless creatures were about to be crushed."

"He must keep you guys in stitches. I'll go see. Can I come by first and talk to you for a few minutes?"

"Sure, but we moved. We're on Telegraph, just into Oakland. How about Sam's Cafe in half an hour?"

"You're on," Rivers replied.

Rivers took a deep breath and tapped the number for Warren Construction, preparing himself for the corporate flak-catchers. His effort was unnecessary. He had barely time enough to say he was from the Berkeley Police when he was connected with Roger Warren. As if to pyramid surprises, Warren assured him that he had expected the call and invited him to a late lunch. Jack's at two. Well, well, Rivers thought, I'm going to get a very good meal out of this.

* * * *

As Rivers maneuvered tuna-sized Dartha through a sea of foreign minnows, he reviewed his brief, but decidedly odd, conversation with Warren. Why was the industrialist so anxious to meet? More to the point, why did this man who controlled an industrial empire of global dimension seem worried? He would have to be patient and wait for the background to fill itself in. In the meantime, he might as well focus his thoughts in a more practical direction — should he have the cold asparagus with hollandaise or an artichoke along with the Petrale at Jack's.

Rivers' food fantasy was interrupted by a bread truck slowly pulling away from the curb. A woman in a maroon Mercedes edged toward the opening space, but Rivers swung Dartha's wheel hard right, cut her off and slid to a stop barely ten feet from Sam's front door. The woman honked and gave him a vicious look. Rivers pretended not to notice. It was a piece of cake. He'd been a waiter in college and to compensate for being clumsy and slow, had mastered the art of walking through a room full of impatient customers as if no one was there. He quickly learned that if you couldn't be competent, you could at least be haughty.

"Not bad, Sherlock," Charles Pierce said, extending his hand as Rivers climbed out of the car.

"It's been a long time, Charles," Rivers replied, shaking hands warmly. "You're looking good. Defending trees obviously agrees with you."

"It does. I like lawyering for a good cause," Pierce replied. "Right now though I'm looking forward to playing Doctor Watson. But James, let me ask you, why did you turn in your bar card?"

"You know those cowboy movies where each side hires a gun-fighter and they shoot it out at high noon? One day in court I saw the whole scene as a quick draw contest."

"So?"

"So, I thought about it and realized I wasn't cold enough or tough enough or mean enough to fight for people and causes I didn't respect. A few days later I sent my gunfighter's card back to the Bar Association and rode off into the sunset."

"You mean you traded it for a real gun?"

"There's more to it than that. It has to do with whether you believe in what you're doing. But let's save it for a time when we have a few hours. How about coffee, or is it too close to lunch?"

"Oh, no. I need caffeine to keep up with you," Pierce said good-humoredly.

The two men sat at a table by the street window, where the sun had warmed the straight-backed oak chairs. Sam's Cafe was an old coffee and egg house that still held out against the onslaught of the East Bay's seemingly inexorable gentrification. Sadly, it too was in danger of becoming newly fashionable now that people who never counted their change had discovered it.

Rivers leaned back, shut his eyes, and felt the sun on his face. Charles Pierce obviously had an interesting story to tell. It seemed simplest to save his questions.

"The roots of the current nuclear plant stalemate began in the mid-70s, when the environmentalists got a tough anti-nuclear initiative on the state ballot designed to change the state constitution to stop nuclear power completely," Pierce began.

"When public opinion polls indicated the initiative might pass, the nuclear industry panicked. They lobbied the legislature to quickly enact a watered-down version of the initiative. Their idea was to keep the brave language, while eliminating the regulatory teeth. They figured that once legislation was in place, the public could be conned into voting against the constitutional changes on the theory that they were no longer necessary. The strategy worked perfectly at first. The legislature passed a weak nuclear safety act and the voters did in fact defeat the initiative. The only drawback from the industry point of view was that in order to get the sup-posedly toothless bill enacted quickly, they had to make some com-

43

promises with environmentalist legislators. Mercifully, when the dust settled it turned out one of the compromises was a dandy from the environmental viewpoint. The conservationists had outfoxed the industry by getting included in the bill a provision which says no nuclear plants can be built until it can be certified that there is a safe way to permanently dispose of the radioactive waste. The result has been no new nuclear plants in California.

"Other states haven't been so lucky and it's by no means sure we won't be building more plants here eventually. The sad and simple truth appears to be that we Americans are the prisoners of our history. For over 300 years, the pioneers used the hell out of the land and the water, cut down every tree in sight, and stripped minerals from the earth. Every time things began to look a little bleak, there was an easy solution—hitch up old Dobbin and head West. When we ran out of West, we substituted technological frontiers."

"Is this a lecture, Charles?"

"You're damn right but it has a point, so bear with me a moment. To over-simplify, we became hooked on the idea that no matter how many natural resources we squandered, science would be there to keep us in the fast lane. In the 50s and 60s, when it became obvious to everyone that oil wouldn't last forever, our politicians looked to the demi-gods of the scientific establishment for a quick fix. Rather than tell people an unpopular truth—that it was past time to conserve—the scientific-industrial establishment trotted out nuclear power as the new miracle, one that by the 1970s had gained the added attraction of sticking it to the arrogant Arabs. Remember when we were kids—good old Ike and his atoms for peace? It sounded great at first and most people applauded uncritically. And even when doubts as to safety began to surface and the evidence of health problems mounted, most people only paid attention long enough to understand that there was no substitute quick fix, just conservation. Then the U.S. Department of Energy was set up to pander to the big science party line that new scientific discoveries will be found to solve any serious radiation hazards before we're all burned to a crisp."

"What about Three Mile island?" Rivers asked.

"I was just getting to that. TMI and other, less serious, accidents have given the public a chance to see how little we really know about managing the atom. Together with a number of disastrous cost overruns at other plants, it's resulted in a slow down in nuclear plant construction.

"But the nuclear industry isn't about to fold their reactors and steal away in the night," Pierce went on. "Several years ago, they made a decision to counter attack. Meetings were held, big bucks were raised and a campaign to sell nuclear power was launched. You've probably seen their so-called volunteers in airport waiting rooms, the ones with the hand-lettered signs that say 'Nuclear Reactors Are Built Better than Jane Fonda.' That's just the tip of the iceberg, of course. The main strategy is to influence key legislators, administrators and judges. That way, no matter what the latest opinion poll may say about the public's increasing distrust of nuclear energy, the important victories will be theirs. Here in California the focus is on replacing the safe waste disposal law with something like 'waste must be disposed of in compliance with all applicable Federal regulations.' As the federal regulations are weak, this translates into 'business as usual.' "

Rivers shifted in his chair.

"Okay, okay, enough background. To get to the point of why you're here, Warren Construction is at the center of the political wheeling and dealing. They've built more nuclear plants than anyone else, and have an enormous financial stake in the outcome. Glomar, Universal Electric, and Behr in Germany build the reactors. Warren Construction pours the concrete, builds the towers and does all the rest. There aren't half a dozen outfits outside the Eastern bloc big enough to compete. Right now W.C. is involved in over thirty projects worldwide. When you realize upwards of a billion dollars can be spent on one plant, it's not hard to see their nuclear business generates more bucks than the budgets of many countries.

"In the 80s, nuclear politics, to use a bad pun, melts down to this: whenever there's an accident or an outrageous cost overrun, the 'anti' side gets a boost. Whenever OPEC raises the price of oil, the pros gain. Although many people have a deep-seated fear of radiation dangers, it's inchoate and undefined. The fear of an energy crisis is as close as the next power bill."

Rivers suddenly realized that the combination of Pierce's deep pleasant voice and the warm sun was putting him on the nod. He shook his head quickly and slid his chair a few feet into the shade.

"Tell me what's happening currently," he interrupted.

"Here in the land of the setting sun, a major issue is whether those few words about safe disposal will be changed. Remember, they were put in by the legislature, not the voters, so they can come out the same way."

"What about the legislature? I thought the conservation lobby had the upper hand in Sacramento."

"Nothing is ever sure when it comes to politicians. The nuclear lobby has about a third of the legislature on their side come hell or high radiation, so they don't need to switch as many votes as you might think."

"You mean buy votes?"

"Don't sound shocked, James. It's not so many dollars for so many votes like in the old days, but yes, I guess you're right—it comes down to buying votes. Given our absence of meaningful conflict-of-interest laws, it's almost impossible to stop. Imagine a medium-sized cement company which supplies a lot of cement to Warren Construction in the Central Valley. They know a big nuclear plant will be built near them if the disposal law is changed. In the meantime, a subsidiary of the cement company is having a perfectly real legal problem with a land purchase. Any one of dozens of lawyers in their area could handle it but the cement company hires the law firm of the local state assemblyman. The work is assigned to a junior partner who does it well and charges a large, but not ridiculous, fee. Several weeks, months, or even years later, the assemblyman votes to support nuclear power. Somewhere along the line, he and his family enjoy a month's tour of the continent. And why not? His law firm is prospering."

"You'll probably think me naive, but aren't there politicians who can't be influenced so easily?" Rivers interjected.

"Of course, but remember, the industry only needs to reach a few. At the same time our hypothetical influence-buying scheme is

46

unfolding in the Central Valley, similar scenarios will be happening in a dozen other places. Not all will be successful, of course, but sooner or later votes will be collected."

"It sounds pretty inevitable," Rivers said.

"It probably would be if it weren't for the counterattack of dozens of conservation and anti-nuclear war groups working to make the public's fear of nuclear power real and immediate. As you know, the anti-nuke struggle has been heating up and Aldo Speldon had emerged from semi-retirement as one of its leaders."

"What happens now?"

"Who knows? If there is any real suspicion Speldon's murder is tied to the nuclear industry, the pro-nuclear people will be stalled at least for a while. Given half a chance, the conservation activists will do everything they can to make Aldo a martyr."

"Let me play the Devil's advocate for a minute, Charles," Rivers said, as he again moved out of the advancing sun. "Could this be another Reichstag fire? Could the conservationists have killed their own man?"

"Shit! You must be kidding!" Pierce replied, the real annoyance in his voice reminding Rivers that possession of the same school tie didn't give one absolute metaphoric license.

"I apologize. But remember, real cops aren't as polite as Inspector Maigret. We're a lot like cats. We poke and maul our corpses. If you really want to help, you'll have to suspend your disbelief."

"Point taken."

"Let me ask you something else. When I called, you said you would bet against the nuclear industry being involved in Speldon's death, but you hedged. Why?"

"Do you want more coffee, James?" Pierce interjected, nodding at the waiter and pushing the mugs toward the edge of the table.

When they were full, Pierce wrapped both square hands around his, making it disappear. Finally, choosing his words with exaggerated care, he said, "It's complicated and I only know bits and pieces of the story, but there's been a nasty personal thing going on between Speldon and Warren for years."

"They knew each other?"

"They've been growling at each other like two male bulldogs

with one steak bone for at least thirty years."

"What's the bone?"

"The future of America. Will it be trees, wild rivers, clean air, and a limited population—Aldo's dream—or will it be bridges, dams, factories, cheap power, jobs and prosperity for all—Warren's dream?"

"When did the personal stuff start?"

"I'm not sure, although I can find out with a few phone calls. It really boiled over, though, with the fight to dam the Grand Canyon in the 60s. But James, I think you'll make a mistake if you only focus on their differences."

"Isn't that your point."

"Not entirely. In a curious way, they remind me of that folk song about the brothers from one of the border states who fought on opposing sides in the Civil War."

" 'One wore blue and the other wore grey, but their widows both wore black,' or something like that?" Rivers sang, stopping abruptly when a woman at the next table grimaced.

"That's the gist," Pierce laughed, "though it's easy to see why you're in Berkeley instead of Nashville. Aldo came from a small town in Central Washington, somewhere near Yakima, and Roger Warren from the same sort of place in Northern Arizona. Speldon's father was a preacher and died when Aldo was small. Warren never knew his Dad. Both had determined moms who held things together and pushed their kids hard. The rest is straight Horatio Alger. Good grades, two jobs in high school, state college on a scholarship, working all the way; top of the class, no money for clothes, parties or girls. They both came roaring out of school with a great hunger for success and recognition."

"They both got it."

"They certainly did," Pierce continued, moving his chair a little to stay in the sun. "Warren followed the traditional American trail to success, piling up lots of money and material possessions, but as the sign says, he did it 'bigger, better and tougher' than almost anyone. He made a million before he was thirty, married ten million more, and never looked back. Warren Construction has made some major acquisitions lately and is well up on the list of the fifty largest corporations."

"Speldon took a different path."

"Maybe it was his parish–house childhood, or the summers he spent camping in the Cascades along the Canadian border when he was in school, but Aldo never gave much of a damn for money or luxuries. He was plenty ambitious though, and wanted to be king of the mountain as much as anyone I've ever met."

"He was certainly literal about it. I read someplace he was one of the great climbers just before the Second World War."

"He was always conquering some new peak. First the Rockies, then the Alps and just before Hitler snuck around the Maginot line, the Himalayas. Aldo may not have been the best of the pre-war climbers, but even then he had a genius for self-promotion through articles and books. During the war he was a paratrooper and then an officer with the ski troops in the Alps. He collected a dozen ribbons and deserved more than half. After the war, he headed several mountaineering and conservation groups. His work was inspired, but he never once forgot to include his picture in the press releases. To the world, he became 'Mr. Environment,' the practical poet who worked tirelessly to save our natural heritage and give us a vision of life beyond materialism."

"He sold me. I've always thought of him as a white-thatched god in hiking boots," Rivers said with a chuckle.

"Don't get me wrong, James. There was plenty of substance to the man. He really did climb mountains, lead ski troops, and help put the environmental issue on the political map. But, as he got older he developed an uncanny knack for alienating people. One moment he was a poetic visionary, a rare man who could simultaneously touch both your heart and mind; the next he was a petty egomaniac hogging credit for someone else's hard work."

"How do you know all this?" Rivers asked.

"One of the news magazines did a detailed profile on both Speldon and Warren when they were fighting over building an airport in the Everglades," Pierce replied, again moving his chair so as to stay in the sun.

Rivers thought for a moment. "You know, Charles, that was such a good story I almost forgot you never got around to telling me why you haven't eliminated Warren as a suspect," he said finally. "Viewed objectively, it would seem damn stupid for Warren or anyone else in the nuclear industry to have killed Speldon."

"There's more. I've been trying to sneak up on the rest. I guess I'm not sure I want to tell you."

"Charles, your life is based on full disclosure."

"Okay, but don't jump to conclusions. Treat what I tell you as just another small part of the puzzle. Agreed?"

"Agreed."

"Warren has a daughter, Sophie; a sort of late-blooming flower child who sings and plays guitar. Good education, good looks, good mind and no patience with building things bigger and tougher. She lived in Europe for a while to support herself as a singer. She's been back a year and a half and is actively involved in the Pacific Rim Society, Save the Sea Mammals, and several other groups. Sophie Warren used to be unknown outside the environmental subculture, but lately, with a couple of hot records and a successful concert tour, she's on her way to being a household word. I really like her. She lives her beliefs; she marches, organizes, licks stamps, gives her money to anti-nuke causes and even gets thrown in jail."

"What the hell are you driving at, aside from the fact you have a crush on her? Even a musical moron like me knows 'Loon Lullaby.' "

"Well then, you probably know that Sophie Warren has a place in the pro-environment power structure."

"Charles," Rivers almost shouted, "I happily concede Sophie Warren is a cross between Linda Ronstadt and Smokey the Bear. Will you please tell me what all this has to do with Aldo's death?"

"The old god in hiking boots, as you call Aldo Speldon, and the young goddess, as I'll call Sophie Warren just to keep our metaphors straight, began to run into each other at rallies and teach-ins. In the beginning, their meetings were accidental, but not . . ."

"Like that, huh?"

"Like that and more. Lately they'd become almost inseparable."

"What about Warren? He can't have been rooting for Aldo to become his son-in-law."

"As far as I know — with one exception — he's been cool."

"Tell me about the exception."

"Aldo baited him. They were on a TV talk show, debating whether an existing nuclear plant, one that was built by Warren's company, is on an active earthquake fault."

"Is it?"

"I would say yes, but it depends on how you define active. Anyway, that's not the point. In the middle of the show, Warren produced some surprise new seismic data that seemed to prove the location safe. This put Speldon on the defensive and he was on his way to losing the debate. He should have taken his licking and hired some other scientist to come up with an opposite conclusion for next time. But Aldo couldn't stand to lose, especially when he was center stage."

"The sort who would start a fist fight fairly, but end up kneeing you in the balls if he couldn't win any other way."

"Exactly. Aldo replied with a crack about Warren having more luck buying geologists than convincing his own daughter. Only a few people watching could have possibly understood the personal side of the allusion, but given the relationships involved, it was way below the belt. Warren went for Aldo on camera."

"What happened?"

"The TV station cut to a jingle about sanitary napkins while a camera operator and assistant producer pulled them apart. The press agents smoothed it over the next day."

"I see what you mean about the personal side being sticky," Rivers said, shoving his yellow legal pad into his woven shoulder bag and reaching for the check.

"Sit still for another minute, James, there's more."

"Okay, but tell me quick or I'll be late for my joust with the black knight."

"Warren is a hunter. He takes almost as much delight in killing animals as Speldon did in saving them. The article I read credited him with winning dozens of target competitions with rifles, pistols, shotguns — everything but sling shots."

"I'm beginning to see why Warren is anxious to see me. One last thing — what do you honestly think?"

"In a funny sort of way, I think Speldon and Warren needed each other."

"Needed?"

"These last few years Speldon has been bypassed, even rudely pushed aside, by a lot of environmentalists. This was partly because of his ego problems, but also because since the 60s poetic types have been out of fashion. It's all scientists and lawyers now. Warren is still on top of his tower, but my guess is he has had similar problems, especially since his company went public. Visionaries aren't popular in business these days either. I'm sure more than one up and coming young MBA is rooting for the old emperor to climb into his jet-powered chariot and roar over the nearest horizon."

"You're telling me they were having the same sort of problems."

"Sure — they were getting old. And the nuclear fight was a tonic for both. It's entered a realm of emotion that the pocket calculator types can't understand and all the environmental impact statements in the world can't contain. For the first time since the big battles over the redwoods and the Everglades, the old leaders are relevant. Both Warren and Speldon must have positively enjoyed sharpening their lances and strapping on their armor for one more charge."

"With Speldon dead, who can Warren battle?"

"That's my point."

6

Tamura decided that it was a double cheeseburger and fries sort of day. After she dropped off the Chief at the police building, she pointed the Nova toward Oscar's at Hearst and Shattuck. She was not expected at Mrs. Speldon's for over an hour, leaving plenty of time to corral her thoughts over a charboiled hamburger.

There were no B.P.D. cars in the parking lot north of the restaurant, the first good omen of the day. She could eat alone without appearing stand-offish. Growing up Japanese-American meant growing up polite. It was difficult for her to be even a little anti-social without feeling vaguely uncomfortable. Except, of course, where her boss was concerned: with Rivers, self-protection meant self-assertion.

As always, Tamura felt defiant when she pushed through Oscar's front door. Many of her friends of the wheat germ and carrot juice persuasion chided her about her junk food lapses. She had taken to replying she would mend her diet as soon as someone came up with a good, organic equivalent for the french-fried potato. That shut them up.

As Tamura moved into the restaurant, she was enveloped by the smell of charcoal and sizzling grease. She happily surrendered to the wonderfully sensual aroma. The young black woman presiding over the grill nodded and smiled as she tossed a fat red patty onto the fire without being asked. Tamura was a member of the family.

Tamura had learned a lot about being a cop right here in Oscar's, under the benign but caring tutelage of Danny Brown, her first and best patrol partner. Even as she collected her medium-rare burger, dripping with cheese, and sat by the front window with its panoramic view of the Fast Gas Station across Shattuck, she could hear Danny holding forth on how to approach a drunk driver. She always sat well away from the table to avoid ketchup splatters when he jabbed his dripping fries this way and that to illustrate the proper technique.

Tamura shivered. Danny had been shot by a drugged sixteen-year-old, and had lost the sight in one eye. They gave him early retirement and last she heard, he was working security for a bank in L.A.

Tamura licked her fingers to clean off the last bit of grease and decided against ice cream for dessert. One excess at a time, she thought virtuously as she collected the Nova and headed for the narrow, winding roads just northeast of the Berkeley border. When she finally found Highland, she parked a few blocks from the Speldon's. There was time for a slow walk in the mid-day warmth of the late autumn sun.

Her destination turned out to have white walls under a red tile roof and an expansive view of San Francisco Bay. The yard was sensibly landscaped with native trees and shrubs requiring little attention. No bermuda grass gobbling up the paths here, she thought enviously as she let the heavy knocker fall against a massive oak and wrought iron door. The entry would have been on the intimidating side of formal had it not been for the seagull of driftwood that smiled down from the lintel.

The woman who answered seemed as whimsical as the gull. She had a small oval face, crowned by loose grey curls, and her pink skin had the look of being cured in the California sun—lined and a little puckered, but glowing. Her outfit consisted of a faded red turtle-neck pullover and red and blue striped Levis, exactly like the ones Tamura had lived in during her last year in high school. The left shoulder seam of the sweater was retreating with dignity, and showed a bit of tanned skin. Her magic was in her eyes. Despite some puffiness from crying, they were young, girlish and full of opal fire. What a pleasure, Tamura thought, to finally meet the Good Witch of the North.

"Mrs. Speldon?" Tamura finally asked, after waiting a minute for the small woman to say something.

"Yes, yes. Who are you?"

"Sara Tamura, from the Berkeley Police. I have identification if you would . . ."

"No, no, please come in. I've been expecting you. Tamura is Japanese, isn't it? I was fooled because you don't look a bit like a policeman, or ... a policeperson, or whatever. I'm not sure what name is fashionable these days. Truly dear, I'm relieved you don't fit the Dick Tracy stereotype. I confess, though, I was about to be impolite when you introduced yourself. Reporters have been banging at my door ever since I got back from that terrible morgue. They act as if they were bred on another planet. I sometimes think of myself as a tough old bird, but I'm soft compared to people who won't allow another being time for a proper cry. It makes me so damn mad. And I can't even retaliate by withholding my quarter. I stopped reading newspapers when they all caved in to that terrible Joseph McCarthy."

"I feel badly about the timing, but I do have a few things I need to discuss," Sara interjected, trying to establish firm footing against Mrs. Speldon's verbal rip tide.

"Of course, I want to help you all I can," she replied in a more relaxed tone. "Your job is to catch the disturbed person who committed this crime before anyone else is hurt. But those media people are different—they're in the titillation business. Fear and greed, blood and gore, anything to depress people so they will buy what's in the ads."

"Isn't that a little extreme?" Tamura interrupted, trying to forestall another tirade as she followed the other woman along a short, tile-floored hallway.

At the door to a large room, Tamura stopped, caught by her own surprise. Plants, lots of plants, were almost everywhere, and everywhere they weren't, an animal stood, sat, hung, or lay, head cocked, to inspect her.

"If you'll sit here by the window, I'll make tea and we can have a talk," Mrs. Speldon said.

Tamura was delighted for the quiet moment to orient herself. She sat near tall wood-framed windows looking west. The postcard vividness of the bay view was pleasantly muted by the unadorned white walls of the room. The menagerie, she now saw, contained only four live animals: an elderly airedale, a collie pup, a longhaired manx cat, and what was surely a skunk. For each creature of blood and bone, however, there were a dozen stuffed or sculpted replications in assorted sizes and colors. Some peeked from behind the potted ferns or small trees. Others hung from the ceiling. Still more crowded every flat surface. It was as if she had stepped into someone's surrealistic dream of a day in the park, in which the funhouse had run off with the zoo to live happily ever after in the arboretum.

"This is a truly magical room, Mrs. Speldon," Tamura said when the older woman returned with tea.

"Please call me Lucy. It's a little too much for most people, but I knew you liked it. You hardly hesitated before coming in. Let me introduce the family. This old orange thing is Peaches," she continued as she plucked the Manx from the top of the portable TV. "She's quite a lazy beast and she drools. The skunk-like one in the potted fern is Peaches' daughter Fooled You. She's six years old and not quite house-trained. The airdale in the corner is Job. He adopted me one rainy day fourteen years ago and has suffered every disease, injury, accident, and affliction ever known to man or beast. And this pup," she added with a smile that made her look scarcely older than the half-grown dog nuzzling her leg, "followed Aldo home a couple of weeks ago. As you can see, he's working hard on getting an invitation to stay."

"Does he have a name?" Tamura asked.

"He didn't for a while, but these last few days I've been calling him George," she replied, almost blushing.

"I guess he's got his invitation," Tamura said with a chuckle.

"Yes, I guess he has at that."

As they chatted, Tamura spotted several carpet remnant versions of Job, matching papier mache umbrella stands with cat's paw feet and Peaches' face, as well as several sculptures of Fooled You made of discarded telephone wire and faithfully painted black and white. Spotting them was like a game of camouflage.

"I'm not completely mad, you know, or perhaps it would be fairer to say that there is method to my madness," Lucy Speldon said following Tamura's gaze. "I have a shop, Lucy's Bazaar, near Walnut Square. I sell my own creatures, as well as those of a few friends. I have one legal partner, but the whole enterprise has turned into a collective. A number of my friends also sell work there and take turns minding the store, which means I have plenty of time to make things. I call it recycled art; everything is done with materials that would otherwise be discarded. I hate waste, and there is so much of it — from cars that only go twenty-five miles to the gallon, to the way we package food, right on down to our daily trash. Some of my friends call me cheap, but I just tell them I was a garbage collector in another life. This being Berkeley, no one dares laugh 'cause I just might believe it — which is a bit of a joke since I'm beginning to after all. Someone had to clean out all those castles where my friends were knights and princesses."

Tamura was beginning to feel as if she were being entertained by a favorite aunt. It was engaging, but it didn't have much to do with the murder investigation. To change the tone, she pulled out her notebook and said, "Tell me a little about your family, Lucy, the two-legged members."

"I guess they'll be in touch soon," she replied, looking her age for the first time. "The kids haven't even heard about Aldo yet. Dennis works for the Forest Service in Oregon. His boss has sent someone to find him in the back country. Emily has been in Italy in a graduate study program. They're on a break and she's traveling in Greece. Things will be easier when they get here," she added, as if talking to herself.

'Lucy, I'm sorry I have to ask questions but maybe it will be best if I plunge in. Perhaps you can start by telling me what happened before your husband went to the radio station and what you did during the evening."

"I don't mean to be evasive," Lucy Speldon replied, still scratching the collie behind the ears, "but before my answers will mean anything, you'll have to understand about Aldo and me. The trouble with so much of the world these days is it's full of terrifying amounts of facts, figures, formulas and what-have-you, but there's so little understanding. To get anyplace in your investigation, you'll have to go beyond Aldo's TV image and understand how things really were for him, won't you? The truth is, Aldo and I haven't been close for almost fifteen years. We lived together — I guess we even liked each other in an old-shoe sort of way — but we weren't intimate, not in any sense of that word.

"It wasn't always like that, of course," she went on, "I was only sixteen when we met, and seventeen when we married. Things were as hot as a hayloft on an August night in those days. Aldo came striding down from climbing in the High Sierra, and stopped for a glass of water at my Dad's summer cabin. I followed him for the next twenty years. And when I say followed, I don't use it as a figure of speech. I chased him up mountains, down rivers, through blizzards and even, God forbid, out of airplanes. A lot of the time I was scared but then so was Aldo—which was, of course, a lot of the reason he did it.

"We had the kids, bought this house, and along the way Aldo became an international celebrity. Eventually, like a sponge trying to mop up a lake, I absorbed all of Aldo I could. I was so full of him, I had no room for myself. Like so many of my contemporaries in what I call the 'last housewife generation,' I needed space to discover who I was. When I asked for it, our relationship simply collapsed. Aldo had a streak of megalomania common to crusaders—he needed his woman to be both foot soldier and cheerleader. When I wasn't always available to uncritically support him, he found others who were.

"You know, it's funny," Lucy Speldon continued. "The fact that Aldo had lots of other women never bothered me nearly as much as the fact that he needed them to feed his ego. It wasn't because he was a hedonist. I know I'm not making much sense but, until Sophie Warren, there seemed to be something false about most of his girlfriends. Anyway, back to the story. I hope I'm not sounding bitter, because I'm not. My decision to be more independent was the right one and I've made a life for myself I'm comfortable with. And don't let me paint Aldo the petty egomaniac, either, because it's much more complicated than that. I always felt we were friends at some deeper level, even when we couldn't talk to each other. If you can understand . . ."

Lucy Speldon's monologue trailed off and she started fumbling in her pocket. Tears traced the lines of her cheeks like spring runoff on an eroded slope. Tamura handed several tissues to the other woman, who was unabashedly sniffling and blinking.

"I don't know why I'm bawling," she said. "It's everything, I guess. A man's life. It's so many years since I've let myself cry for Aldo."

"Do you want me to come back tomorrow, Lucy?" Tamura asked, feeling awkward.

"No, no, I'll just make more tea. The bathroom is in the back if you need it. You're actually doing me lots of good," she added, attempting to smile through her sniffles.

Tamura set out in search of the bathroom, mostly to give Lucy Speldon a chance to collect herself. When she returned the older woman sat calmly by the window looking toward the Golden Gate. The sun was lower now, but it was still a fine, clear afternoon. Tamura noticed that despite her grey hair and wrinkled face, Lucy Speldon had the slim figure of a much younger woman.

"Well, to finish," Lucy said with a smile, "Aldo and I evolved what your generation would call an open marriage. We were old-fashioned—or I guess the slang now is 'uptight'—so we spared each other the details. Aldo went his way and I went mine, no questions asked or answers volunteered. It took a while to get comfortable seeing other men; these days your average high-school student has more experience than I did. But after a few years and a few incidents that would surely make you laugh, I worked it out. Lately I've mostly been dating Malcolm Curry, the photographer. We get together once a week or so, and now and then we take a short trip. He's been in New Zealand doing a magazine piece the last few weeks."

"Did your husband know about the relationship?"

"I'm sure he did, although we never talked about it. Malcolm specializes in nature photography and he and Aldo have known each other for years. The truth is that when Aldo finally realized the old days of my worshipping him were over, he didn't care what I did. He loved our kids, this house, and was comfortable with me running the domestic side of his life while he took his pick of any number of young ecology groupies. In a way, he had it made."

"Had things changed recently?"

"Yes, lots. The nuclear issue, of course, has been snowballing into the major political fight of the decade, and Aldo was in the thick of it. It offered him a chance to put his vision and experience

59

to work. He was one of the few who understood that at bottom the struggle isn't just about electricity, or even about pushing the button, but about a concept he called 'ghiah,' the interconnectedness of man with all natural systems in one great organism. Have you read J.E. Lovelock, Sara? No? You should. Anyway, after several years leading a dwindling band of followers, Aldo found he had the magic touch again."

"And then came Sophie Warren?" Tamura interrupted, interested, but afraid she might be subjected to the tirade of a true believer.

"Yes, then came Sophie, his true love. I don't mean to be flip. I do think it was the genuine article. Sophie was good for Aldo—so good that I think it must have been mutual. Anyway, between his excitement about demonstrations—at Seabrook, Arroyo Seco, Livermore—and Sophie, Aldo was born again. Even his figure benefited. It was out with the Scotch and chocolate cake around here and in with carrot sticks and Calistoga water."

Tamura leaned forward to pour herself another cup of tea. "Can you tell me more about Sophie Warren?"

"Only what you probably already know. She's a good poetic singer. Her work is simple and honest. In a funny sort of way, I was proud of Aldo for having the good sense to appreciate her."

"I gather that from an ecologist's point of view, Sophie's father is a top bad guy and that he and your husband weren't exactly enthusiastic about each other."

"Like the Capulets and the Montagues, Roger Warren and Aldo loved to hate each other."

"Do you think your husband got involved with Sophie Warren to spite her father?"

"I've asked myself that," the older woman responded, looking bothered. "Maybe, I just don't know. There are so many things involved and life can be so resistant to explanation. Oh, well . . ."

Tamura had sat quietly listening to Lucy Speldon ramble on about Aldo Speldon, Roger Warren and the environmental battles of the last two decades. Now, for the first time, she heard a false note. Everything had seemed quite straightforward and spontaneous until Aldo's motives had been questioned. Now Lucy was floundering. Why?

Instead of sitting back patiently and waiting for the cat to gradually back out of the tree, Tamura, sensing a possible breakthrough, interrupted with another question.

"Lucy, could Roger Warren have killed your husband?"

The color drained from the older woman's face and her normally animated fingers became stiff, almost clawlike. "I'm sure he didn't," she said with exaggerated determination. "Roger's whole life is built on tackling things head on. He isn't the type to shoot someone in the back. I absolutely don't believe he is capable of doing what was done at the radio station. He just couldn't have."

"You seem to be saying that Roger Warren could have killed your husband, but not from ambush?" Tamura added, her heart sinking as she realized she was compounding a serious error. She had tried to grab the cat, missed, and was now chasing it far out of reach.

"I most definitely am not," Lucy Speldon responded fiercely. "Don't you put words in my mouth. I'm saying Roger, that is Mr. Warren, simply couldn't have been involved. Just because his ecological views are distorted, doesn't make him a murderer."

Tamura didn't know what to think or say. Damn, she should have let Lucy Speldon ramble. Now, that she was on guard, there was nothing to do but try another approach.

"What about other people who might have wanted to hurt your husband?"

"As I've said, Aldo wasn't the easiest person to get along with," Lucy Speldon replied, sitting back and seeming to relax. "He had no patience for people he considered fools. His friends understood a lot of his vanity was a cover for shyness and made allowances, but there were definitely people who avoided Aldo. And I guess I should mention Walter."

"Walter?" Tamura questioned.

"Yes, Walter Bell. For years he was Aldo's chief assistant—you might almost say disciple—until they had a bitter falling out. It made me sad; I always liked Walter. It was about the time Aldo and I were going our separate ways, so I never understood all of the details."

Tamura glanced up from her notes and saw the older woman looked exhausted. "Lucy, I know you must be tired. I just need a few more facts and I'll let you get some rest.".

"No need to rush; you've been a good diversion. And I haven't been a very good hostess. Let me cut you a slice of tofu-cottage cheesecake. I invented it over the weekend using perfectly good left-overs."

Before Tamura could think of a polite way to beg off, Lucy Speldon was off to the kitchen. Old Job, hearing the refrigerator door, wobbled after her, licking his toothless gums.

7

Jack's on Sacramento Street at the edge of San Francisco's financial district gives the impression of a genteel, slightly dowdy, establishment going downhill with dignity. The presidents of corporations, senior partners of law firms, and officers of banks who make up much of the clientele, like it that way. It's the sort of place which couldn't exist in the cash-equals-flash canyons of Los Angeles, but is right at home in a city where rich and powerful are so deeply entrenched it pleases them to masquerade as unpretentious and plain.

Rivers was ten minutes late because he stopped to buy a necktie at a shop next to the parking garage. Jack's, he had remembered just in time, was so smug they refused to accept either open collars or credit cards. He cheerfully spent $25 on a rep tie with a muted stripe that would have been appropriate for lunching at the Yale Club and ambled into the restaurant, pretending he was a senior partner in Interest, Annuity and Dividend.

The elderly head waiter wasn't fooled. With a lifetime invested in separating parvenu from plutocrat, he barely glanced at Rivers' preppie tweed jacket or Brooks Brothers' shirt, letting his gaze drop immediately to Rivers' cowboy boots. I wonder if they have a shoe rule, Rivers thought: wingtips and penny loafers may enter, boots and sandals are sent to the modern steakhouse down the street.

Before Rivers had a chance to elaborate his theory, the old man turned and limped toward a table near the rear of the large *belle époque* room. Rivers followed, taking short steps so as not to run up the old man's heels, and letting his mind flash back twelve years to the last time he had lunched at Jack's. He had been celebrating passing the bar exam with three ambitious law school classmates. It had been a schizoid time; part of him wanting everything Jack's stood for, while another part wanted to grow his hair long and live simply in the country. After more than a little mental anguish, he had chosen the latter. True, he had long since quit the woods and many people thought his present job was a cop out in more ways than one, but he had no regrets. By conventional standards, he wasn't much of a success, but at least he had escaped the indignities suffered by his three friends. One was a slightly alcoholic partner in an establishment firm that represented a prominent Asian dictator, another a state senator who would shake hands with anyone, and the third had just missed going to jail on a political corruption charge after making a pile of money as a lobbyist for an asbestos company.

It was almost two fifteen. Jack's was fast clearing out. Only one man occupied a table in the right rear corner. Still full of caffeine, Rivers felt like a greyhound being led by a tortoise. Finally, as they crept close to their destination, the man at the table stood. He was a couple of inches over six feet, with a grizzly bear chest. A soft tweed jacket and blue paisley tie accentuated his ruggedness rather than taming it.

Rivers' extended hand disappeared into a vise of firm flesh. He had to tense all his YMCA weightroom muscles to keep it from being crushed.

Perhaps Pierce was right about the MBAs with their computers waiting to put Warren out to grass, Rivers thought as he met the man's steady, bleached-blue gaze, but it would take some tough MBA with a hell of a big pasture to do it. Close up, Rivers could see deep lines in Warren's ruddy face and folds in his heavy neck, but the older man had a firm belly, his own teeth, and a thick head of closely cropped grey hair.

"Glad you could come, Lieutenant. I thought this would be more pleasant than my office. Will you have a drink?" Roger Warren asked in a surprisingly mild voice.

"Yes, thanks," Rivers replied, admiring how Warren played host with a dignity approaching courtliness.

Warren nodded. An elderly man in a black suit and white apron approached. Jack's had obviously cornered the market on old white waiters with dour expressions.

"Scotch and water for me, John. And you, Lieutenant?"

"A dry gibson up, please."

"Do you eat fish, Lieutenant?"

"I've been looking forward to the petrale ever since we talked."

"Ah ha, you've been here before. You surprise me."

"No blue uniform and nightstick?" Rivers remarked with a smile.

"Let's just say you seem somewhat different from the police officers I've known." Warren's eyes wrinkled at the corners as he added, "And I say that even though I caught a glimpse of the price sticker on the back of your tie."

"Touché. Maybe I can paste it on my nightstick," Rivers replied laughing.

When Rivers thought about the lunch later, it was with real pleasure. Everything had been good—the drink, the food, and especially the verbal thrust and parry. Roger Warren had a dancing intellect, not a bit slowed by the soft pedantic homilies that can so often accompany a man's seventh decade.

After the last bite of fish, Warren put a pin in the balloon of small talk.

"You've come to find out whether I killed Speldon," he stated bluntly.

"Did you?"

"I guess I asked for that. No, I didn't kill Aldo, and I didn't hire anyone to do it either. If I had wanted him dead, I wouldn't have butchered him from ambush."

"You seemed anxious to talk when I called. Is that what you wanted to say?"

"Yes, and to admit that this whole business has me upset. I hated Aldo's guts but I wasn't remotely ready to have him stretched out on a slab. And I'm not delighted half the world woke up this morning and started pointing at me before they found their teeth."

"Forgive me, Mr. Warren, but you don't strike me as a man who gives much of a damn what anybody thinks of you," Rivers responded, pouring more coffee from the heavy silver pot.

"You're right. I'll skip the bullshit. There is more to it. I wanted to see you quickly to discuss some facts that are ... well ... personal and delicate. It's not that you won't discover them—it's just that ..."

"Does all your prefacing mean we're going to talk about your daughter Sophie's relationship with Aldo Speldon?" Rivers asked quietly.

Warren leaned forward in his chair, eyes narrowing. "You did your homework before you came out to play, I see. Well, even though you've obviously heard a version of the story, I'd like to have my say. For a number of years, Sophie and I have been estranged," Warren said, the old-fashioned word reminding Rivers that, chronologically at least, Warren was an old man.

"She has hated much of what I stand for and, the truth is, she probably even hated me for a while," Warren continued. "During the last couple of years I've been trying to tear down some of the walls between us. She has taken some conciliatory steps, too, and lately I've been thinking we were on our way to being friends. Her becoming involved with Aldo didn't make it easier, but I've learned to live with tougher things."

"And Speldon's death?"

"I don't expect to make more progress with Sophie until the dust settles."

"Until the killer is found, you mean?"

"That would do it, but I'm not naïve, Lieutenant. If you don't already know who killed Aldo, you may never find out. I deal with statistics and probabilities every day and I know enough about law enforcement to understand that you do too. If a murderer isn't caught standing next to a corpse, the odds of ever finding him aren't terrific unless he walks into a police station and confesses. Realistically, that means I've got to be able to convince Sophie that in the present political climate, Aldo Speldon is the last person I would kill. Do you understand anything about energy politics, Lieutenant?"

"Enough to know that you and lots of other powerful interests have bet a big pile of chips on being able to cover the country with nuclear power plants and that your daughter and Aldo Speldon were sitting on the other side of the table. Here in California you've been working on getting pro-nuclear law changes through a — how shall I say it? — through an adroitly lobbied legislature."

"You're ahead of me again, Lieutenant. I was going to tell you a long story, but you seem to have grasped the essentials. And even though you're probably a bird watcher at heart, I hope you will try to be objective. As far as the legislature goes, I won't pretend my hands are absolutely clean, but please understand unless we go nuclear in a big hurry, lights really will go out, factories will close and adequate heating will be a memory before the year 2000. When the big generators stop, it will be the so-called conservationists who have egg on their frozen faces, Lieutenant."

"Perhaps so, Mr. Warren, but I'd rather have a solar collector on my roof than live next to Three Mile Island. Just the same, I can assure you I've reached no conclusions about anything. But the fact that Speldon's death won't help you build reactors isn't conclusive of much. History is dripping with people whose emotions caused them to do things contrary to their financial self-interest. A recent incident in a TV studio comes to mind," Rivers added quietly, almost as an afterthought.

Warren didn't blink. "I can't deny that one. Aldo was a first-class bastard. He could pump out Olympian visions and poetic bullshit by the barrel, but in a fight he would kick you in the balls any time things weren't going his way. Even so, I never expected him to drag Sophie into a TV debate. For a moment I lost my head. It was stupid—uncontrolled violence always is. It was especially stupid right then because I'd won the debate and very few viewers could possibly have known what Aldo was talking about."

Warren leaned forward again and looked Rivers directly in the eye. "Lieutenant, I went for Aldo face to face. I didn't take him from behind in the parking lot."

"Do you have other children, Mr. Warren?"

"I have a son, Mark. He's a lot like me. He accepts the world as it is and tries to do practical things to improve the quality of life. He runs our operation in Canada, and maybe one of these days he will . . ."

"Is he there now?"

"In Vancouver. I talked to him this morning. He hates—I guess I should say hated—Aldo worse than I did. Mark grew up with Aldo's pettiness and dishonesty, but never enjoyed the battles. My son is not a killer, Lieutenant."

"And how do you explain your daughter?"

"I don't need to explain Sophie to you or anyone else. She's none of your damned . . ."

"I thought Sophie was the main reason we're sitting here," Rivers replied, forcing himself to mirror the older man by leaning forward and narrowing his eyes.

"Do you have kids, Lieutenant?"

"Two. Grade school age."

"Do you understand them?"

"I'm too busy picking up after them most of the time to even try."

"Has it occurred to you that, even when they're old enough to pick up after themselves, it won't change much? The wonder of being a parent is you can never understand them, and they can never understand you. Sophie has never realized it takes crap to produce a chrysanthemum. My life has been spent roaming the world, shoveling the shit. Sometimes I pile it up and sometimes I flatten it out, but I'm long gone when people come along to smell the posies. When Sophie was tiny, I was like a king to her. Even during her teens we were close, especially after her mother died when she was thirteen. But some time during her first year in college, I lost her. Or perhaps it would be fairer to say that she decided I was no longer worthy of her friendship. Almost overnight everything I stood for, was proud of, made her furious. When she found out I was hoping to build a hydro project the ecology fanatics claimed was in the Grand Canyon, she tried one last time to get me to understand what a Neanderthal I was. Instead of accepting that she and a lot of other people had a point on that one, I went down with all my guns blazing. We didn't talk again for over fifteen years. She's been in Europe much of the time and I've had plenty of time for regrets."

"But you haven't changed your politics. Warren Construction is not only a big part of the pro-nuclear lobby, it's involved in construction projects worldwide."

"No, I haven't changed my basic views. I never will. I'm a builder and I'm proud of it. I've made dams, roads, power plants and factories that have changed the face of the world for the better. The plain fact is that more than half the world is starving, Lieutenant, and you won't find many starving people who prefer miles of empty wilderness to good jobs and a full belly. But I've learned a little humility, too. No matter what you may have heard, I don't believe in clear-cutting the last redwoods. It's even occurred to me that technology can cause problems and science may never supply all the answers."

Rivers didn't say anything and Warren continued.

"I won't live forever, Lieutenant, and I want to enjoy the love and respect of my daughter before I'm too dead to appreciate it. Partially because of Sophie, I've been trying to trim my sails for quite some time."

"What about your stockholders? Dams in the Grand Canyon— or even *almost* in the Grand Canyon—can't be too popular, even with folks who use Warren Construction stock dividends to pay their dues at the country club."

"There you are, Lieutenant. The world has turned a few times since lefties like Woody Guthrie wrote hymns of praise to the Grand Coulee Dam. In the last few years, we've brought in a bunch of scientists and lawyers to see that we don't stub our toes again like we did on the Colorado."

"And you hate them, don't you?"

"Some mornings I do. I've never had much use for people telling me what I can't do, even if it's for my own good."

"Where were you last night at nine o'clock, Mr. Warren?" Rivers asked, again raising his eyes to meet the older man's.

"So, Lieutenant, the gloves come off. Will you be disappointed if I don't shift in my chair, wipe the sweat from my brow and confess? The truth is I was home alone in Mill Valley and no one can back me up. There's a young couple that live in a bungalow on my property; they do the gardening in exchange for their rent. They went to Yosemite for a long weekend. I was reading and had unplugged the phone."

"What were you reading?"

"The Co-Evolution Quarterly and bits and pieces of the Sunday New York Times."

"C.Q.'s strongly pro-solar, isn't it?"

"I learn more reading the other guy's propaganda than I do my own."

"Why did you unplug your phone?"

"Haven't you ever noticed how quiet it gets when the phone can't ring, Lieutenant?"

"Not a very sociable world view, is it Mr. Warren?"

"Come on, Lieutenant, who I talk to on the phone, when I take a crap, and how I wind my watch are my concern. If you have anything relevant to ask me, ask it so we can get out of here before supper."

"How many guns do you own?"

"I figured you'd get to that. Three dozen, if you count some antiques I'd be afraid to fire."

"How many workable shotguns?"

"Eight or so."

"Twelve gauge pump?"

"Perhaps half."

"Are they all in your possession?"

"I have a couple, maybe three, and my son has the others."

"Do the people who live at your place know where the guns are kept?"

"It's no secret. They're locked in a rack in my shop and the key is in my desk."

"Will it be okay if I send someone to your house to pick up the guns this afternoon? I can have them back in a couple of days. Also, I'd like to have one of my people talk to your employees. What are their names?"

"Patterson and Bostic—Hal Patterson and Barbara Bostic. They think living together without a license is sexier than getting married."

"They're probably right," Rivers said with a grin as he wrote the names down.

"They may be at that," Warren responded.

"Is it okay to pick up the guns? It's your right to say no. I don't have any evidence that would qualify me to get a warrant."

"I'll call Barbara and tell her to cooperate. If I had anything to hide Lieutenant, it would already be hidden."

"I'd prefer to have Lieutenant Orpac stop by unannounced, if you don't mind. They can call you to get authorization."

"As you wish, Lieutenant. Incidentally, I was shooting skeet yesterday afternoon and used two of the shotguns."

8

Tamura was sitting on the corner of her desk talking on the phone when Rivers came into their shared office a few minutes after four. Her work space was in the darkest corner of the room, an arrangement which neither she nor Rivers liked. Tamura thought they should share the workspace. Rivers wished he could make her disappear altogether.

"Oh, here's James now. We'll be right down," Tamura assured the plastic mouthpiece.

"Yes, inside ten minutes," she added.

Rivers thought she looked like a college kid making a date—excited and alive. He was crashing. The alcohol and coffee had worn off and he was feeling every minute of last night's lost sleep. On an ordinary day he would have made up a reason to sneak home early and sack out. However, it would take a first class excuse to escape today, and he was too wasted to concoct one. Instead, he collapsed into his swivel chair, lifted his feet to the edge of the scarred oak desk, and shut his eyes.

"James, don't flake out," Tamura almost yelled.

Rivers' eyes remained resolutely closed.

Tamura tossed a stuffed calico cat in his direction. Both her aim and velocity were better than she intended and the velour feline smacked its sprawled target firmly on the chin.

The cat was a memento of Rivers' first successful murder investigation and had become one of his two dozen good luck talismans. Now and then, when the tension between Tamura and Rivers thawed for a moment, they called the cat Ralph and made up Polish cat jokes. Once, when Tamura was in a particularly good mood, she had brought in a plastic fish for Ralph, sparking an argument over whether cats can safely eat fish bones. They didn't talk to one another for the rest of the day.

After an extended pause, Rivers partly opened one eye. Moving his right arm with exaggerated slowness, he felt along the floor on the right side of his chair until he found Ralph. He set the fuzzy toy carefully on his lap, opened the other eye, and began picking pieces of lint from its tail. With a melodramatic squint in Tamura's direction, he said, "One more attack on me or my animal before our nap is through and I'll file a P.C. 597. And because you probably don't know what that is, I suggest you go look it up and leave me in peace."

He folded his long arms around Ralph, settled even farther back into his old-fashioned swivel chair, and resolutely shut his eyes.

"James, you're impossible," Tamura snapped, as she stomped toward the door. "That was Lorenzo. He and Mary found a third body. So while you dream about making up phony cruelty-to-animals complaints, I'm going to deal with a real murder, which, in case you've forgotten, is defined in Penal Code Section 187 as 'the unlawful killing of a human being with malice aforethought.' And just in case you're interested, Mary and Lorenzo think there may be a connection with Speldon's killing, so they've been standing around in the mud holding the body for us."

By the time Tamura reached the bottom of the narrow back stairs to the parking lot, Rivers was a step behind. "Let's pick up some coffee on the way," he said as they pushed through the door into the late fall afternoon.

"Don't you think they've been kept waiting long enough?" Tamura asked irritably.

"Don't you think I'm the Lieutenant and you're my assistant?" Rivers snapped back, finally letting his annoyance show.

"Yes sir," Tamura replied, realizing with pleasure she had penetrated his Mr. Mellow facade. Rivers was famous for his aversion to departmental brass who won arguments by pulling rank and often claimed that standing on authority was the last resort of a small mind when its position was untenable.

Rivers got his to-go coffee at ¡Ay Caramba!, the burrito place on the corner of Grove. Tamura then continued west on University Avenue to the Berkeley Marina. She directed the car to within a few feet of the Bay before turning north on a frontage road. They passed a mooring area where the masts of a hundred Saturday afternoon fantasies crowded together like pins on the shoulder of a forgotten tailor's dummy, and then a boatel-motel complex, before turning west again. Now they were on a narrow lane bisecting a landfill jetty which jutted west into the Bay. Junipers, green-black in the fading light, tightly lined the north margin of the road.

"I run here a lot," Rivers said. "I've seen a few egrets lately and last week I saw some brown pelicans down past where the boats are moored."

Tamura relaxed a little as she pulled the Nova behind a patrol car and coroner's van a hundred yards beyond the KILO driveway. Rivers could surprise you once in a while she thought, glancing at the tall, slim man sitting next to her. Their eyes met for an instant. She noticed that his hazel eyes looked like brown-green mud. He was clearly exhausted.

No one was around, so they slammed the car doors to attract attention. Mary Finnegan immediately stepped from between two of the bushy trees and motioned for them to follow.

About twenty feet into the half light of the landscaped forest, they saw the driver of the morgue wagon leaning against a tree, smoking a cigarette. Lorenzo Jones was standing a few feet away, next to a lumpy tarp, his chocolate-toffee face almost invisible in the gloom. He slipped his foot under a corner of the grey plastic and casually flipped it back, revealing a small, thin black man, lying face down on a cushion of fir needles. He looked as peaceful as a sleeping child.

"Do the honors," Rivers said.

"Meet Willie Thompson — pimp, dealer, petty crook, et cetera," Jones replied. "He caught a knife in the gut. We rolled him to see if there was anything underneath, but he's back the way we found him now."

As he talked, Jones moved around the body, ending up next to Tamura. She felt herself enveloped by the scent of lilac. She could block out Lorenzo's aftershave, but when she felt his hand playing along the small of her back, she decided she couldn't ignore him any longer. A new man wasn't the furthest thing from her mind, but that didn't mean she was ready for a lilac-scented lady-killer whose

73

idea of romance was nuzzling over a corpse.

Leaning forward, as if to get a better view of the body, Tamura kicked Lorenzo Jones on the right ankle.

He suppressed a grunt and withdrew his hand as if he'd been stung. Tamura moved to the other side of the body, kneeling down to look closely at the dead man's carved belt buckle. She hoped she hadn't kicked too hard. It was one thing to keep Lorenzo at a distance, but she didn't want to make an enemy.

Tamura was somewhat relieved when an apparently unfazed Jones began to sing in a melodic baritone, "Oh don't spurn me, my Asian daffodil, don't cast me aside, my Oriental hummingbird . . ."

"Cut the crap, Lorenzo!" Rivers turned away from the corpse. "There's enough to do without your flirtatious bullshit. Understand?"

Jones looked surprised, and, swallowing a smartass reply, he snapped, "Yes, sir," with drill sergeant briskness.

Rivers' hands were curled into tight fists. He willed them to relax. Why had he come down on Jones so hard? Tamura could obviously take care of herself. And even if she couldn't, what was it to him? Maybe he was short-tempered because he was so tired, he thought, as he forced himself to focus on the problem at hand.

"What do we know, Mary?" Rivers asked.

"The killing occurred some time early last evening. We'll get a more complete report in the morning, but, considering the exposure, it will be hard to pinpoint the time. Carl poked around for quite a while and Phil and Ben just left."

"I think there's an obvious connection between this corpse and Speldon and Rathman," Lorenzo Jones interrupted with an assertiveness which dared anyone to disagree.

Tamura noted wryly that Lorenzo had apparently made the transition from aspiring lover to aspiring lawyer with little damage to his ego.

Rivers smiled to himself. Even though Lorenzo had just begun night law school, he had apparently learned that how you say something is more important than what you say.

"What's the obvious connection, Lorenzo, other than the fact that all three men were killed on the same night within a couple of hundred yards of each other?" Rivers asked politely.

"Obviously," Lorenzo continued in his best professorial tone, "the killer shot victim number one and victim number two at the radio station and then needed to absent the scene. To accomplish that objective, he ran around the muddy area near the studio and headed into these trees. Coming through, he met victim number three—this body here—and had to kill him too, because he— victim number three, that is—could identify him as being at the scene of the homicides of victims number one and two."

"Where did the killer get a knife?" Tamura interrupted. "As you pointed out, Speldon and Rathman were shot."

Jones didn't pause. "Of course, I gave that problem my considered attention. The killer was well prepared and brought the shotgun to do the original crimes and a knife just in case it might come in handy," he continued, obviously impressed by his own reasoning.

"Why was this Boy Scout running into the trees? Why didn't he just park in the KILO lot and leave by the main road?" Tamura persisted.

"Parking down here would be safer. There's nothing past KILO but the Bay. No one would be likely to come poking along on a rainy night. And, if the killer was parked down here, it would be a lot quicker for him to cut through the trees to get back to his vehicle than to go out through the parking lot and down the road," Lorenzo finished with growing confidence, sure that he was scoring points.

"What do you think, Mary?" Rivers asked.

"I admit it's natural to want to connect the killings, and I guess it could have happened the way Lorenzo described, but I doubt it. Willie Thompson was a small-time pimp when he could get that together. When he couldn't, he was a small-time anything else that came along. Lately it's been mostly drugs, I think."

"So, on a bad day he can't afford his Ripple. What's that got to do with his catching a blade?" Jones said, forgetting his law school voice.

"Lorenzo, what would Willie Thompson be doing standing around a bunch of wet trees on a rainy night?" Mary Finnegan asked.

"It's a pretty good bet he wasn't trying to spot a rare species of owl," Rivers added.

"He must have been down here to do some personal business, and I'd bet that's what got him the knife," Mary Finnegan continued, her soft voice drawing them all close together in the fading light.

"Isn't it possible there was more than one killer and that Willie here was in on killing Speldon and Rathman?" Jones asked.

"Phil and Ben discussed that," Mary Finnegan continued. "It doesn't seem likely. For all his faults, Willie's never been the kind to kill. And even if he was going to turn homicidal, killing Speldon or Rathman doesn't make sense. They lived in different worlds. Willie's only concern with the energy crisis was how to con PG&E into keeping his meter turned on. Remember, no wallets were taken and the killer wore big hiking boots. Incidentally, the boot tracks do head in this direction before the mud gives way to pine needles. Maybe we'll find something to change my mind, but I'll bet there was no direct connection between the killings."

"Sara?" Rivers queried, uncharacteristically using her given name. The caffeine had started to work and he was feeling better.

"I'd say the killer came through this way," Tamura said. "If the timing was right, Willie might have spotted him. But I find it hard to believe Willie would have been spotted in these trees—a black man wearing dark clothes on a rainy night. He may not have been a genius, but he had lots of experience at hiding. I just can't see him trying to bum a cigarette from a guy with a shotgun. Willie must have been involved with his own deal. Maybe it went wrong somehow and someone paid him off in a way he didn't expect. A lot of drug deals go down in these trees. It's secluded and you can see anyone coming."

Tamura turned to Lorenzo Jones. "What does patrol know about Willie?"

"What's there to know?" Lorenzo said with visible distaste. "He was just another loser trying to hustle a living from the streets because he didn't have the guts to go to school and take some responsibility for his life. When Dirty Frank Johnson got put away, it left a hole in the San Pablo Avenue pimping business. I heard Willie was trying to get something going with a couple of Frank's foxes, but he never had much of a chance. He just wasn't big or mean enough for the heavies to take seriously. Willie was born a small-timer."

"Death didn't improve him any," Rivers said quietly. "Mary, you and Lorenzo put in all the overtime you can stand. This could be our first break. It's your beat, so you should have a good idea who to talk to. I'll come up with help by morning."

"Our first big break?" Tamura asked with surprise. If it hadn't been for his matter-of-fact, slightly weary tone, she would have thought Rivers was being sarcastic. "I thought you agreed Willie probably wasn't involved in the Speldon killing."

"You suggested the reason. Whoever killed Willie may have seen Speldon's killer, his car, or something else that could help us."

"Catch the black pimp's killer, cut a deal, and catch the man who killed the important white dude. Is that it, Lieutenant?"

"Save your cynicism for law school, Lorenzo," Rivers replied. "With a little luck, maybe we'll catch them both. Anyway, let's rehash it when the sun's up. I'm going home before my kids forget they have a father. Tamura, will you check with the kid who's minding the phones? If there's anything even lukewarm, call me. By the way, did you learn anything from Mrs. Speldon?"

"Maybe, but it can wait until morning."

9

It was past six when Rivers got home. There was no light upstairs, so he parked Dartha in the driveway at the side of the brown-shingled house, walked around to the back and climbed the few wooden steps to Jeannie's back door. He had barely knocked when he was pulled into the kitchen, hugged firmly, kissed soundly, and told his kids were happily watching Star Trek reruns with Brian, Jeannie's son. Rivers yelled hello to the kids, gratefully accepted an invitation to supper in forty-five minutes, went back out the door and slowly climbed the narrow curved stairs that led from Jeannie's deck to his own smaller one above.

He paused for a moment and looked across the bay to the bright spires of the City of Saint Francis. He wondered if the black knight was sitting at the top of his tower looking at Berkeley. Somehow, Rivers felt he was—that Roger Warren's tough aggressive intelligence was assessing him. Friend or enemy, only time would sort it out. He slipped his key into the back door lock and pushed the rain-swollen wood with his shoulder. When it finally popped open, the force of his push propelled him halfway across the kitchen. Finding himself facing the refrigerator, Rivers opened it to make himself a very dry double "margib," a martini with three onions and two olives. Rivers carried his drink into the bathroom, where he ran the tub water hot.

One of the things he liked best about the big, square, turn-of-the-century house—owned half-and-half with Jeannie—was the bathroom. The tile was real, the sink was made of honest porcelain, the fixtures were brass, and the long tub stood on lion-claw feet. His grandmother would have described it as commodious, meaning it was big enough to absorb life's varied odors and vapors without resort to fans, room fresheners or other modern paraphernalia.

Next he padded into the bedroom and found a clean pair of jeans and a cotton sweater. Finally, he pulled the phone plug. Yes, Mr. Warren, he thought, I do know how quiet it can be when the phone doesn't ring.

As always, Rivers felt slightly guilty when he disconnected himself from the world. However, it was a condition easily cured by hot water and a couple of sips of gin. As Rivers stretched his long legs to the end of the tub, he fished an onion from the bottom of the glass with the tip of his tongue. He always ate the onions before the olives.

So many questions and so few answers, he reflected as he let his tired eyes close for a minute's rest. Could they be dealing with a political killing, some weird offshoot of the worldwide nuclear madness? Was Tamura's hunch right, that the killer was some punk searching for macabre fame by slaughtering a celebrity? Or was the reason for the killings more conventional—lust, fear, greed, revenge, or one of the other biblical motives which could set friend against friend, wife against husband? So far, they hadn't enough decent evidence to decide. Until they did, their chances of catching the murderer would remain someplace between slim and nonexistent.

Almost an hour later, Rivers awoke to find Jeannie tugging his shoulder.

"James, amigo, at least get in bed before you conk out. What will the papers say if the ace Berkeley criminal investigator drowns in his own bathtub stinking of gin?"

Jeannie pushed up her sleeve and pulled the plug. "Come on now, you bad-tempered lout. Get yourself into bed."

"Uh huh . . . what time is it?"

"It's close to eight. Now move. I know how to get boys out of bathtubs and I'll twist your ear if you shut your eyes again. The kids can hang out downstairs for a couple of hours and then I'll tuck them in."

10

Rivers woke at 6:30, a crafty minute before the alarm crowed. It was still dark, but the air was light, promising another clear, cool morning. Within five minutes he had slipped into his sweats and shoes, was out the front door and jogging up the big hill that rises a thousand feet along the eastern margin of the city. He zigzagged along residential streets by the still dozing houses until he reached the Municipal Rose Garden, a lovely floral amphitheater terraced into the hillside in the 30s by the WPA. It stood as a graceful reminder that soup lines aren't the only way to deal with a depression.

After pausing a moment, Rivers continued jogging up the steep streets. The sun hadn't yet cleared the top of the hill when he did. From Grizzly Peak, the road which snakes along the crest, he looked down at the small city, a quilt of patchwork pastels scrubbed clean by heavy dew. Further west, the twin towers of the Golden Gate Bridge poked through a wall of fog, just then squeezing past the headlands back to mother ocean.

Rivers lowered his gaze. Almost unconsciously, he picked out the baroque stone City Hall, now used by the school district, and next door the 1950s plastic courthouse, both just west of the old downtown. Behind them he spotted his office window in the Coolidge-era police building. It brought him up short. Who the hell had killed Speldon and Rathman? Perhaps today a few of the knots would begin to unravel. Even a blind elephant is bound to find a peanut sooner or later if he keeps trunking, he remembered his daughter assuring him when he was stumped on another case.

Rivers smiled, stood on his toes, and raised his arms over his head. The act of stretching shifted his gaze to the Marina. On the north end he found the little spit which was home to KILO. He stared at it hoping for an inspiration. His mind was blank. After a long moment he shrugged and began an easy lope down the hill. Descending was his favorite part. Normally he named the dogs and sometimes the old trees and pretended life was easy. This morning, however, he ran fast, concentrating only on where he put his feet.

By the time Rivers showered, gulped down two glasses of fresh orange juice, half a grapefruit, and a bowl of Skinner's raisin bran, it was past 7:30. He moved quietly so as not to wake the kids, clutching a big mug of black coffee as he tiptoed down the front stairs. Jeannie would have to get them off to school one more morning.

Tamura was at her desk when he walked into the office ten minutes later. She looked rested and bright in a denim skirt and red flannel shirt, unbuttoned to the waist. Under the shirt a lavendar leotard outlined her breasts like cellophane over plump oranges. For perhaps the two-hundredth time, Rivers wondered if all Japanese women had constantly erect nipples, or if Tamura was special.

"It's a nice morning and I thought we might start with a truce," Rivers said, feeling slightly euphoric from his run.

"Okay, if you'll throw in a blackboard," Tamura replied.

"A truce is not enough? Vat do you hef in mind?" he asked in the thickest New York Jewish accent he could fake.

"Before we blunder on, I thought we should review what we think we know. I want to write the suspect's names—even the most remote ones—on the board."

"Sort of like the first day of grammar school," Rivers remarked, suppressing a laugh.

"Give me a break, James. You're the one who proposed the truce. Here is my idea. We put Speldon's and Rathman's names at the top of separate columns. Underneath I'll put the names of the people to whom they were most closely connected. Listing everyone isn't going to magically produce our killer, but it may turn up connections between people we've missed. It's a little trick I learned from 'Hill Street Blues,' " she concluded with a chuckle.

"Suppose the killer isn't on your list? Suppose he's just someone off the wall?" Rivers queried. "You made a good point yesterday when you said that media killings are more likely to fall outside normal patterns. In fact, you were so convincing I've been almost

81

ready to turn in my ball of yarn."

"Was that a backhanded compliment? It was a good point, and thanks for recognizing it, but it obviously makes sense to follow up the idea that the killer knew Speldon or Rathman. Even heroes can have personal enemies. Really, James, I'm convinced we can keep better track of the possibilities with a little graphic help."

"It seems like life mimicking art, but why not? Maybe a media crime needs a media solution. Design your list while I read Speldon's obits. When everyone arrives, you can explain what you're trying to do. Oh damn, I promised Mary I'd stop and get some decent coffee."

"Not to worry. It's all made," Tamura said cheerfully, nodding to a table in the corner as she walked out of the room.

Tamura was so delighted she almost hugged herself. Maybe Rivers was right; maybe she was trying to run the investigation like a detective movie. Why not, though? Movies were fun and it wasn't as if Rivers had a better idea on how to get organized.

The morning meeting got going less than fifteen minutes late. Tamura cajoled the officers into a ragged semicircle facing the blackboard, while Mary Finnegan passed the Dream Fluff donuts. Rivers got so interested in something Carl Burnett was saying, he missed the chocolate old fashioneds and had to settle for a French and a powdered jelly. If nothing else, Rivers had to admit Tamura was a beautiful printer and despite himself, he began to get interested in her exercise.

Tamura stood by the blackboard with a pointer. Her black hair bounced almost to her waist. Her smile signaled high spirits.

Carl Burnett thought it was a shame they hadn't had teachers with bodies like hers in Greenville when he was a kid.

Lorenzo Jones wondered if he should try a different aftershave.

"We're ready, Mrs. Miniver," Phil Orpac piped up in his best falsetto.

"I'll trust you all to stop smirking and pay attention or I'll rap your knuckles," Tamura said severely, ignoring Phil.

"Ooh, start with me, teacher," Lorenzo moaned to a chorus of laughter.

"I spent a few hours with Lucy Speldon yesterday," Tamura

ALDO SPELDON

Frank Speldon	Emily Speldon	Lucy Speldon	Sophie Warren	Other Lovers
(son)	(daughter)	(wife)	(lover)	(fill in for 5 years)

Roger Warren	Walter Bell	Malcolm Curry
(old antagonist)	(friend, turned enemy)	(wife's lover)

Opponents—	Enemies inside the
pro-development,	environmental movement
(fill in for 5 years)	(fill in)

Others?

FRANK RATHMAN

Mr. & Mrs. Sheldon Rathman	Susan Rathman	Eileen O'Hara
(parents)	(sister)	(roommate & lover)

Enemies at KILO?	Other enemies?	Other lovers?
(fill in)	(fill in)	(fill in)

WILLIE THOMPSON

Where do we start?

began quickly before a new outburst could begin. "She's over 60, but looks younger and seems about as sinister as my Aunt Keiko. Lucy and Aldo were married for forty-plus years. According to her, they'd evolved a fairly civilized 'you go your way and I'll go mine' lifestyle since the kids had grown up. She runs the arts and crafts store near Walnut Square and supports herself. Speldon had been doing an aging satyr number for several years, but she claims she learned to live with it. Apparently she was about to divorce him a few years ago, but liked the lawyer she consulted less than Aldo's current lover, so she didn't go through with it. Lucy has a lover named Malcolm Curry, the prominent nature photographer. I put his name on the list, although I must say she pretty well convinced me their relationship wasn't the stuff of murderous gestures.

Besides, he's in New Zealand. I'm having that checked, of course.

"On Sunday evening Lucy Speldon claims she curled up to watch Masterpiece Theatre at 9:00, but was interrupted when a friend called soon after, which must have been about the time of the murders. I talked to the friend, who is also her partner in the store. She confirmed the call. One of the Speldon kids, the son, is working for the U.S. Forest Service in Oregon, and the other, Emily, is a student traveling in Greece. Naturally, I'm trying to confirm that both of them were where they were supposed to be Sunday evening.

"As far as money is concerned, Lucy Speldon apparently has a good deal more than her husband did. She inherited a chunk and her shop makes a little. With Speldon's death, she automatically inherits the house, because it's in joint tenancy. Speldon's savings and other property, which includes royalties from several books that are still selling, goes half to the kids and half to several conservation organizations. She thinks it might all be worth a couple hundred thousand, but no more. Speldon didn't seem to take money very seriously and made no effort to cash in on his fame.

"In short, I'd be surprised if Lucy Speldon has a shotgun under her bed. There was one odd thing though. Everything was straightforward until I asked her whether Roger Warren could possibly have been involved. All of a sudden she made about as much sense as a speech at the United Nations."

"What does all that have to do with the blackboard?" Carl Burnett asked.

"As we go over each possible suspect, I'll put a mark next to their name—a plus if anyone suspects them, a minus if no one does, and a zero if we aren't sure. Unless there are any dissenters, I'll mark a tentative minus next to the Speldon kids and Malcolm Curry. If it wasn't for the fact that I'm sure Lucy was lying to me about Warren, I would mark her name with a minus too, but let's be conservative and give her a zero."

"Did Lucy Speldon know about Sophie Warren?" Rivers asked, focusing his eyes on Tamura's to stop them from making a quick detour to her breasts. Why was it so hard to keep his mind off her tits, anyway? He was old enough to know that even if her nipples were sweeter than cherry wine, it didn't make up for her vinegar tongue.

"Lucy told me about her before I asked," Tamura replied. "She claimed she thought Sophie had been good for Aldo."

"Lesson one in the homocide business is to pay close attention when anyone claims they're immune to the ravages of the green-eyed monster," Phil Orpac remarked.

"Talk to her yourself, Phil, but I'm convinced," Tamura responded.

"Phil, what did you get?" Rivers asked to forestall an argument.

"I dug into Rathman's personal life before I began chasing shotguns," Orpac said with a sour glance at Rivers. "Carl, with all due respect to your great grandpappy's murderous slaves, I couldn't come up with a whiff of anything out of the ordinary. Rathman lived with Eileen O'Hara. She's a freelance fashion designer, 28, bright, attractive, high strung, on the edge of making it. Under different circumstances I'd be delighted to take her to dinner or, for that matter, any place else she wanted to go. She and Rathman had been together a couple of years and were just beginning to talk about having kids, even though neither had any interest in marriage. On Sunday evening she was at a folk dance class at the International House with forty others. And unless I'm easier to fool than I think I am, she's genuinely broken up about Rathman's death."

"Did Rathman have any money?" Rivers asked.

"About what you'd expect. He owed on some school loans. His property consisted of a four-year-old VW Rabbit with a banged-in rear end, a water bed, a $1,500 sound system, half of which belongs to Eileen, and a houseful of flea market furniture. He never made a will, so in theory his parents in Rhode Island inherit, and Eileen gets nothing. But apparently, the Rathmans have already told her to keep everything. She's leaving tomorrow for the family funeral in Rhode Island. Next weekend Rathman's friends are planning some sort of memorial service. I'll dig some more but I've already talked to a dozen friends and neighbors without finding anything but shock and grief. Looks like his only worry was his job. KILO was recently sold to some people from L.A. and rumors are flying. Whenever a radio station changes hands, heads can roll in a hurry.

Just to be on the safe side, Rathman was in the process of making demo tapes to send around to the San Franciso stations."

"Demo tapes?" Ben Hall asked.

"In an electronic business, you use electronic resumes. When you're scouting job possibilities you send tapes to the stations you're interested in."

"Okay, Rivers said, "I gather we need to do more checking on Rathman. Does anyone disagree or have anything to add? If not, Tamura, why don't you add a few more minuses."

Holding out his cup to Lorenzo Jones, who had taken charge of refills, Rivers added, "Phil, I was going to suggest you follow up with Warren but that will have to wait. We obviously have to concentrate on Willie Thompson. My idea, and believe me, suggestions are welcome, is that you — Mary, Lorenzo, and Ben — coordinate sweating every pimp, prostitute and dealer in town. No rough stuff, but we need to move fast."

"Sounds like the Gestapo," Tamura remarked.

"How many civil liberties are those three corpses enjoying this morning?" Carl Burnett commented quietly from the back of the semicircle.

"I agree," Phil Orpac said, clasping his hand behind his head, his compact body hunched forward in his chair. "Anyway, Sara, nobody's going to get hit with rubber hoses. We'll just call in favors, make threats, and hope for the best. I'll be surprised if someone on the street doesn't tell us something soon so we'll quit interrupting their movie."

"Enough philosophy, who knows anything about KILO?" Rivers asked, glancing at the wall clock.

"KILO, the heavy one at 86.5 AM and 107 FM. We turn you on," Lorenzo contributed in his lilting baritone. "They used to be into sex, drugs and rock and roll. When they were really down to seeds and stems on Haight Street, they were playing the Commander Cody song on KILO — if you get my drift. Lately they've been going through a musical identity crisis, trying to find something that will fly in the 80s. Then this L.A. outfit with big bucks stepped in and bought a chunk . . ."

"Sounds like you've been sweet-talking some lady deejay, eh

Lorenzo?" Tamura asked.

"I get around, that's all," Jones replied, sounding uncharacteristically embarrassed.

"Cut the bullshit, Lorenzo. Ben's been spending time we don't have checking out KILO. If you know something, open up," Rivers demanded.

"Okay, okay, counselor," Jones said, looking at the floor as he pulled a rolled-up magazine from the back pocket of his sharply pressed uniform pants. He passed it to Rivers without unfolding it.

"I don't think I've ever seen a black man blush before," Mary Finnegan said. "What is that, Godzilla meets Hustler?"

"It's the October issue of *The Black Capitalist — The Business Magazine for Black Americans,*" Rivers read. "The feature article is about Federal Communications Commission policies designed to encourage minority ownership of radio and TV stations. Lorenzo, I appreciate your showing this to us. When the rest of these cynical bastards are picking up early-retirement checks and guarding banks for beer money, you'll be laughing all the way to your penthouse. I gather KILO is mentioned in . . ."

"Yes," Jones interrupted, and smiling at the others as if he were already board chairman. "A few years ago, the federal government set up a loan program to help minority applicants qualify for licenses to operate new stations and a fund to help buy existing ones. A group of black and Spanish — I mean Chicano — entertainment types got a license in L.A. Their format was a combination of reggae, salsa, and a kind of modern jazz called 'fusion.' Before you could say Bob Marley and the Wailers, it went from being a tailender to the top of the FM rating book. The same group, with some Bay Area partners, bought into KILO. They're monkeying with the format and moving the studio to a big warehouse south of Dwight on Ninth."

"It would have helped if you had told me that yesterday, Lorenzo, but I guess I still would have been down there talking to the employees," Ben Hall sighed.

"Did you learn anything worthwhile?" Rivers asked.

"Yes. It turns out I did a favor for one of the engineers a few years back when I didn't see a couple of joints lying on the floor of his pickup after a traffic accident, so I had an in. KILO's a pretty integrated place, but there is some racial tension. Even so, Rathman was generally thought of as a decent guy. He had a habit of tumbling the ladies though, and that got him into hot water a couple of times. There are about twenty-five employees, not counting the freelancers, who I haven't looked at yet. I ran the regulars through the computer. If you eliminate traffic and minor juvenile, you're left with two. Two garden variety drug possession busts and the armed robbery of a gas station fifteen years ago. I am going to dig some more today, but I agree Willie Thompson is more important."

"Thanks, Ben. You too, Lorenzo," Rivers said. "Sara and I will show the flag later this morning. Before we quit, let's finish our chart. At least for now, I suggest we put a zero next to the nuclear industry people. There is no evidence they were involved and even the media is downplaying conspiracy theories this morning."

"By the way, James," Tamura interrupted, delighted that "Sara's chart" had become "our chart." "I cut the obits out of the San Francisco papers. We'll have the *New York Times* later in the morning. If anyone comes across other material on anyone related to the case, tack it on the wall. Since we don't know what we're looking for, we may as well be thorough. I . . ."

"Sara," Mary Finnegan interrupted, "Roger Warren, Sophie Warren, and Walter Bell, whoever he is, still have no checkmarks."

"Bell's an old friend of Speldon turned adversary. He works for Global Oil in Richmond."

"After we finish at KILO, you should talk to this guy Bell," Rivers said to Tamura. "Or, on second thought, maybe you'd better arrange the meeting for after work. I'll tackle Sophie Warren later today."

"What about the old man, James?" Phil Orpac asked.

"Oh, he's a suspect all right, but I'm inclined to ignore him for now. Let's see how he does in a waiting game."

"Quick, James. You're down to your last silver dollar. The coin is in the air, double or nothing. Heads Warren did it, tails he didn't," Carl Burnett almost whispered, reaching for the last donut.

"Tails," Rivers said, wondering if he needed to remind anyone he had never won the office football pool. "What do you think, Carl?"

he asked instead.

Burnett dipped half of the donut in his lukewarm coffee, munched quietly, then wiped his fingers on a paper napkin. "Phil has just about got me believing Rathman wasn't the main target, although we obviously need to take a look at some of his lady friends and, even more important, their friends. I don't make sense of it with Speldon either. You asked me to think about how the killing was done. The more I do, the stranger it seems; almost like whoever did it wanted to prove he was important. All that gore just isn't a stylish way to kill someone. A pro will go for a single shot or two from up close with a small gun, while amateurs generally prefer the more exotic methods—poison, fire, a faked accident or something else designed to look like natural death. All I can come up with are two words: hate and crazy," Carl continued, his quiet voice commanding attention. "I see those men with their heads almost blown off and I think of the killer acting out of some crazy anger. One question especially bothers me. How premeditated was it? In a way, it seems almost spontaneous. It's as if a passerby sauntered up to the window and blasted away. I don't mean it happened that way, but you asked me for what amounts to a gut reaction. I'm telling you it seems cold-blooded and casual, as if General Patton had commanded his tanks in shorts. I can't help thinking that if the killer had had time to plan, he would have gone about it in a different way."

"The killing obviously wasn't completely random. There must be some connection to Speldon or Rathman," Mary Finnegan interjected.

"I'm with you on that, Mary," Burnett answered. "The killer didn't go out on Shattuck Avenue and take potshots at secretaries on their lunch break, or try to shoot a rock star at the Cow Palace. He apparently had some reason—even if it was crazy—to shoot at that particular window. Just the same, I'm not sure we're going to figure it out the way we're going about it."

"What the hell else should we be doing, Carl?" asked Rivers, with more than a little annoyance in his voice.

"Suppose the killer is nuts. He hears Rathman on the radio a few times or reads something controversial that Speldon wrote and goes snap for some completely off-the-wall reason. Is there anything we're doing now that would lead us to him?"

"Carl is right," Phil Orpac said, as he stood and stretched. "In this town, people have been killed because the moon is in Scorpio. And while we're talking about crazies, let's not forget to follow up on the calls that Lassiter is getting. Ralph the Rooster has confessed again, and so has old Annie McAlpirin. There are some odd calls too; one from someone claiming he's a grad student who apologized for killing the wrong people."

"What about him?" Rivers asked, looking at Lassiter.

"The conversation only lasted a few seconds. He sounded kind of desperate. His voice was just a whisper," Lassiter answered. "He apologized and hung up. Lieutenant Orpac told me to call the University to see if they have anyone named Strange registered. It was closing time and they said they would run it down this morning."

"How do you know his name?"

"I don't. Like I said, he was whispering. I'm not sure what he meant when he said Strange, but I think he was referring to himself."

"How did Warren's guns check out?" Tamura asked, gathering her papers.

"Two had been fired recently. One of those was a twelve-gauge Remington pump which could have been the murder weapon. Warren had a good supply of the common types of shot, including the brand used Sunday," Burnett replied.

Rivers stood up. "Let's quit for now. Tamura, don't wander off. We'll leave for KILO after I brief the Chief. Oops! Wait a minute Mary, Lorenzo. There's one more thing. Carl has a good point; maybe it was something said on the air that set the killer off."

"We listened to the tape of Sunday night's show while we were waiting for you," Tamura responded as she moved over to the coffeemaker again, trying hard not to spoil a good moment with a grin.

"I . . . Well, good," Rivers responded a little lamely.

"It's easier to see white folks blush, isn't it?" Jones said, making no attempt to hide his grin.

"It seemed so ordinary, and when things got busy I forgot to mention it," Tamura said, not wanting to end up with Rivers mad at her again. "It's on the machine on my desk. I was going to suggest you listen to it, just in case I missed something."

"While we're at KILO, let's get everything Rathman said on the air for the last six months, assuming they keep it," Rivers responded, ignoring her. "Also, someone should call Lucy Speldon and get her to dig up Speldon's calendar for the last year, as well as any recently published articles. Carl, would you wade through the material for a start? I know it's outside your job description, but if there's a red flag anyplace, I know you'll spot it."

The large, rumpled, impassive man was the only person in the room still sitting.

"James, I deal with fingerprints and footprints these days, not vague suspicions. Still, you obviously need all the help you can get, so I guess if this is an exception, I'll . . ."

"And then there's your Great Grandpappy hanging the wrong fellow, isn't there?" Mary Finnegan added matter-of-factly. "It embarrasses you, doesn't it?"

Carl Burnett turned and looked right at her, round eyes wide and expressionless. It was his dead fish look, the one that always scared Tamura when it was directed at her.

Mary Finnegan stared back pleasantly. For what seemed like an impossible length of time, neither blinked.

Finally, with a hint of a smile that Rivers thought was to cover embarrassment, and Tamura thought was cute, Burnett said, "Yes, Mary, it does. I haven't much more use for lawyers than Mrs. Speldon does, but I've never advocated hanging them indiscriminately to deal with the surplus."

"I should hope not," Lorenzo Jones boomed indignantly.

11

Rivers thought Chief of Police Roger Bacon was an opportunistic, manipulative bastard. Now and then, when he caught himself admiring the man, he thought it must be time to turn in his badge, pack up his kids, and shuffle on down the turnpike of life.

"Well, James, it's good of you to drop by," Bacon said as he strode briskly into his outer office at 9:15 and shook hands firmly. Rivers hunted for a reply as Mrs. Fosdick, the Revlon-red-crowned dragon who had guarded the inner office through the incumbency of five police chiefs, looked on curiously. Was the Chief's remark a sarcastic comment on the fact that Rivers hadn't reported the day before, was it just small talk, or both? It was an understatement to say Roger Bacon had a sorcerer's knack for blurring the straight-forward with the disingenuous.

"Morning, Roger. I would have come up yesterday, but when we discovered the third body, the day got away from me," Rivers heard himself reply heartily.

Rivers had worn his best outfit: a blue blazer, indigo-dyed Italian denim pants, and a grey shirt with a muted red stripe. He had even polished his cowboy boots. At the morning meeting, in contrast to Phil, Carl, and Ben, he had felt almost regal. As he started to brief Bacon on the day's agenda, however, he realized that next to the Chief's bespoken grey suit, blue silk shirt (exactly the same shade as his eyes), soft black Italian shoes, and red paisley tie, he looked like a house moth at the court of a Monarch butterfly.

Bacon directed him to the sofa and chair near the window and they sat down. The Chief had installed the furniture at his own expense, apparently to demonstrate he didn't need to hold the world at bay from behind a typical police bureaucrat's battered fortress of a desk.

Rivers outlined the case, careful to be thorough. Bacon said nothing but sat easily, ankles crossed—no skin showing between trouser hem and dark grey socks.

Rivers was not sure how his narrative was being received, and he was relieved when Mrs. Fosdick entered with a tray holding a diminutive copper coffee pot.

Bacon poured. The coffee was Turkish—bitter, aromatic and good. Little lumps of sugar nestled in a cut crystal bowl. After several sips, Rivers forgot his selfconsciousness, finding it unexpectedly pleasant to finish his rundown and conclude with an outline of the day's assignments.

After a pause, Bacon nodded. "Very good, James, very professional. You have my complete confidence. I don't mind telling you that clearing this thing up is important. Of course you know that for fifty years, going back to Vollmer, Berkeley was rated as the top small city police department in the state, perhaps even the nation. I see my role here as leading us back to that high ground. We lost a lot of credibility during the political disturbances of the 60s and early 70s, but we're definitely on the upswing now. As you know, I believe a force the size of ours can be more effective than a big city department—or even a national police organization, perish the thought. We may not have every sophisticated piece of hardware, but we can make up for it with intelligence, closeness to the community, and the speed that comes with being small and less bureaucratic. My job—our job—is to prove that a city the size of Berkeley can take care of its own law enforcement problems efficiently, even brilliantly."

Rivers didn't respond. He couldn't think of anything to say.

"If we fail to find Aldo Speldon's killer, it won't help us prove that, will it?" Bacon asked rhetorically.

Rivers stood up, hoping that if he acted as if the meeting were over, it would be.

Bacon stood too, offering his hand. "One more thing, James. I made a few calls to old friends who enjoy, shall I say, influential positions in several of our nation's security agencies. Given the crucial importance of the nuclear issue, I knew they would be keeping an eye on developments within the industry. Perhaps the information they've sent along will surprise you," Bacon concluded with a smile.

The smile, Rivers thought unkindly, was similar to the expression Jeannie's cat Artemis got when he deposited a freshly killed mouse in the kitchen. Just the same, Rivers was curious and had to restrain himself from following when the Chief moved over to his rust-colored standing desk.

Bacon extracted a single sheet of blue paper from a vertical storage bin. Rivers remembered the Chief's memos were color-coded but couldn't remember what the colors signified. Some detective I am, he thought, as he wondered idly if Bacon ever regretted not having a sitdown desk. Probably not, he concluded.

"I'm sure you remember blue is the color I use for highly confidential information," Bacon said in a tone that indicated he had read Rivers' mind. "This is a summary, of course. Do what you think necessary."

Rivers was almost out the door before Bacon continued. "Oh, by the way, James, I've had a call from Roger Warren."

Rivers paused and decided not to take the bait but to wait for Bacon to go on.

Instead, after a polite interval, the older man simply smiled and invited Rivers to drop by the one o'clock press conference.

"Fucker," Rivers muttered to himself as he walked down the hall.

12

On their way to KILO, Rivers and Tamura acted as if they had mutually decided silence was the best way to maintain their spirit of conscientious neutrality. Rivers even refrained from grimacing at Tamura's less than orthodox traffic maneuvers. She, in turn, suffered in silence when he insisted on a stop for coffee. When they reached the station, things were miraculously harmonious. Rivers suggested Tamura tackle managing director Dorsey while he wandered about chatting up the hired help. She told him it was a good idea. The two officers even managed to exchange slight smiles before going their separate ways at the studio's front door.

Tamura took the steps to Dorsey's second floor office two at a time. As she bounded up the last couple with no shortness of breath, she decided to postpone the jogging program she had agreed to start with her friend Terri. No sense chasing myself in circles if three glazed donuts don't slow me down, she told herself cheerfully.

The door to the small, empty reception room was open. Tamura walked in. The door into the next room was open as well. Tamura was waved through by a huge black hand.

As she entered, Tamura saw that the great hand was connected to an even bigger arm, and the arm to a correspondingly massive shoulder. Opening her eyes wide, she was able to see that the oversized body parts were connected in the normal way to form a well-proportioned, if huge, man. She took him to be Charles Dorsey.

Dorsey sat in a large padded swivel chair, feet up, talking into a white phone. His expensive new desk, built on the same scale as the man himself, would have been at home on the executive floor of the Transamerica Pyramid. Instead, it was jammed into a small, tacky room, the walls of which were papered with a rogue's gallery of predictable rock stars.

95

Tamura sat and examined the performers arranged cheek by jowl. They all looked as if they would just as soon have been elsewhere, with the exception of Jimi Hendrix, who didn't seem to care.

Tamura's musings were interrupted when Dorsey, seemingly in one continuous movement, cradled the receiver, lifted his legs off the desk, stood, and gave her a toothy grin. Impressed, Tamura forgot the sleaziness of the surroundings, smiled assertively, and extended her small hand.

"Well, dear sister, I'm supremely appreciative for the discerning sensitivity and unimpeachable sagacity of the powers that be in our local gendarmerie that has resulted in their dispatching you to conduct this tête-à-tête rather than that insufferable prick, Rivers."

Although Tamura had often described Rivers in much the same terms, she found herself bristling a little at this outsider's attack. Her annoyance wasn't sufficient to overcome her ingrained Asian tact, however, and she said nothing. She concentrated instead on retrieving her hand from Dorsey's grasp, which she was surprised to find was as exciting as it was powerful.

"How can I be of help?" the muscular giant purred.

Tamura censored an almost flirtatious response, hoping her face hadn't given her away. This was a murder investigation, not a singles bar, she reminded herself as she gave her hand a jerk only to find Dorsey had let go a split second before.

To get things on a more businesslike track, Tamura reached into her shoulder bag and grabbed notepad and ballpoint. "You could start by giving me some background on KILO, then follow up with any current politics or gossip that might possibly be relevant. I can tell you frankly we have no suspect, so it's important to sift as much general information as we can."

"Just the gossip would fill volumes," Dorsey laughed, wetting his prominent lips slowly and winking.

Tamura concentrated on the green lines of her empty notepad.

"KILO is an intimate, oddly isolated, and above all, highly verbal, subculture," Dorsey continued, settling into his chair and transferring his gaze from Tamura to the middle distance. "But you said you wanted background. I'll give you a short, sweet history which, as it happens, borders pretty close to the truth.

"KILO was one of the few good things to start the year Nixon beat McGovern. Since then, we've proven once again that if a rag-tag bunch of have-nots work their asses off, they can eventually make it in the land of opportunity. When we started, the established AM stations had divided up what they assumed was the market. There were a couple of news stations, several that played pop, a couple that played top-40 rock, one with a talk show format, and so on. They all had nice, safe relationships with the ad agencies, record companies, etc. Not surprisingly, they didn't have the welcome mat out for hungry black folks who wanted a seat on their gravy train.

"Our only chance was to be different. Almost by default, we became the FM radio voice of the left-outs—the hippies, students, blacks, Chicanos, and even..." Dorsey added with a nod at Tamura, "a hip Asian or two. Our sound changed a lot from year to year: funky folk, what we used to call 'movement bluegrass,' a little acid rock, a dash of Motown, and plenty of new-style electric jazz."

Tamura listened to classical music, now and then switching her dial to a country station to indulge her passion for Willie Nelson, Emmylou Harris, Jimmy Buffet, and other neon cowpeople. How could KILO get away with presenting such an odd combination of music under the same call letters? She was about to ask but decided it was better not to interrupt a monologue gathering momentum.

"More than a little of our success has come from our public affairs and news programming," Dorsey continued, absorbed in making triangles with his enormous fingers. "Music stations have traditionally invested as little time, energy and creativity in words as they thought the FCC would allow. The result is the repetitious hourly headlines and boring late night public affairs interviews you're used to. With every second person in Berkeley having a university degree and the rest being alumni of one or another anti-war, civil rights, or eco-freak organization, we gambled there was a market for a more intelligent format.

"We started in '72, doing a little of our own investigative reporting, and specializing in interviews with every controversial, wigged-out personality who passed through the area. It worked so well we're still at it. The main difference is that now the people who work here take themselves more seriously. The jive-ass brothers, radical feminists, and inscrutable Asians who put our news and public affairs programs together don't agree on a damn thing except they all want to grow up to be Dan Rather. Anyway, to keep this short history short, listeners liked our combination of good music and good reporting almost from the beginning. With a dip or two, our audience share has been up every year. Two years ago, we shocked the socks off the establishment stations when we broke into the top dozen or so outlets in the market. Of course, by then radio had changed. The big AM stations who were trying to appeal to everyone were going the way of the *Saturday Evening Post,* and our competition was mostly FM—specialty stations with stereo broadcasting equipment. In fact, the AM market took such a dive around here, we bought an el cheapo band as a hedge against the future. But our success created its own problems; we were literally getting too big for our britches."

Dorsey's sweeping gesture and contemptuous glare took in the whole studio.

"We were trying to play in the same league with Cox and Golden West, using what amounted to a couple of tin cans and a piece of string. For example, we could easily have tripled our audience, except for the minor problem that our signal couldn't be heard past Vallejo. If you have ever been sailing, you know that you can make a small boat go faster by adding more sail only up to a certain point. If you add too much, you simply dig a hole in the water. Things never got to the point where we were bailing, but we have badly needed a bigger boat for a long time. To survive it, we were forced to toss a lot of stuff overboard. Or to put it more accurately," he added with a chuckle, "we were forced to chuck what was left of our radical-bluegrass, folk and R&B in favor of a faster beat and a pile of money. It's really okay, though, since it was time for a format change anyway, and the venture capital we collected is buying both a new transmitter and a new studio."

"You mean you sold the station?"

"That's it precisely. Since I announced the sale a few months ago, things have been a little tense around here. But don't read too much into that. I can't imagine any employee holding a grudge large enough to off one of my best people."

"You sold the station, yet you're still here?" Tamura wondered out loud, realizing it was obviously Rathman's death, not Speldon's, which loomed large to Charles Dorsey.

"Of course I'm still here. Except maybe for this new desk, I'm the most valuable item at KILO. The new people bought my brains and my talent as much as the station," Dorsey said smiling a wicked smile. "Oops, I see by your delicately disdainful expression that I've offended. So sorry, but modesty doesn't become me. In the NFL, a large brazen man beats a large modest one every time. If you're small *and* modest, you're a spectator. The business world may be a bit more subtle, but the idea is the same."

"Who exactly bought your station, Mr. Dorsey?" Tamura asked sharply, deciding not to be mocked.

"All right, Sister. I could tell you had some juice. Some very slick brothers from L.A. They also dabble in record companies and sports franchises. I kept a big hunk of KILO stock, of course, along with a five-year management contract, at a figure even I couldn't refuse. If you come around this side of the desk, I'll show you what their Midas touch has produced."

Tamura didn't get up. Instead she craned her neck to see what Dorsey was pointing at. Beyond the blood-red sail of a small boat moving in the direction of the Albany shore, a steel tower was under construction.

"In this business, the power is in the tower. When that thing starts booming, seven million people will be able to pick us up. We've already moved our two-bit AM operation to a corner of our new studio building on Parker, just across from Fantasy Films. The FM studios, offices, and my suite still need a lot of work, so we won't move the main operation for another three months."

"But you admit your employees weren't too happy with the switchover?" Tamura asked, still feeling combative.

"I don't *admit* a damn thing. This is Berkeley, sister. You know what that means? Lots of sound and fury over everything and nothing. Two WASPs who — when they weren't stoned — claimed to be Marxists kicked up such a fuss I had to ask them to walk. Big deal. Sure, they had talent, but talent hangs from trees in this neck of the woods. And anyway, since the Soviet Union began beating up on little countries, their politics have been pretty passé.

"Let me lay it on you straight, my friend," Dorsey said with a big sigh. "Intense, visionary manipulation is what this business is all about. I happen to be very good at it. Change is not part of the game, it *is* the game. Ask yourself this: who still listens to the big middle-of-the-road stations that used to make dudes like me deliver at the back door? So I put in a new sound. So some people resisted. So the radical fringe acted weird. So what else is new? Sure, some listeners will bitch about too much new wave and turn us off. A few more employees will leave. The truth is though, that most people are just naturally fickle. They'll be lapping up our sound before the new year."

Dorsey's gaze drifted back towards the new tower. Tamura again leaned forward. He was right. The truncated steel structure did have a certain raw beauty.

Dorsey's voice was softer when he spoke again. "Nasty, grey day. Nasty murderous madness. Frank was a good man. A friend. He had a good education and a genuine streak of creativity. More important for KILO, he knew how to get along without making anyone feel he was better than they were. It's a goddamn waste. Mostly you let yourself forget about all that craziness churning away out there. But when it brushes this close, it spooks you. It definitely spooks you.

"Ask all the questions you want about KILO, and about Frank Rathman, but I don't think you'll find the answer here. What happened to Frank was just part of a random, senseless eruption that's in danger of consuming us all. When the religious freaks tell me Armageddon is just around the corner, I listen, sister, I listen."

Tamura looked up in surprise. First the up-front flirting, the heavy success rap, and now Watchtower rhetoric. Who is this man?

Dorsey winked, sensing her question. "My father was a minister; Church of the Divine Holiness in West Oakland. As much as I loved him, I always laughed at his messages of death and destruction. Now I'm not so sure. He may have had a pipeline to the great black

Jesus in the sky after all. But let's get back to business. I don't really know what to tell you. Frank was a genius at avoiding confrontation. Whenever people were uptight, he was always trying to get them to talk things out."

"You're doing fine," Tamura said when Dorsey seemed unsure whether to continue.

"Frank simply didn't engage in backbiting. If he had a fault, it was his refusal to be judgmental. I really don't believe he had any enemies, except maybe the Marxists, at the end. If one of the consultants helping with the format changes had been put down it would at least make a crazy sort of sense. But then, why should killing Frank Rathman add up to anything? The news services assume the great white environmentalist was the target and that Frank was just an unlucky piece of background. Isn't that what you think too?"

"Aldo Speldon may turn out to be the target, but we have to cover all the bases," Tamura replied, realizing vaguely she was borrowing clichés from the wrong games. "Let me ask you about Rathman's activity with the union," she added quickly.

"I get you now. But you're wasting your time. There's nothing sinister about it. Until recently, we were one of the few Bay Area stations with no union. When we were new, we simply couldn't afford to pay AFTRA scale. Most of the employees understood and didn't hassle me. In turn, I ran this place a lot looser than any union shop. The Mediamix deal changed all that—although it took me a while to realize it. Suddenly we had enough money to pay people better, but I decided to get rid of the worst of the oddballs first. There was no bloodletting, but there were just enough changes for a lot of people to get needlessly paranoid."

"Job insecurity plus a pay grievance equals union," Tamura interjected.

"You got it. Frank wasn't the leader of the pro-union drive, but he was for it. He was never obnoxious though, like the radicals, who acted like we were involved in round one of the revolution. In fact, Frank got into a nasty argument with them in September when I let them go. They claimed I was guilty of discrimination because of their union activity. Frank agreed with me that they were so irresponsible and unprofessional they deserved to be fired. Anyway, a month ago I realized having the union wasn't as bad as the all-out fight it would take to keep it out. Besides, the pay raise they demanded was slightly less than what I'd already budgeted. Two weeks ago I signed the papers. We even popped a couple of champagne corks and agreed to get on with the 1980s."

"It will be a big help if you can get me a list of everyone who has worked here in the last two years, including regular freelancers," Tamura said as she stood. "Note those who might possibly have a grudge against anyone or anything connected with the station, no matter how minor. I'll be downstairs for a couple of hours."

"Now, can I ask you something?" Dorsey said, still reclining in his chair.

"Sure."

"How about dinner?"

"Ask me again when the killer is caught," Tamura said over her shoulder as she made her way through the receptionist's office toward the stairs.

* * * *

Rivers was having a good time downstairs. KILO was as active as a beehive on a hot spring morning. He didn't understand much of what was happening, but he enjoyed the buzz. He was amazed at how quickly information came in, was repackaged and passed on. It was as if KILO was its own small planet, with only an electronic window to the wider universe. Or, perhaps more accurately, it was like a news and entertainment factory producing a version of reality structured for an audience that distrusted the alphabet-soup media conglomerates.

Rivers circulated through the honeycomb of partitioned work spaces. People were too involved in their personal movies to pay much attention to him. He had the feeling that as long as he didn't trip over a word processor, or bump into a news ticker, he could stay for a month. He paused by the window to a studio. A zaftig announcer in tight jeans and a semi-transparent silk top was confidently manipulating dials on a recording board while talking to two people. He opened the door and tiptoed in.

In danger of learning more than he wanted to know about trichomonas and non-specific urethritis, Rivers exchanged winks with the announcer and headed toward the heart of the electronic hive, an ON-AIR studio at the opposite end of the building from the one that had been wrecked Sunday evening. Here, a young, caramel-colored disc jockey in a white jacket and red beret joked with a bearded Caucasian newsman during a commercial break. Rivers realized after watching for a few minutes that while they didn't acknowledge his presence behind the glass, the men were playing a weird version of "electronic chicken" for his benefit. Their exchange of outrageously lewd and insulting banter during the taped commercials stopped a millisecond before the newsman went back live with the day's events. The object of the game was to squeeze in the final insult without letting one of the seven forbidden words loose on the air.

Rivers hung out by the studio door for a while after the news, enjoying the deejay's off-the-wall rap. Before long, a bearded, barrel-chested man in Oshkosh overalls pushed by, arms filled with notebooks and newspaper clippings. The newcomer slipped into Red Beret's chair as the latter stood, lifted the mike, did a jig and said: " 'Til midnight, my people, when yours truly is transformed from a mild-mannered morning man into that sweet-talking, soul-swinging casanova of the airways—Dr. Do Right. Now, here's the original Peking Man, Dusty Dan, to brutalize your senses for the next hour."

Rivers caught Red Beret as he stepped out the door. "Excuse me, I'm James Rivers, Berkeley Police. I'd like a few words . . ."

"Sure, man. The name is Christopher Ahmed Youngblood, but everybody calls me Jango. I'm no snitch, dig, but anything I can do to help, well man, consider it done."

"I don't really have anything specific to ask you, Jango. Maybe you can tell me what you think about what happened Sunday night."

"I don't know the names, man. But I do hear the voices of death. Normally I work the weird shift, midnight to four; the hours of the wolf. This morning I'm filling in. You're a cop, so maybe you can understand that there's a lot of heavy hate stewing out there."

Rivers nodded.

"I'm alone down here, so even one crazy-ass voice can fill a lot of space. It doesn't seem to matter how harmless my rap is, man. Sometimes I get the feeling some dude might blow me away if I insult his favorite rock group. I don't mean to badmouth everyone. Most of my callers are just lonely insomniacs making sure someone else is alive. They're not who I'm talking about; it's the ones who've lost their souls that get to me."

"Jango, have you ever gotten any weird calls while you were discussing pro or anti-nuclear politics?"

"Understand me, man, I play music and I rap some, but I stay off anything heavy. You know, shit like 'If you're diggin' on your best friend's old lady, should you let it loose, or go with it?' Or, 'Should you drop out of school and take a job or hang on until you get a degree?' That sort of thing. At two in the morning, no one wants to talk about radiation, man. The world's too quiet for heavy shit. But I take your meaning. If one of those crazies starts mouthing off anything you might like to hear, I'll get you a tape."

"Thanks." Rivers fished out a card and wrote his home phone number on the back.

"Oh, one more thing," Rivers added. "Can you tell me how Frank Rathman fit in around here?"

"Not me. I'm a lone wolf howlin' in the night. By the time the sun comes up, I'm curled up in my den."

After Jango slapped his hand up, down and sideways, Rivers wandered off in search of the pleasantly plump young princess he'd seen earlier. He found her sipping a Tab in a closet-like room full of vending machines. He tried not to smile as he introduced himself.

"Hey, I'm Ellen. What's up? You're the guy who threatened to handcuff Charles to the post, aren't you?" she responded in a breath.

"That's me," Rivers replied. "I caught your act with those V.D. clinic people and thought maybe we could talk for a minute."

"I don't have herpes, clap, or any other communicable disease, and I regularly inspect my . . . Oops, sorry. It takes me a few minutes to come down after I finish taping. You want to talk about what happened Sunday night," she said, collapsing into a faded blue lounge chair as if she'd been shot.

"God, that was awful," she continued, seeming genuinely distraught. "When I think about it I get completely freaked, so I keep busy. Yesterday we were all walking around like zombies—I mean, catatonic. Today everyone's sublimating their feelings with hard work. Nobody . . ."

"Tell me about Rathman," Rivers interrupted, sitting on a battered coffee table next to her chair. He adjusted his position slightly, taking advantage of the light that penetrated her purple blouse. He had a passing flash that he was turning into a incurable breast fetishist, but shrugged it off. Growing older decently, someone wise had said, meant raising your neuroses to the level of eccentricities.

"The killer couldn't have been after Frank, could he? I mean no one, except maybe half the women in the building, had any reason to be after him," Ellen began with a sigh.

"What do you mean?" Rivers asked. He was a little surprised, but remembered Ben Hall saying something about Rathman's being a ladies' man. "I thought Frank Rathman was serious about the woman he lived with."

"I don't mean to sound flip, especially about someone I cared about as much as Frank, but he really was a legend around here. Sure he was serious about Eileen. Who wouldn't be? She's great. Frank just didn't believe in categories: going steady, getting engaged, monogamy, marriage. When it came to sex, he was a happy-go-lucky snake. Show Frank a hole and he'd crawl right in. There weren't many women around here he hadn't hypnotized at least once."

"How old are you?" Rivers asked, confused by her switch from Lolita to Auntie Mame.

"Twenty-three, almost. I'm the Public Affairs Director. I guess I should say Acting Director. It can be a load of manure, doing PSA's for everything from sickle cell anemia to workshops for the sensuous paraplegic, but I love radio and Charles has promised me a news spot soon. In this business," she assured him seriously, "you make it by the time you're 26, maybe 27, or you're . . ." She finished the sentence by drawing her right forefinger slowly across her jugular vein.

"Tell me more about Rathman and his admirers," Rivers said. "But first—if I can be blunt—were you one of them? And second, was there a jealousy problem?"

"To your first question, yes, on and off," she answered proudly. "And to your second, not that I know of," she replied more seriously. "You have to understand. There is so much ego ambition around here, people don't have energy to waste being jealous over someone who was both an easy lay and totally unobtainable. I mean, a little nookie after lunch isn't the same thing as introducing someone to your father. It would have been different if Frank had been available, but no one had any illusions. At least, I don't think so. I can check it out if you want."

"Please. And don't forget about husbands and boyfriends. Maybe some of them didn't have such a tolerant attitude toward trespassing snakes. Now, what about politics? I understand some employees are upset about the station being sold."

"There was a mass freak-out at first, but Charles is still in charge and no matter what he says about getting rid of this one or that one, he almost never fires anyone. Sure, the Marxists are gone, but if you ask me, they baited him into it. They had some words with Frank and some of the rest of us because we only wanted a pay increase, not worker control. If they hadn't left over the station being sold, it would have been over the capitalist exploitation involved in raising the price of rootbeer in the vending machine, or something equally stupid. I mean, what can you expect from a Marxist rootbeer freak?"

Rivers' glance dropped to the Tab can in Ellen's hand. With some effort, he kept his mouth shut.

"You don't know anyone who might possibly have had it in for Frank, do you? Maybe professional jealousy or something like that?" Rivers asked.

"Nope," she replied, springing to her feet in a way Rivers guessed was calculated to get the maximum bounce from her cupcake breasts. "I'm late to tape the weekly calendar. I'll work on the Don Juan angle, but don't get your hopes up."

"Thanks."

"Sure, call me tomorrow. Bye," she said as if they commonly

came in a sentence and took off down the corridor.

Rivers took a deep breath and set off to find Tamura who, as it turned out, was in the business office surrounded by a cluster of male engineers and advertising salesmen. He caught her eye and motioned her over. Before joining him she said something to the men which made them howl with laughter. As they walked together to the front door, she fished in her bag and handed him the car keys.

"Stay as long as it takes to finish here, and then get one of the patrol people to run you back to the office. And just concentrate on the facts, please, ma'am."

Why James, Tamura thought to herself, if I didn't know you better, I might think you were jealous.

13

Rivers illegally evaded several street barriers and exceeded the speed limit in an effort to get to the daily press briefing no more than fashionably late. He failed. Bacon was already striding back and forth providing the TV cameras plenty of opportunity to catch the cut of his suit.

Rivers stood at the back of the room listening to the Chief's rap. If he hadn't known better, he would have been convinced the Speldon murder investigation was making great progress — with Roger Bacon calling the shots. Rivers had a brief but strong urge to shout, "Bullshit. Don't believe a word of it! I'm running the case and we haven't come up with a damn thing."

Easy James, he lectured himself. Bacon's personal identification with the case was probably beneficial. At the very least, it meant the investigation team would get all the departmental support it needed. But there was an obvious danger here, too. If Bacon was positioning himself to claim credit for catching the killer, he was also setting himself up to be labeled a failure if they came up empty. Rivers knew he didn't want to be around the day Roger Bacon failed.

Bacon picked off questions with the aplomb of a trained seal catching herring, responding to them with care and detail. He created an illusion of openness and honesty. In fact, his answers were outrageously padded with information having no bearing whatsoever on the murder investigation. Seduced by Bacon's style, the reporters seemed at first not to notice the lack of substance. But finally, when the Chief responded to a question about the murder weapon with a rambling description of the structure of the Berkeley Police Department, a couple of reporters realized he was jiving and started tip-toeing toward the exit.

Bacon stopped them in their tracks. He mentioned as if it were of little consequence that the Department believed there might be a connection between the killing of Willie Thompson, a suspected dope pusher and pimp, and the Speldon/Rathman murders.

The reporters were uncharacteristically silent. Apparently no one wanted to admit they had no idea who Willie Thompson was. In fact, only the reporter from the local Berkeley paper had noticed the death of the obscure black dealer, and although she had filed a brief "third killing in two days" story, she hadn't guessed there was a link between a run-of-the-mill ghetto homicide and the Speldon case.

Bacon swept the room with his best imperial gaze. Then, pretending the absence of questions meant everyone knew exactly what he was talking about, he nodded regally, tucked his pigskin case under his arm, and strode off as if the Governor was waiting for him in the next room.

Rivers' first thought was that going public with the Thompson connection was a mistake—at least until they'd had a chance to drag the streets. Reconsidering, he realized Bacon might be right. Running the possibility of a deal up the flagpole and waving it to the world might produce someone with valuable information.

On the way out of the room Rivers received a second surprise. One of the news people, who knew he was running the investigation, asked what he thought of the reward being offered by the Nuclear Industries Association. Several TV reporters paused to listen.

"What reward?" Rivers asked, realizing too late the reporter was getting rid of his bruised feelings by playing the same game on him as the Chief had just run. Clearly he was in for a load of crap.

"You mean you aren't aware of the latest developments?" one of the TV women asked.

Rivers shrugged.

Everyone laughed.

Finally an Oakland reporter he was friendly with handed him copy from one of the wire services. The gist of it was that Roger Warren, speaking on behalf of a nuclear trade association, had offered a $50,000 reward for information leading to the conviction of Aldo Speldon's killer.

Warren's move is as brilliant as it is irritating, Rivers reflected.

The nuclear association gets worldwide publicity they could never buy for $50,000 and Warren comes off as the avenging angel, halo firmly in place. It wouldn't do him any harm with his daughter either.

Rivers tossed his woven shoulder bag on a straight chair as he entered his office. Then he retrieved it and fished through a pile of loose paper at the bottom. Finally finding the right scrap, he dialed Sophie Warren's number. It was busy. He dragged the phone over to the wall, where someone had neatly tacked the *Times* obit. He was the only one in the building with a long cord. When the budget people had rejected his request for the cord, he had written an impassioned ballad entitled "Ma Bell and the Smith and Wesson," about how the BPD had plenty of bucks for guns and none for communication. His impulse had been to post it on the bulletin board in the squad room. Instead, he tossed it in the wastebasket, borrowed ten dollars from Phil Orpac and took himself off to Radio Shack. When he returned, he locked his door and got to work. Presto, a thirty-foot cord and no confrontation.

He sometimes thought of the cord installation as a turning point in his police career. He had joined Violent Crimes intending to resist neanderthal police attitudes and politics. It had taken him far longer than it should have to understand that the fascistic attitudes he was out to battle were neither prevalent nor a problem. In the meantime, his misplaced concern nearly blinded him to the real enemy: bureaucratic stupidity.

Rivers dialed Sophie Warren's number again. A woman answered on the third ring, saying "847-2100," with the detached authority that meant answering service.

"I'd like to talk to Sophie Warren," Rivers said politely.

"So would every other ghoulish reporter in the northern hemisphere," the woman answered sarcastically. "Warren isn't taking calls."

I bet she'd bite me if she could, Rivers thought, wondering if there was a way to handle the situation tactfully. When nothing occurred to him, he fell back on bluster.

"Look, Ms. whatever-your-name-is, I'm not representing the press of either hemisphere. I'm Lieutenant Rivers from the Berkeley

Police, and I need to talk to Ms. Warren immediately."

"Who said she would talk to a pig any more than a snoop?" the woman snapped back.

"Lady, your philosophy is your business. You can sing it, scream it or choke on it, but take down this number while you're at it: 848-4000. Tell Ms. Warren she has exactly five minutes to call me. If she doesn't, I'm going to send a police car to haul her down here. And if by any chance, any chance at all, I can't find her, I'm going to have them pick you up instead."

"How dare you. What right do you have to harass an innocent citizen?" the woman said, her voice rising an octave.

"None at all, lady, and I'm not going to. Just the same, if I conclude you are covering up the whereabouts of a key figure in a criminal investigation, it will certainly give us something to talk about for an extended period of time."

With that, Rivers hung up, leaned back, put his feet on the desk and shut his eyes. It was ten minutes before she called. He had guessed fifteen.

"This is Sophie Warren. Sorry you had trouble getting me," she began simply.

"Ms. Warren, I'm in charge of investigating the murder of Aldo Speldon and Frank Rathman. I'd like to talk to you at your earliest convenience," he said, doing his best imitation of a proper police officer.

"I'm pretty upset. Can't it wait until tomorrow?"

"I don't mean to be impolite, but no. Two men are dead, and at this stage of the investigation, every minute is precious."

"I'm going running at four o'clock to try and clear my head. Perhaps just after that," she offered.

"How about my running with you?"

"I go a ways," she replied uncertainly.

"My flat feet and varicose veins slow me down some, but why not give me a try?" he answered with a laugh.

"Do you know the fire road in the canyon that starts by the Space Sciences building?" she asked.

"Strawberry Canyon? Sure."

"It's close to eight miles round trip," she said, implying he might want to reconsider.

"I know."

"Well, okay then. See you there at four o'clock. How will I recognize you?"

"Leave that to me — I'm the detective."

Rivers looked through his mounting pile of phone messages. Nothing urgent. Phil Orpac had set up a system to follow up any tip that looked half-alive. The rest of the calls could wait.

On his way out of the building, Rivers looked in on Orpac, who, with Finnegan, was presiding over a bedraggled assortment of hung-over and withdrawn street people. Orpac noticed him standing by the door and shrugged. It wasn't an enthusiastic shrug.

Rivers picked a crumpled *Chronicle* sports section out of the wastebasket at the bottom of the back stairs, found his car, and drove to the Shattuck Co-op market. He parked under a sign that announced, "Parking for patrons only." It didn't say when you had to be a patron, he rationalized, as he skipped across Shattuck against the light. Anyway, the truckloads of milk, peanut butter, and bananas he had bought for his kids over the years should qualify him for a space with his name on it.

As Rivers climbed the stairs to the Kafenko coffee shop, he saw the sun was still warming the outside deck. There was only one other customer — an Indian wearing a tired-looking black suit, smoking Gauloise, and reading *Der Spiegel*. Rivers tossed his blazer over the back of a chair and continued through the open glass doors into the small restaurant. He was glad to see K.T. Archer behind the counter. They had made friends a few years before in a modern dance class. On a sunny Tuesday after class, they had gone to the beach, smoked a joint, and made love behind a sand dune. Rivers had enjoyed it a lot and wondered why they hadn't done it again. One of these days he should ask K.T. if she knew.

"Well, if it isn't Wyatt Earp," the solidly-built, thirtyish woman said good-humoredly. "Is this a friendly call or have you come for the Dalton gang?" she added, her curly black hair bouncing.

"Nah, I corralled them before breakfast. But if you should happen to see the Kid . . ."

K.T.'s laugh filled the small cafe. Then, becoming serious, she

112

said, "You look beat, James. I guess this recent mess has you jumping. What can I get you?"

"Half a jack, avocado and sprouts sandwich on light rye with mayonnaise, and a bowl of bean soup if it's really hot, and a Calistoga water."

"Okay, but I read that the nutritive value of sprouts has been greatly exaggerated," she replied, standing with her hands in the pockets of the red-and-white-striped apron that stretched across her sturdy hips.

"I like them."

"How odd. I bet you like raisin bran and wheat germ, too," she said with a chuckle.

"Come on. My taste ain't all bad."

"Why don't you go sit on the deck and I'll bring your food out," K.T. answered, blushing slightly.

Rivers glanced at the first page of the sporting green, shook his head, and sadly chucked it into a trash bin. No sense in dissecting how the Warriors blew a twenty-point lead in eight minutes, he thought as he fumbled in his back pocket for the crumpled blue memo Bacon had handed him with such phony drama.

MEMORANDUM

TO: Lieutenant James Rivers
    Head of Violent Crimes Division (Acting)

FROM: Roger Bacon
    Chief of Police

RE: Speldon/Rathman Murder Investigation:
    Nuclear/Industrial Conspiracy Aspects

The following is a synopsis of information supplied to me by certain well-placed acquaintances within our national security apparatus. As it is officially outside the legal purview of the various agencies involved, this material is strictly off the record.

PRESENT SITUATION: A systematic attempt to displace Roger Warren as head of Warren Industries is being launched by an internal corporate faction which seems to be led by Douglas Heisman, past president of Biosphere, a multinational company acquired by W.I. last year. The goal of the dissident group appears to be the replacement of the one-man command structure by a high-level management committee. (This would give more power to a half dozen senior vice presidents who are covertly sympathetic to it.) The takeover bid is being manipulated on two fronts.

Front One: Overt argument, privately directed at existing board members and aimed at convincing them the day of the one-man corporate empire builders like Roger Warren is done. The insurgents have made some headway with this, but so far have failed to gather sufficient votes to take control.

Front Two: OPERATION SENILIFICATION is simultaneously being put into effect on a covert level. Based on the premise that certain traits commonly associated with the aging process mean sure removal for a corporate leader, Roger Warren is being made to appear forgetful, foolish, capricious, and dictatorial. In a word, senile. To illustrate:

1. Inter-company directives have been issued using Warren's personal computer code (but in fact without his knowledge) on a range of mundane topics from proposed job-sharing plans to dress codes to pay raises. His subsequent ignorance, denial, and anger at what appear to be his own orders have been effectively exploited to cast doubt on his competence.

2. Leaks to the press. Several items have been planted in a local humor/gossip column widely read on Montgomery Street, portraying Warren as an aging buffoon (i.e., Curious Case of Cooked Goose—Can it be true that a noted S.F. industrialist and fowl fancier shoots a Canadian goose a week in retaliation against the bird-watching environmentalist who has been seen cooing about town with his daughter? Or: Low level latrinalia at Warren Construction: This company needs a leader *for* the 80s, not *in* his 80s). In fact, Roger Warren is in his early 70s.

3. Information supplied to the financial community hinting at cost overruns and construction delays on several big proj-

ects. Although the "difficulties" are serious, they are not unusual in the construction business. Nevertheless, the constant negative rumors have depressed the stock somewhat.

The covert strategy has enjoyed considerable success. R.W.'s attempts at denial and vindication have, if anything, been counterproductive. There just doesn't seem to be a good way for an older person to stand up and say, "I still have all my marbles," without people figuring if it was true, there would be no reason to say anything. There is a feeling in certain financial circles that maybe Roger Warren should step aside. This view has gained acceptance by between six and eight members of the seventeen-person Board of Directors.

OBVIOUS QUESTION: Is it possible the internal political fights within Warren Industries could have resulted in murder? In other words, could Aldo Speldon and Frank Rathman have been killed as part of an elaborate dirty trick designed to set Warren up? When I asked my source this question, I was treated to much throat-clearing. Of course, security personnel often take refuge in coughing, throat-clearing, and wise looks when asked sensitive questions. Sometimes this indicates they know something they can't or won't tell you, but more often it's because they don't like to admit they haven't the foggiest idea.

* * * *

Rivers sat back and watched the cars promenade along Shattuck Avenue. Ridiculous, he thought. The Feds have been reading too many bad novels. Absurd or not, he couldn't dismiss the memo out of hand. You don't last long as an investigator unless you are willing to accept that the ridiculous occurs regularly and the impossible only slightly less frequently. No matter how discouraging the prospect, he would have to send someone across the Bay to look for dirty white collars.

He tore the thin blue paper into little pieces and then wondered what to do with them. Was it safe to drop them in the basket, or should he eat them along with his alfalfa sprouts. Just then K.T.

came along with his food, and he stuffed the bits of paper into his shoulder bag.

"Believe it or not, you got into my dreams the other night, James. You were dressed in black with a big pistol on your hip. It's a little hazy, but I think you were sitting on a tall stool, like a piano stool, turning slowly back and forth."

"What were you doing?"

"Hummm . . . maybe I'll tell you some other time," she answered with a wink.

Rivers laughed with her and then asked, "How's Danny? Are you guys still together?"

"Yes and no. Our relationship is about to die of politeness. Danny has the mind of a railway conductor. Everything is done according to schedule. So much time for writing, so much for exercise, so much for his male friends, so much for me. I care for him a lot, but I'm too much of an anarchist to settle down with AMTRAK."

"Half the people I know are having trouble balancing freedom and commitment," Rivers responded kindly.

"The fact lots of people are in my boat doesn't help plug the leaks. I'm still stuck with how to get through tomorrow; alone, or with Danny. Maybe I should try to catch someone new," she added with mock suggestiveness.

"Put me on the back burner," Rivers laughed. "If we ever do get a hold of this Speldon thing, I'm going to sleep for a week and then spend some time with my kids. Do you know what time it is?"

"Three o'clock," she replied.

"Oops, I'm off to see if I can keep up with the Miss Scarlett of my little 'Clue' game."

"Happy trails," she called after him.

Rivers stopped at home to change into his running clothes. In the morning he had run in tattered gray sweat pants, but now he slipped into his white shorts with the faded blue edging. He peeked in his full-length mirror. The shorts made his long legs look lean and graceful. He and Tamura were alike in one way, he had to admit—neither could pass up a mirror. If they ever adopted a law banning vain detectives, Berkeley would have some openings.

116

Dartha strained all her horses chugging up the steep, winding Strawberry Canyon road in second gear. Rivers sat back and tried to relax as a stream of Hondas and Rabbits passed. Disgusted, he punched up Hoyt Axton on the tape deck and listened to him sing about Geronimo's Cadillac. He was racing compared to the old Indian chief. Just the same, he reviewed his decision not to get a new car. It had long been his position that since he didn't know where he was going in life, there was no point in hurrying. Just the same, he had to admit that in his current role as fleet pursuer of justice was inconsistent with a top speed of 20 mph.

Dartha finally ambled over the last rise and eased into the parking lot by the Space Sciences building. A slim woman was doing yoga exercises at the beginning of the fire road. She faced away from the parked cars toward the greening hill. Rivers watched as she stood on her toes, hands over head. He thought of a young deer nibbling a high branch.

Rivers clambered out of the car and introduced himself. He was about to say more when she inclined her head toward the road. He nodded and they picked their way down the first steep incline to where the dirt track catches the ridge line and snakes south for a couple of level miles.

They settled into a comfortable pace. Out of the side of his eye, Rivers inventoried his running partner. Sophie Warren was thin, almost delicate, in spite of being close to 5'8". She reminded him of a Maxfield Parrish print that had hung in his grandfather's woodshop when he was a kid.

As the road unwound through groves of eucalyptus and evergreen, and then along chaparral-covered slopes, Rivers let his mind drift. The woman next to him seemed completely lost in the rhythmic movement of her easy eight-minute-a-mile lope. When joggers approached from the other direction, they moved to the right together like a matched pair of carriage horses who had trotted side by side for years.

A mile or so along the road, the hillside rounded to the west, affording a panoramic view of San Francisco Bay. The sun hung

117

just above the rose-tinted fog that swirled about the twin towers of the vermilion bridge. They each turned to check the other's reaction. Rivers grinned. Sophie Warren conceded him a small, tight smile in return. Rivers admired her light, muffin-colored skin and the bits of blonde hair escaping from her impromptu runner's ponytail.

Rivers was annoyed when he realized he was also admiring her upthrust ass and rosebud breasts. It was a lot easier to handle a murder investigation if you didn't fall for your suspects. On the other hand, Phil Orpac maintained that being sexually turned on by an attractive female murder suspect was almost inevitable when you figured you became a homicide cop in the first place because you were attracted to death and, by extension, to killers. The theory smacked of the night courses Phil was taking to get his master's degree in Community Psychology, but Rivers had to admit that on the basis of a head nod and a small smile, he was on his way to being hooked on Sophie Warren.

Sophie Warren picked that moment to say, "Do you suspect me of killing Aldo, Lieutenant?"

Like father, like daughter, Rivers thought, remembering Roger Warren asking him the same direct question.

"No, or to be completely honest, not much. Of course we suspect you more than we do most of the world, but that doesn't mean we're ready to lock you up and bury the key," he replied with a laugh, hoping to lighten the mood.

"What do you mean, more than most people?" she asked sharply, not amused.

"Do you know anything about murder investigations, Ms. Warren?" he asked seriously, realizing she was on a ragged nervous edge and not wanting to tip her over.

"My friend Aldo has been dead less than 48 hours, that's all I know."

"Well, we, the police, that is, usually assume that when someone is killed, someone who knew the victim did the killing."

"That's a little paranoid, isn't it?"

"Maybe, but that's not the point. Statistics show that killers and their victims usually know each other."

"So when you say you suspect me more than most of the world,

118

it's because I knew Aldo?"

"That, and to be frank, a little more. Murder is usually an intimate act. Casual acquaintances rarely kill each other, which is why murder investigations are sometimes easier then you might think."

They were off the ridge and running downhill through the tree-lined canyon now. Sophie speeded up and Rivers had to lengthen his stride. He gave her a quick glance. Her fists, doubled tight, were punching the air.

"You've decided the killer must be either me or my father, is that it?" she asked with a husky edge to her voice.

"No, have you?"

"What do you mean?"

"Do you suspect your father?" Rivers asked her.

"Am I really supposed to answer that?" she responded angrily.

Rivers was quiet for several paces. When he spoke, it was as gently as he could. "Neither you nor your dad is at the top of my list, although your father isn't at the bottom, either."

"Why not?"

"Just my gut feeling that your father could kill if he or someone he loved was sufficiently threatened."

"If he ever did, he would be justified," she said defiantly.

"I thought he was your candidate for public enemy number one. Besides, aren't you morally committed to the right of all creatures to live — from baby seals to two-toed salamanders?"

"Don't mock me, Lieutenant. I honestly don't know how I feel about him half the time. Dad's an idiot in lots of ways, but he is my flesh and blood. I guess I am finally starting to admit that I love him despite his caveman politics and . . ."

"And what?"

"How can I be open with you? You're a cop, after all. When push comes to shove, you put on your helmet and flak jacket and bash war protestors, environmentalists, and . . ."

"Give me a break," Rivers interrupted, thoroughly pissed. "This isn't 1967 and I'm not on the tac squad. It's my job to investigate two brutal murders, one of which happens to be that of your best friend. I like my job. In a world where black and white all seem to be blurring into gray, one of the few things clear to me is that killing another human being is wrong. And if it's worth anything to you, I don't like the MX, MIRVs or acid rain any better than you do. Now, do you have something you want to tell me?"

"Not really, but Dad did call me yesterday."

"And?"

"Nothing, really. He said he was sorry about what happened to Aldo and if there was anything he could do to help me, he was there."

They had come four miles and reached trail's end. Rivers stopped, planning to take a couple of minutes to relax and stretch before running back. Warren stopped when he did, but as she turned, he saw that it wasn't to rest. Tears wet her face and her body shook violently.

Rivers had no handkerchief or anything else to offer. For a moment, he hesitated. Then he took her hand, wondering if she would pull away. Instead, she almost collapsed against his chest. He wrapped both arms around her. She grabbed hold as if he was a lone log in a sea of sharks.

Warren cried in earnest. Their sweat and tears mixed, almost gluing them together. A few other runners came down the hill, looked at them curiously, but said nothing. This was Berkeley, California, after all, where people crying in public were probably involved in some wacko new therapy.

"It's getting a little chilly. Shall we jog back before it gets dark?" Rivers asked finally, when Sophie's tears had subsided to an occasional snuffle.

She nodded, turned her back to Rivers, and pulled up her T-shirt to wipe her face. Then together they began jogging back up the road through the dim light of the over-arching forest. As they moved higher along the canyon and out of the trees, the last glow of the sun lit the evening fog.

14

Rivers got back to the police building a little before six, still wearing his shorts and running shoes. It was unnaturally warm for November, a sure sign rain was on the way. As he climbed the back stairs, he felt every step of his two long runs in the complaining muscles of his lower back. The pain reminded him he hadn't done his stretching exercises for two days.

When he entered his office, Rivers saw Carl Burnett and Tamura sitting at the small library table next to her desk. He collapsed in his swivel chair with a grunt intended to substitute for a greeting. Tamura's uncanny ability to work long hours with neither complaint nor hair out of place made Rivers feel vaguely guilty and apologetic. He stopped himself from explaining he too had been working—not just jogging. Instead, he pulled out his right-hand bottom drawer, fished behind a thin rack of files, and found a pair of old jeans, a long-sleeved blue sweatshirt with the neckband torn out, and an Almond Joy left over from Halloween. He felt better as he pulled the soft denim over his knees.

"What's happening?" he asked, proffering part of the unwrapped candy bar.

Carl broke off a full half.

Tamura wrinkled her nose and said, "Coconut," in the same disgusted tone that his kids saved for "liver."

"Carl was showing me some of Speldon's articles and speeches," Tamura continued more pleasantly. "Fortunately, his secretary is in love with her file cabinet. Every article, memo or speech he ever wrote is indexed both by date and subject. Going through the speeches looked like it would be a big job until Carl realized Speldon delivered the same ones over and over, changing just enough details to be current. There's the 'spaceship earth' theme, with lots of references to the need to conserve, recycle, and establish a harmony with the earth. His point being that without radical changes in attitude, the world is on a collision course with environmental disaster."

He was right, of course, even if he was a repetitious old bore," Carl Burnett mumbled, still reading through the pile of papers.

"Isn't there anything about nuclear plants running amok and turning the planet into a radioactive cinder?" Rivers asked, a little surprised to find that Carl was a closet conservationist.

"That's the second speech. In the last couple of years he talked a lot about what would happen if a nuclear reactor went haywire in a big way. Apparently, one did just that in the Soviet Union a number of years ago, and the facts about how radiation killed everything for miles around are just coming to light."

"Does he get into international politics, defense spending or nuclear weapons systems?" Rivers asked.

"Yes. He's all for environmentalists getting involved with anti-war activities and recently gave a big speech at one of the weapons lab blockades," Burnett replied, letting the paper he was holding drop to the table.

Rivers, sensing the big man had more to say, tried to catch his eye. Burnett had rolled Tamura's desk chair back from the table out of the circle of light cast by her desk lamp.

"You don't suppose someone in the Pentagon or one of the security agencies decided Speldon's activities were so threatening to national security that they took matters into their own hands, do you James?" Burnett asked.

Rivers was unable to suppress an involuntary shiver. Perspiration was still drying on his back, but the real chill was in Carl Burnett's voice. Damn it. First Bacon with his ideas about corporate subversion and now this ex-CIA man acting as if someone had stolen his decoder ring.

Rivers took a deep breath as he tried to make out Burnett's expression in the deep shadow.

"I guess I can imagine situations in which our government would kill a civilian," Rivers replied. "But this just isn't one of them. Aldo Speldon may have been a pain in the ass, but he wasn't nearly influential enough to threaten any fundamental government interest. But if you think he was, or even half-suspect anything like that, I want to hear about it."

Carl Burnett didn't move. His big body slumped in the chair. He said nothing. Finally, just as Tamura was ready to throw something at him, he rolled the chair back toward the light. He looked first at Rivers, then Tamura.

"You don't have time for the confessions of this tired old agent. Just understand that I've had a bellyful of grown-up preppies playing lethal ego games in the name of patriotism. I became a technician here to escape the stink of democracy rotting by the Potomac. I promised myself straightforward police work from now on. I mean to keep that promise. I think that's what's involved here, but if either of you doubts it, or thinks I might still be connected with the agency, I want out. Over the years I've done some . . ."

"Let's talk about Speldon's articles, Carl," Tamura interrupted, hoping to defuse the tension and get him back on track.

"They fall into a couple of broad categories. The majority are specific attacks on nuclear power—doom and gloom about meltdowns, the end of the world in a nuclear shootout, and so on. He also wrote a lot about the politics behind the government's consistent refusal to adequately police nuclear power plants."

"What did he say?" Rivers inquired.

"That the oil, coal, and nuclear companies have merged into several conglomerates whose combined political clout is so great that short of a monumental disaster, no effective government regulation is possible or . . ."

"Isn't there anything more pointed or personal?" Rivers interrupted. "Hundreds of anti-nuclear activists say the same thing every day without getting their heads blown off. Did you find any hint he had discovered any particularly sensitive radioactive skeletons?"

"Not really. Speldon saved a lot of his venom for fellow environmentalists who didn't agree with him. Take a look at the lines I've marked in red," Carl said, proffering a small stack of paper.

Rivers moved across the room, feeling a quick, fiery pain in his lower back. He pressed it against the side of a three-drawer file cabinet as he read bits and pieces from the environmentalist publications. Ah ha, he thought. Here's a sample of what Charles Pierce had been talking about—the flabby underbelly of the god in hiking boots.

Speldon obviously had an old king's fear that the princes of the next generation were riding too close to his castle. Walter Bell appeared to be the person highest on Speldon's shit list. Bell was pilloried for stealing Speldon's ideas and for stabbing him in the back in several political fights, but most strongly for selling out to big oil. Bell's name wasn't the only one on the list, however. A number of others appeared more than casually and would have to be checked.

"I thought you were going to see Bell this evening, Sara," Rivers commented after a few minutes.

"I am, and I have to get moving if I'm going to get to Richmond by 7:15."

"I'll walk you out," Carl Burnett said, bringing his soft bulk upright as gracefully as a dancer.

"Oh, James," Burnett added from the door. "Roger Warren's secretary has been trying to reach you. The great man wants to give you another audience."

Returning to his desk, Rivers found the slip with Warren's number on top of the growing piles of messages. He punched out the seven numbers. As it rang, he glanced through the notes. The mystery man had called again, but since the University hadn't been able to identify anyone named Strange, and he had sounded crazy, he was being consigned to the "kook" category.

Someone identifying himself as Warren's personal assistant finally answered. She told Rivers Mr. Warren would be pleased if he would join him for supper.

Rivers hesitated. The thought of changing his clothes and driving to the city exhausted him.

Before his tired mind could dredge up an excuse, the smooth voice continued. "Mr. Warren would be happy to meet you in Berkeley if you prefer, Lieutenant, but he would like to speak to you this evening."

"Tell him Augusta's on Telegraph, just north of Ashby, at 8:00. It's got a neon fish in the window," Rivers added.

It was just past 6:35 according to the grammar school style wall clock over Tamura's desk. He decided he was too tired to go home and change. Instead, he called Augusta's to make a reservation, and then called Jeannie to check on the kids. She explained they were in their usual Star Trek rerun trance and couldn't be disturbed, and she was busy trying to get the pesto sauce together with the pasta and had no time to bother with him either. He made a couple of kissing sounds into the phone before cradling the receiver. Next, he dug a Baby Ben alarm clock and a patchwork quilt out of a file cabinet. He set the alarm for 7:45 and went into Rafferty's darkened office, where he curled up on the oversized couch.

15

To get to Richmond on time, Tamura had to drive close to the speed limit, a pace she considered reckless. The Global Oil Refinery was one of the several oil and petrochemical complexes grouped along the east shore of San Pablo Bay to form a refinery row. Although she had even less use for oil refineries than she did for cars, Tamura had to admit at night the countless little lights on the tanks and towers transformed industrial ugliness to a small hamlet of fairy castles.

The guard at the security booth consulted a list and waved her through, pointing toward a boxy, three-story, 1930s-style stone building with tall steel-sash windows that looked like regional headquarters for the Department of Agriculture. Bell's office was on the top floor, and had a three-inch, gold-lettered sign bolted to the door which said, "Walter Bell, Environmentalist." Apparently, the security guard had announced her approach, because the environmentalist himself opened the door before she could knock. Tall, thin, balding, and late-fortyish, he looked like a cross between the "before" picture in the old Charles Atlas ads and a poorly nourished crane.

Tamura introduced herself and extended her hand. Like a mollusk which wanders too close to an anemone, it was entrapped by moist and slightly sticky tentacles. It took a good tug to get her hand free, and still more effort to resist the urge to wipe it on her skirt. Tamura accepted Bell's offer to sit down on an uncomfortable-looking couch in the window corner of his square, beige-carpeted office. When he turned to move a captain's chair from the other side of the room, Tamura quickly wiped her hand on the stiff couch fabric.

Before Tamura could say anything, Walter Bell picked up a paperweight from the modern coffee table between them. Tamura noticed the little object was a pewter sea lion. Bell began to talk as if he had been rehearsing his speech all day.

"I'm sure you've been told that Aldo and I were enemies, and that's why you've come. That's not really true. I could never accept his calling me a traitor, but I still wanted him to see my motives were good. Now he's dead," Bell continued, absent-mindedly placing the sea lion on the table before flexing his long, arthritis-gnarled fingers in what Tamura thought looked surprisingly like a strangling motion.

"Now he's dead and I'll never make him see," Bell repeated the phrase several times, as if it were a mantra that would lead him to enlightenment.

Tamura felt the weight of her long day. Bell obviously needed help with his feelings of guilt and despair, but she wasn't up to it. She was just a tired cop at the end of a twelve-hour shift who wanted to ask her questions, take her notes, and go home to a hot bath. But what could she do? As her old partner Danny Brown had once told her when trying to explain the proper techniques for questioning a suspect, "you can't push a river."

With a swallowed sigh, Tamura decided to go with the flow and encourage Bell to rap. She was too tired and hungry to come up with any decent questions anyway.

"Mr. Bell, I need to know about your relationship with Aldo Speldon, how it started, and what led to your, ah, discontinuing your association."

Bell rubbed his hands through the straight black strands of his thinning hair. This time he picked up a sculpture of a whale carved out of some sort of bone.

"Aldo had tremendous power. He could hypnotize you with his words; sometimes just with his presence. I heard him speak for the first time at a rally one Sunday afternoon back in 1959. I'd been working for two years with the Army Corps of Engineers, my first job after getting my Ph.D. in mechanical engineering. I was already appalled by the Army's blindness to the destructive environmental consequences of their acts. They really believed progress was synonymous with damming things up and cementing them over. Aldo appeared in my life at just the right moment. It was almost as if I invented him to lead me out of a career I had come to hate.

"It's hard to explain today, but back in the 50s, when most people believed in Eisenhower and the eight-cylinder Buick, Aldo was a visionary, almost a saint to the few who saw that the planet was being ruined. From the very first time I heard him speak, his ideas seemed to be the only rational ones in an upside-down world. I quit my job and joined him. At first, I was mostly a disciple, although I was helpful in exposing some of the Army Corps' worst abuses. I was very happy. It was as if I had found the true path — as if I'd finally come home.

"All the environmental issues were black and white then," Bell continued, hunching forward in his chair, talking rapidly, hardly pausing for a breath. "We fought corporations and governments, none of which had any sensitivity to what they were doing to the environment. We were right and good, they were wrong and evil, and before long the public began to enlist on our side. By the mid-60s we'd begun to win some victories. It's no exaggeration to say we saved forests from the saw, rivers from being trapped behind walls of concrete, and so on. But most important, we promoted an awareness that man isn't omnipotent on the planet."

As Bell rambled on as if he were a keynote speaker on Earth Day, Tamura tuned out the words and watched the man. His hands, cupping the whale, no longer looked like claws. His eyes stared into some private world. Even his expression had become peaceful. Tamura allowed the rise and fall of Bell's voice to induce a mild hypnotic trance. It took a blazing flare from a refinery stack to rouse her.

"What happened to change your relationship?" she asked quietly, feeling curiously refreshed.

Bell was silent for several seconds. "Time — the passage of time more than anything," he said finally. "I'm not a strong person, but I'm not stupid. Corporations that laughed at the Sierra Club, or the Wilderness Society, or our organization in 1960 became more sophisticated by the middle 70s. They were ready to do things to minimize environmental impact, at least when it didn't cost too much. Things were becoming more complex in other ways too. Suddenly there seemed to be a dozen sides to every issue, rather

128

than just two.

"Aldo never changed. He was always the purist. To stop further environmental degradation, he started a 'no-growth' campaign in the mid-70s. I explained to him a hundred times that no growth at all made no sense to large segments of our population. Blacks and Chicanos wanted a decent place to live and work; middle-class Americans wanted their kids to have a better job and a fuller life than they did, and so on. But Aldo was Mr. Clean. In a sense, he wanted the entire world to take a bath.

"It was sad. We began to alienate old friends. Even worse, we were so doctrinaire we began to make government and corporate people who weren't pro-environment at all sound sensible. I begged Aldo to ease up. When he finally got it through his head that I meant it, he called me a Judas. That was too much, and I quit. Surprisingly, I got dozens of job offers. Aldo's attacks resurrected me as a moderate. I ended up here, where my job is to keep Global's name off the environmentalists' shit list. Aldo continued to denounce me with every vile name he could think of. He reduced our relationship to a morality tale: 'Beware of nurturing a snake at your breast.' "

"Weren't you furious?" Tamura asked, getting caught up in the story.

"I probably should have been. The truth is Aldo's attacks made me feel guilty, even though I knew I was a considerable influence for good in the energy industry. In between the flak-catching they hired me for, I've set up a model environmental program for large refineries which is being adopted all over the world."

Beginning to get excited, Bell knocked a knee against the coffee table, upsetting a pelican. He tried to right the delicate wooden bird, but his hands were shaking and it toppled again.

"Even though I get awards and recognition, I feel awful inside. Can you understand what I'm saying, Officer?"

Bell's look of mute appeal was so naked, Tamura found herself responding. "I came to Berkeley as a freshman philosophy major in 1967, when I was sixteen. I showed up at every anti-war demonstration, churned out peace posters by the thousands at Guerrilla Graphics, and really believed the revolution would bring a better, more just world. For a while, it seemed like my career was getting hauled out of campus buildings by men with crash helmets and tear gas guns. After I graduated, I drifted through graduate school and several jobs for almost ten years. Then one day I found myself wearing the uniform I had despised. Most of the time I think working in Violent Crimes is as righteous a job as any. No one likes murderers. But guilty? Sure. Sometimes I get the feeling I've sold out."

Bell's face relaxed for a second time.

"Thank you. You know, I kept hoping that if my work here brought enough dramatic changes in oil industry policies, Aldo would accept me again, but now . . ."

"I only have a couple more questions for you," Tamura interrupted to forestall another monologue. "Can you think of anyone who might have had a motive for killing Aldo Speldon?"

"So many of Aldo's enemies are dead or have mellowed, and I wasn't close to him since the anti-nuclear issue got hot. I'm a dated environmentalist. People in the know treat me as if I had been in the cabinet three presidents ago. They shake hands, give me a big smile, and tell me they would love to chat, but there is someone across the room they must talk to about the outer continental shelf. But if I had to name Aldo's bitterest enemy, it would be Roger Warren."

"Do you think Warren murdered Speldon?"

"He and Aldo have certainly had some vicious fights over the years, but I really don't think so, unless . . . No, I really don't think . . ."

"Unless what?" Tamura demanded, forgetting her bedside manner.

"I don't think Roger Warren would have killed Aldo for political reasons."

Tamura grabbed the sea lion paperweight before Bell could.

"Why the qualifier, Mr. Bell? What other reason do you suppose Warren might have had for killing him? Perhaps because Speldon was friendly with Warren's daughter?"

"There was that," Bell hedged.

"Stop pussyfooting. Can't you be direct?" Tamura said impatiently, deftly nailing the remaining paperweights before they were claimed by Bell's outstretched grasp.

"I guess so," he said softly, "but it might hurt an innocent person."

"I'll do everything I can to protect the privacy of anyone who isn't involved," Tamura said, returning the small talismans to the table and leaning back on the couch.

"Roger Warren and Lucy Speldon were lovers," the environmentalist said, picking up the sea lion and squeezing it in a cupped fist.

"You're not serious?" Tamura blurted.

"I don't want to make trouble for Lucy, Officer Tamura. She was always wonderful to me. Even after Aldo started attacking me, she was kind. But I know what I saw."

"And what was that?" Tamura asked.

"I was in Grenoble, France three years ago for an international conference on air pollution from stationary sources — that means factories as opposed to vehicles. One evening I was sitting alone in a sidewalk cafe reading the *Herald Tribune,* when Roger Warren and Lucy Speldon walked past. I paid the check, and went after them to say hello. I hadn't caught up when they turned into a small hotel."

"You followed them?" Tamura asked.

"My curiosity simply got the better of me. I waited a few minutes and went in. They were registered as Mr. and Mrs. Roger Warren. I left Grenoble the next day and never saw them together again, so that's all I can tell you."

Tamura reflected for a moment. So Lucy Speldon had been lying, or at least not telling the whole truth. Lucy Speldon's relationship with Roger Warren might not be shocking in itself, but considered side-by-side with her husband's love match with Warren's daughter, it sounded like daytime TV.

"There's one last thing, Mr. Bell," Tamura said, interrupting her own thoughts. "Where were you last Sunday evening? You understand it's a question I ask everyone connected with the investigation."

"Yes, of course. I was getting ready to catch the early morning plane to Los Angeles to give a seminar to a group of sleepy oil executives on the petroleum industry's responsibility to protect the coastal waterways. So much for impact, Aldo would have said."

"Did you see or talk to anyone?"

"Not after 8:30, when I got home from an early supper with friends."

"Thanks for telling me about Grenoble," Tamura said as she stood and made her way to the door.

Bell didn't respond. He was still sitting in the director's chair, clutching the pewter sea lion.

16

Tamura paused for a moment as she stepped out of the Global Oil Building. The heavy, sulphurous refinery air did little to lift the blanket of guilt and sorrow she had acquired inside. But it had been worth it, she thought, her spirits rising a little. She had learned something valuable, a strand of information that when pulled might unravel the entire mystery.

Tamura thought about Lucy Speldon on her way home. Could she have been involved in killing her husband? At the very least, Lucy had a lot of explaining to do. Perhaps when the explanation was made they would be nearer the truth.

When she got to her cottage, Tamura twisted her key in the lock, shoved the door open, and waited. All was quiet. Still she didn't move. Forty-five seconds elapsed. Tamura felt her muscles grow increasingly taught. Finally, a small triangular orange head peeked around the door jamb. Tamura let out a small whoop of triumph as she scooped up the startled feline, cradling her in the undignified manner one holds a baby.

"I'm not so tired I can't outwit a silly-face samurai cat," she gloated.

Once inside, Tamura collapsed into her overstuffed brown velvet chair. She had bought it at Goodwill for $25, a good price considering the bottom was only giving way on one corner. She felt both exhausted and hyper as she watched Annie pick crumpled wads of paper from the wastebasket and drop them at her feet. After beating the small red beast at the door pounce game, it would be impolite to turn down an invitation to play catch-the-mouse. Obediently she tossed a few paper balls before focusing her waning energy on dinner.

Here it was after 9:30, and she hadn't had supper. Why was it the heroes of detective fiction never experienced this problem? Maigret would be sipping Calvados at the corner cafe, while waiting for his plump andouillettes. Inspector Van der Valk would be at home with his feet up, concentrating his mental energies, while Arlette whipped him up a tasty batch of cassoulet. Even Martin Beck would have had the presence of mind to make himself a sandwich and open a bottle of Swedish beer. Being a detective was so much more civilized on the Continent. And to make it even worse, she was out of popcorn, which with soy sauce, melted peanut butter, and garlic powder had passed for dinner more than once. What she really needed was an attentive house-husband, someone to order the particulars of her day, create succulent suppers, and fill her nights with passion.

Reluctantly she decided it was unlikely Prince Charming would appear with a piping hot pepperoni pizza. Pulling on a white wool sweater, she went outside and tapped on the door of the adjoining cottage. Her friend Terri, a small woman with a mop of curly brown hair, opened the door, clutching flow charts in one hand and a statistics text in the other. Terri was studying for one of the seemingly endless exams involved in getting her MBA at Cal. Convincing her to take a food break was about as difficult as getting Rivers to take a nap.

Considering the hour, they decided on hot turkey sandwiches and Irish coffee at Berkeley's least pretentious landmark, Brennan's. Even though it was Tuesday, the old pub, with its oval center bar, ranks of battered tables, and portraits of blue ribbon cows from some 1950s era state fair staring down from faded green walls, was crowded with its usual odd assortment of humanity, talking, laughing, eating, and drinking as if TV had never been invented. By the time Tamura put away her second drink, along with a piece of blueberry cheesecake, she forgot the murder investigation and was enjoying her friend's chatter.

Terri was engaged in her ritual wail over the lack of available men in Berkeley. This led them both to what they called the sexual fantasy game, a diversion they had invented when they were roommates at Cal. It was as simple as it was sophomoric: if you could invent the perfect lover, who would he be and what would he be like?

Over the years, it had ceased to be a game, becoming instead a way of sharing. Terri, whose parents were Jewish and wealthy, tended rather regularly to fall for Asian men, while Tamura, who had grown up in a mixed minority neighborhood on the fringe of Watts, was almost always attracted to clean-cut WASPs and Jews. They both claimed to want a settled relationship but not, as Terri often said, if they had to scrub a house in the suburbs to get it.

Flushed with her second Irish coffee, Terri began to tease Tamura. "I saw a picture of your boss in the morning paper. From all your horror stories I thought he'd look like a cross between Richard Nixon and Gomer Pyle: someone you couldn't imagine liking. But he's pretty cute, Sara, just your tall, Caucasian type. Why, I might even trade the phone number of an assistant professor of Korean Studies who hates Jewish women for an introduction."

Tamura started to joke back, then realized she was at a loss for words. Why, she wondered, am I acting like a clam, and why does it make me so uncomfortable to fantasize about Rivers? To distract Terri and cover her own confusion, she changed the subject, declaring a new allegiance to Japanese men.

"I don't believe it, you mean you met a sexy Asian?" Terri responded.

"Nope, but I saw *In the Realm of the Senses,* that Japanese film you've been telling me about for years. Fuji Tatsuya is pretty cute, even if he does lose his penis in the end."

The two women polished off the evening with a last round of Irish coffee and a detailed discussion of Cliff Wong, Terri's current lover, and how his ability to deliver in bed partially made up for the fact he was cheap and forgot her birthday.

"Sara, you haven't said a word about your big murder investigation. Can't you at least tell me how it's going?" Terri asked as she drove her faded green Honda station wagon toward Sacramento Street.

"What would you think if you knew that one of the victims had been sleeping with the daughter of his most bitter enemy, at the same time the enemy was sleeping with his wife?"

"The dead man's wife, you mean?"

"Exactly."

135

"Sounds like you ought to round them up."

"The weird thing is, all three seem like pretty decent people. It's so damn frustrating. Everyone we meet seems to have a motive, but when we follow up, poof. Take this afternoon. A couple of people told us Rathman, the radio guy who was killed with Speldon, had a nasty argument with some radical employees at KILO before they were fired a couple of weeks ago."

"Sounds promising."

"Sure, so I spent a couple of hours checking them out. Some Marxists! Turns out they run a tofu falafel wagon up by Cal — and even charge extra for hummus!"

"Closet capitalists!"

"That's it. The stand was so successful, they needed to work full time. That's where the fight with Rathman came in. They wanted to get unemployment benefits too."

"I don't follow."

"If they quit, no benefits. They could only collect if they were fired, so to accomplish that, they acted outrageous."

"That's disgusting, Sara. I hope you turned them in to unemployment."

"Terri, I'm in murder, not welfare — although I may be collecting a check soon if I don't smarten up."

"Sorry, it just makes me mad. I'll try to be more helpful. Why were the killings done during a radio show? Have you figured that out?"

"We keep coming back to that question, too. So far, all our answers are duds."

"Maybe it was something one of them said," Terri persisted, as she turned right onto Sacramento.

"We're checking that," Tamura replied tiredly, wondering why she was mixing business with pleasure.

"It's funny what will set people off," Terri continued. "A few weeks ago Cliff tried to listen to a program on NPR. A minute after it started, he was ready to break the radio. Finally he realized he had the wrong station and was listening to one of those right-wing religious shows. Of course, Cliff is always making stupid mistakes."

17

Rivers reached Augusta's a few minutes past eight. Roger Warren was sitting in the small reception area, holding a glass of red wine. He wore an Irish wool sweater over corduroy pants and looked as comfortable as anyone could in front of the Avedon poster of Penelope Tree.

"There are usually fewer people up the steps in back. Let's see if we can eat there," Rivers said, after they had exchanged hellos.

When they were settled at a small table, covered with a cheerful blue checked cloth, Bonnie, the restaurant's owner, stopped to say hello. Rivers chatted for a moment, without introducing Warren.

"What's best?" he asked.

"The clams in wine sauce are heavenly, if you don't mind my bragging. So is the fresh salmon with beurre blanc. But if you really want a treat, try the mussels; they're petite and very sweet."

Rivers ordered the mussels and Warren the salmon. Warren praised the house red, so they ordered a carafe, along with an antipasto to share.

"Thanks for making time to see me this evening," Warren began when the waiter had left. His delivery was polite and he was smiling, but Rivers sensed the underlying arrogance of a powerful man who has learned to cover an iron fist with a velvet glove.

"It must seem a bit of a reversal for the suspect to be hounding the police, but I'm worried about my daughter and I'm determined that this whole mess be cleared up as quickly as possible," Warren continued.

"I saw your daughter this afternoon," Rivers replied, hoping to throw Warren off balance.

"I know. How is she?" Warren replied, neatly pulling the rug from under Rivers' maneuver.

Rivers made a quick decision not to ask Warren how he had

learned about his meeting with Sophie. The industrialist's power apparently extended to knowing what the Berkeley police were doing, step by step. Rivers felt like Muhammed Ali must have on that hot night in Manila, with the mighty Joe Frazier prowling the ring, eager to meet him toe-to-toe. Ali's strategy had been to cover up, lean on the ropes, counter-punch now and then, and wait for the later rounds. There was no harm in trying the same approach. It had worked for Ali.

"She seemed confused and upset to me, but I think underneath it all she's okay. Having her lover killed and her father a suspect can't be easy, but if you want my opinion, I don't believe she thinks you had anything to do with Speldon's murder," Rivers replied guardedly.

"What about you, Lieutenant?"

Rivers shrugged.

"So, I'm still a suspect?"

"More so since that grandstand play of offering the reward," Rivers answered, delighted to land his first jab.

"That wasn't in the best of taste, was it? I'd been getting pressure from industry people all over the world to defend myself, and when the PR department came up with the reward idea, I finally decided to go along."

"Finally? I'd hate to see you move fast."

"Look, Lieutenant," Warren replied sharply, "the ecology groupies have convicted me of murder in the press without a shred of proof. There's always a lot to be said for a good offense when the going gets tough."

"Has your board suggested you step aside until the dust settles?" Rivers asked quietly.

"That idea isn't as far beneath the surface as I'd like it to be," Warren replied. "In the construction business, no one is above pressure from the banks and insurance companies."

"And from inside Warren Construction?" Rivers asked.

"Stop the innuendo and say what you mean, Lieutenant."

"Via-soft and Biosphere," Rivers replied simply.

"They're wholly-owned subsidiaries of Warren Industries, the holding company which . . ."

"But not totally controlled subsidiaries. When you acquired them, you beefed up the latent dissident faction on your board. More to the point, you strengthened a clique of executives who want you out. And from what I hear, they've been playing rough."

"So what?" Warren challenged.

"So maybe you didn't kill Speldon but are being set up by the people playing dirty tricks inside your company. I have no idea what's really going on in that black tower of yours, but I'm planning to turn over a few rocks and see what crawls out."

"Don't waste a lot of time on it."

"Why not? You're not leveling with me."

"Lieutenant, I've known for a year that at least one of those acquisitions was a mistake—that we tried to gobble too much in one bite. Some of the new people who came with the mergers resented us. A few are out to get me and don't give a damn how they do it. My first thought was to fire a few disloyal idiots as an example. Fortunately, I didn't. Once I thought it over, I realized I was being set up, and the blatant villains were only bait."

"Bait?"

"Yes, small fry—or perhaps I should say middle-sized fry— dangled under my nose. The people behind the power play hoped I would fire the lot. Of course if I had, there would have been more dirty tricks and more obvious villains, who in turn would have had to be fired. The idea was to continue to bait me until I became enraged, lost my sense of proportion, and struck out wildly. When I looked sufficiently ridiculous, the boys with the clout would come out of the woodwork, cluck a few times about how no one is indispensable, before getting the board to give me a Rolex, while everyone whistled, 'So Long, It's Been Good to Know You.'"

"It didn't work," Rivers interjected.

"Damn right it didn't. I may not be able to run a five-minute mile any more, but I can still cross the street by myself. I bought a couple of their peons, let the dirty tricks continue, and gathered evidence. I even reacted outrageously to several of their ploys to encourage them to be more brazen. Finally, a couple of weeks ago, I got everything I need to directly implicate some executives who are also board members. At the January board meeting, I'll lay it out and squash the whole traitorous bunch," Warren summed up with satisfaction.

"Maybe your enemies figured out what you were up to and killed Aldo Speldon to put the monkey on your back," Rivers remarked.

"Believe me, Lieutenant, when I heard about Aldo on Monday morning, that was my first thought. But by the time I lunched with you, I realized there were too many holes in it."

"Such as?"

"First, my informants hadn't heard a thing. Second, several of the people at the top of the conspiracy were out of town and out of touch. Third, no one had made any attempt to capitalize on the fact I'm an obvious suspect, and most important . . ."

"Nothing was planted on you," Rivers interrupted.

"Why Lieutenant Rivers, you surprise me. You almost sound as if you think I'm innocent. But you're right, that's the key. If I was really being set up, any fool would have done a better job. My scarf or gun at the scene of the crime, some of the right kind of mud on my tires. With a few creative touches we would be having this chat in an iron cage, wouldn't we?"

"Sure, but you haven't convinced me not to poke around Warren Construction. What do you plan to do next?"

"I don't plan to confess, if that's what you mean. I've been hoping you would come up with something, but since you haven't my next step is to turn my own security people loose and ask the Feds to come in," Warren answered, taking the last bite of his salmon.

"It sounds as if your private mafia is already operating; you knew I'd seen Sophie this afternoon. I can't stop you from asking for FBI assistance, if you can show this is a federal matter, which I doubt. But Feds aside, if I get the idea that your people are interfering, I'll . . ."

"Simmer down," Warren interjected peremptorily. "I hate to deflate your conspiracy theory of the capitalist pig with spies everywhere. It has a certain sophomoric appeal. But I knew you were with Sophie because one of your people told me. When I called, the young officer who took the call, Lassiter, I think, remarked on what a coincidence it was that you were off talking to another Warren. It

140

didn't take a detective to figure out it was Sophie."

That idiot, Rivers thought. Just then someone touched his shoulder. He jumped, dropping his salad fork on the floor.

"What is it?" he snapped at an athletic young waitress whose carrot-colored hair was tied in a bun.

"I didn't mean to startle you. There's a phone call from a Lieutenant Orpac. He says it's urgent."

As Rivers walked to the reception table by the front door, he realized his head was aching. The pressure of the investigation was starting to show. He would have to make time to do his yoga. He took a deep breath and shook his hands at the wrists to relax shoulder and neck muscles.

As he passed the redheaded waitress, Rivers touched her freckled arm. "I didn't mean to jump at you. Is there a more private phone?"

She smiled and motioned him to follow her down a short hall toward the restrooms, where she opened a closet door. She pulled a small phone from under a pile of tablecloths and plugged it into a jack behind the vacuum cleaner. Rivers laughed. The young woman laughed too and left him alone.

"Hey, Phil, what's up?"

"Maybe a lot."

"Where are you?"

"Oakland Airport. I'll be on the 9:30 to L.A. to see our eyewitness."

"You mean the person who killed Willie Thompson?"

"Careful, James, remember we have no evidence on that, and we agreed if we got some real help with the Speldon and Rathman deaths, we wouldn't be too fussy about where it came from."

"Yeah, I remember," Rivers replied grumpily. "I don't really like it much more than Tamura does, but it's probably our only chance. But Phil, we're not letting anybody go who's still clutching a bloody knife."

"Cut the Girl Scout act. This was your idea and it's the best we've got. Besides, I have a plane to catch, so we'll worry about ethics later. Here's what's happening. Lorenzo got hold of a dealer named Jerry Muñoz, a sort of latter-day flower child, complete with beads, bells, and Guatemalan shirt. Muñoz won't deal hard stuff, only grass, psychedelics, and a little coke—all of which he claims are good for people. The point is, he says there was supposed to be a big coke buy Sunday involving Oscar Williams."

"Oscar Williams? Not the Oscar Williams who plays basketball back east?"

"He's the one, but adjust your tenses. Williams tore up his knee in the playoffs last spring. It finished his career, but apparently he's started a new one—dealing to athletes. The important thing now is that Sunday's buy didn't go down and Williams has disappeared."

"So?"

"So, Muñoz says Willie Thompson was a part-time gopher for Williams and was supposed to be bag man Sunday night. But with that much dust on the line, he's sure Williams wasn't far away."

"Your being at the airport is connected to all this?"

"Williams comes from L.A.—near Watts, not too far from where Tamura grew up. Late this afternoon we sent a teletype to Los Angeles and some other places like New York and Boston, where Williams has roots. A short time ago the phone rang. Someone asked if we wanted a fast break."

"Williams?"

"Swish. He told us he was at his mother's and we agreed to talk. In the meantime, I told him I'd ask the LAPD to keep an eye on him from across the street. He said okay, as long as they stay outside the three-point line and don't try any backdoor plays. I agreed."

"How did Williams know to call?"

"Some of his high-school basketball buddies are cops down there. But listen, Williams is no fool. He isn't going to say a word unless his attorney is present. We either produce an Oakland mouthpiece named Wilbur Lincoln and someone from the D.A.'s office high enough to make a deal stick on our end, or we're back to square one. And James, it has to go down tonight."

"How the hell can we do that?" Rivers asked, stubbornly hanging on to the idea of getting to bed early.

"Not we, boss. You. Get some No-Doz and take a cold shower. The last flight is at midnight. You have plenty of time to find Lincoln and get him to the airport. I'll have someone from the LAPD pick you up."

142

Rivers leaned against the closet door and allowed himself three silent "motherfuckers." Then he fished a couple of dimes from his shoulder bag and called Lorenzo Jones at home. The patrol officer answered on the second ring and cheerfully agreed to do his best to find Wilbur Lincoln and have him at the police building by ten. Rivers hung up, feeling more cheerful. What the hell, I can always sleep fifteen or twenty hours tomorrow, he thought as he called John Hanrahan from the D.A.'s office and got him to agree to stand by.

When Rivers rejoined Warren, the entrée dishes had been replaced by a large piece of chocolate cake and black coffee.

"The woman who seated us sent the cake. It's the last piece and she wanted to be sure you got it," Warren said.

"Did you know some scientist discovered that chocolate and sex have the same chemical effect in the brain?" Rivers replied, reaching for his fork.

"Yes, I read that too. But at my age they work at cross purposes."

"How's that?" Rivers asked, his mouth full of cake.

"Three bites of the first and I'm too bloated and lazy to be much good at the second."

Rivers laughed as he gulped down the coffee. "I don't mean to be impolite, but I've got to scoot. Things are finally moving."

"Your mood has lightened. Can you tell me what's up?"

"No, and that's not only because I don't trust you; it's because I don't know yet. But I'll make you a deal. I'll keep you informed if you'll promise me something in return."

"No freelancing."

"You got it. Keep your people out and resist the urge to try to control events. In other words, sit tight."

"I can't promise you that."

"Listen, Mr. Warren. I don't have time for a long speech so I'll tell you the last line first. Do it my way, you stubborn bastard. The meal's on me. Ciao."

Rivers stopped by his flat for a five-minute shower. Remembering what Orpac had said, he turned the water on full cold for the last thirty seconds. He toweled off briskly, checked his belly in the mirror to be sure the cake didn't show, stepped into clean brown cords, and pulled on the same faded cotton sweater he had worn at dinner. The chocolate-coffee rush was still lifting him as he peeked in on the sleeping kids and headed back to Grant Street. He arrived a few minutes past ten, just as Lorenzo arrived leading a very short, very stylishly dressed black man in his mid-30s.

Rivers cursed silently. Tall or short, white or black, witness or suspect, everyone involved in this case dressed like Pierre Cardin's brother.

"Listen, Lieutenant, I don't enjoy being rousted out in the middle of the night by your man here," Lincoln began, even before Lorenzo completed introductions. "Unless I'm under arrest, and I can't imagine I am, I would like an immediate explanation. If the explanation isn't entirely satisfactory, I will file a lawsuit . . ."

"We're merely seeking your cooperation," Rivers interrupted, suppressing his desire to kick the man. "If Officer Jones has appeared to act hastily, it's because we're facing an emergency which you, as an officer of the court, will surely appreciate. At this moment, there is a man in Los Angeles who is, shall we say, the beneficiary of the concerted attention of several members of the Los Angeles police force. This gentleman wants very badly to talk to you."

As Rivers continued, he realized that although Lincoln's goatee suited his moon face, his razor-thin moustache was almost as offensive as the Phi Beta Kappa key dangling ostentatiously from a gold chain stretched across his pot belly.

"And who may I ask is this citizen in distress, Lieutenant?" Lincoln asked, rocking back on the heels of his elevator shoes.

"Oscar Williams. He used to play some basketball. Does it ring a bell?"

"Yes, yes. Like the First Baptist Church on Easter Sunday. But you will have to excuse me. I have to be in court early tomorrow and I need my rest."

"Perhaps you don't understand, counselor. Williams is under heavy police surveillance and wants to talk to you."

"I have perfect hearing, Lieutenant, and an IQ sufficient to grasp a simple declarative sentence. Oscar Williams is one of the most charming men who ever wore short pants, but he already owes me $8000 for services rendered. Unless you're willing to guarantee my normal fee of $200 per hour plus expenses, I don't think we have anything to discuss."

Rivers swallowed an urge to tell Lincoln exactly how much he thought he was worth.

"Sit tight for a few minutes, counselor; let me check the piggy bank." He walked into Rafferty's office and called Hanrahan. Rivers explained what was happening and got Hanrahan to agree to meet them at the airport in time to catch the last flight.

"Do we absolutely need that twerp?" Hanrahan asked.

"Phil Orpac says yes. Remember, John, this is our first lead of any kind. Paying Lincoln may be obnoxious, but it's not as bad as failing to turn up Speldon's killer."

"Okay, but I wouldn't pay the Chief Justice $200 per hour. Tell him $750 total and we'll have him back by noon. If he so much as blinks, make it clear he either cooperates or he'll be so far down my shit list he'll have to move his sleazy law practice to San Jose."

18

The plane was half empty and the flight was uneventful. Rivers and Hanrahan sat together in the rear of the 727. Lincoln muttered something about never sitting in the rear of anything, and chose a seat up front.

Hanrahan was a balding man in his middle 40s with a lightbulb nose. He liked scotch, golf, and bathroom jokes, and was sure to be appointed to the bench now that the Republicans had their man running things in Sacramento. As a deputy public defender, Rivers had opposed Hanrahan a dozen times, quickly learning that despite his hearty exterior, he was one tough, quick-minded Irishman. Every cop in the East Bay positively revered him as the author of "Hanrahan's rule": "Everyone arrested is guilty of the crime charged, and even if they're not, the arresting officer should still be congratulated because they're sure to be guilty of something else." This was supported by Hanrahan's even more popular first corollary: "All prisoners showing signs of physical abuse have been damaged while assaulting an officer, resisting arrest, or both—there are no exceptions."

Hanrahan's public relations flair wasn't limited to making himself popular with cops. He had a genius for making a media splash. A good example involved a recent trial where he convicted four teenagers of killing a blind newspaper vendor who helped support her eighty-year-old mother. Rivers knew, of course, that a deputy D.A. who regularly tried the killers of eighty-year-old nuns and sweet-spirited quadraplegics had to be getting a hand from further up the power ladder. It was something to keep in mind. If things turned dicey and someone ended up marooned at the end of a shaky limb, it wasn't likely to be John Hanrahan.

Rivers reviewed the case for Hanrahan before lying back and nursing a double brandy. The final shape of any deal offered Williams was up to Hanrahan, he thought, as he shut his eyes and consciously relaxed his muscles — first the feet, then the ankles, and so on. Deciding there wasn't much the cops could do if Hanrahan was too chicken to move boldly, Rivers lapsed into his favorite activity, not waking until the wheels of the 727 scratched the flood-lit belly of LAX.

The three men were met at the gate by a plainclothes officer. She led them to an unmarked car, illegally parked in a white zone in front of the terminal. Williams' mother lived only fifteen minutes from the airport. Their drive along an asphalt corridor through urban dreck was interrupted only once by Los Angeles' closest approximation of open space, the huge asphalt parking field surrounding the Hollywood Park racetrack.

Rivers, feeling dreadful after his short nap, perked up when he spotted a twenty-foot-high donut, appropriately perched atop the "Big Do-Nut Drive In." He mumbled a request for coffee, but the driver ignored him, turning right on Hoover and then right again on 115th, a residential street. They continued past a row of modest bungalows, pulling in behind three tan sedans with the pinch-penny look shared by unmarked police cars the world over. A uniformed officer kept a few curious neighbors, complete with housecoats and pincurls, a hundred feet or so up the street behind a smog-stunted palm. On the whole, everything looked quiet, low-key, and sleepy, Rivers thought. He noticed that while the paint was peeling off most of the houses, there were new-looking bars on their windows.

Phil Orpac stood by the curb. Rivers introduced him to Lincoln and Hanrahan before nudging him to the side and muttering, "Phil, you know what's going on. I'll follow your lead."

Orpac moved to one of the LAPD cars and dialed a number on its radio phone. He exchanged a few words and gestured to Lincoln to take the phone.

Orpac walked up the cracked sidewalk a polite distance to where Rivers was standing with Hanrahan. Lincoln looked left, right, up and down, as if he was playing the lead in a James Bond movie, before mumbling a few words and hanging up. Orpac, Rivers, and Hanrahan had a good laugh. The call was not being recorded.

Lincoln addressed the trio in stentorian tones, "I demand to speak with my client."

"That's what you're here for, counselor," Orpac responded. "It's the third house down with the porch light on."

"What do you think, Phil?" Rivers asked as he watched Lincoln strut up the walk, pigskin briefcase complete with gold initials swinging from his short right arm.

"Williams obviously wants to talk. After all, he called us. My guess is he knows something about the Speldon killing but wants to be sure he saves his own skin in exchange for the information. Are you the one who decides whether his offer is good enough, Mr. Hanrahan?"

"I don't have the authority to let him walk away if he confesses to a murder but, unless I'm missing the point, I don't think he has the slightest intention of doing that. Let's see what he wants before we speculate. Frankly, I'm still not as clear as you two seem to be as to why he called us."

"We put out a bulletin about Williams late this afternoon after we got a tip he was involved with Willie Thompson in a coke buy set for Sunday night, which of course was when Rathman, Speldon, and Thompson were killed. Apparently Williams has a buddy in the LAPD who alerted him."

"Is this all your theory?" Hanrahan interrupted.

"Nope, Oscar came right out with it. And, for what it's worth, he also said that even if we hadn't connected him to the case, he would have gotten in touch with us when the dust settled."

"Don't tell me he wants to do his civic duty," Hanrahan said with undisguised cynicism.

"He said he doesn't like nukes and dug Speldon for having the balls to stand up to the plutonium fuckers . . ." Orpac responded politely, ignoring Hanrahan's tone.

They were interrupted by the buzz of the car phone. Orpac picked it up. After listening for a moment, he put his hand over the mouthpiece and said, "Williams is ready to talk to the officer in charge and the D.A., but he wants to record the conversation."

Rivers looked at Hanrahan.

The Irishman shrugged.

Rivers nodded.

Orpac uncovered the mouthpiece and said they would be along.

"I feel a little like we're the Lone Ranger and Tonto walking into the outlaws' den," Hanrahan muttered as the two men started up the short walk.

"Speak for yourself, Kemosabe," Rivers replied, "I'm just delivering the newspaper."

"I hope the headline isn't about the latest escapade of a seven-foot killer in short pants," Hanrahan added with a chuckle.

Rivers laughed too and felt his tension ease. He would never like this cynical bastard, but somehow it was nice to know he had the guts to go along with his brains and political connections. Maybe he wouldn't be such a bad judge after all.

As Rivers and Hanrahan stepped onto the narrow wooden porch, there was a sharp crack. Both flinched before realizing it was only Lincoln ineptly tugging at the front door, which was slightly swollen by dampness. On the third pull he got it open, and they entered a small front room. Lincoln motioned them along a three-step hall and into a freshly painted yellow and white kitchen. The brightly lit room with its starched white curtains reminded Rivers of visits to his grandmother's kitchen thirty years before.

A tall, clean-shaven, light brown man stood and offered his hand. Rivers shook it.

Hanrahan nodded noncommittally.

Williams wore a pair of loose drawstring pants and a tight purple T-shirt. His torso looked like an ad for a Nautilus machine; a heavy silver chain with a shark's tooth encircled his large brown neck. He still looked like one of the starting five.

"Would you gentlemen like a beer?" Williams asked with a smile.

Rivers was thirsty and nodded.

Hanrahan shook his head.

Without bothering to ask Lincoln, Williams moved to the refrigerator, limping slightly. He took out three bottles of Bohemia, holding them all easily in his right hand.

When they were seated at the yellow formica table, there was a moment of silence.

Finally, Williams picked up a green glass vase containing one plastic daffodil, leaned back on two chair legs, and started to speak in a low, melodic voice.

"I have a chance to spend some time in Europe studying art for the next couple of years. I have one little problem though. For reasons perhaps you gentlemen can guess, it may be inconvenient for me to leave the country just now. It seems that there are people who want to talk to me about an incident that allegedly occurred in Berkeley this past Sunday evening. All clear so far?"

Rivers inclined his head.

"Now, suppose I was able to help the Berkeley police with some information about the murder of two prominent citizens? Would it be fair to suppose they wouldn't inquire too diligently about the circumstances under which I came across this information?" Williams had removed the plastic flower from its container and was rolling it gently between his large hands.

"It would depend on the information and the circumstances," Hanrahan said abruptly.

"My client is a man of great good faith and obvious respect for the law or he wouldn't be voluntarily proffering his evidence," Lincoln interposed. "I am sure that you can have the utmost confidence in his veracity, candor, and . . ."

"Thank you, Wilbur, my man, but it's too close to dawn for lawyer talk," Williams interrupted. Then, turning a heavy stare on Rivers and Hanrahan, he said, "It's as simple as this. If I help you, will you help me? I know something valuable, but there's no way I'm going to run it down until I get your word I can fly away from here. Since I got hurt, I got mixed up in a bad movie. What's gone down in the last few days has opened my eyes. I want out of that movie before I'm part of a sad ending. The only way I know how to do that is to get away from the California pressure cooker altogether. I took a few art courses in college, enough to know I have talent. I got it from my daddy, who could have been a fine painter if it hadn't been for a few bad breaks—like being born poor and black in Alabama, and then having me and my sisters to support."

After an extended pause, Williams added, "I want to do something I know he would have approved of."

No one said anything. After a minute Williams spun the yellow plastic flower between his hands like a pinwheel and dropped its stem into an empty Bohemia bottle so fast Rivers was tempted to ask for an instant replay.

"Do I have your cooperation or don't I?" Williams asked. "I can't see it's such a big deal. You've got no evidence to hold me. And the fact is, I wasn't the one who stuck Thompson, although I have a hunch I'll live longer if I don't talk about that part of it. But then I have an even stronger hunch. You don't give much of a damn about the death of a no-account nigger pimp anyway."

"Let's get down to it," Hanrahan snapped in a voice hard enough to cut glass. "What exactly are you offering?"

"It's simple," Williams responded mildly. "First my attorney starts his cassette player and mumbles a few legal generalities about how we're all here voluntarily. Then you and Lieutenant Rivers introduce yourselves. I'd appreciate each of you telling good buddy Sony here how much you appreciate my voluntary cooperation. I will also be beholden if you'll say something pretty clear about how you're immediately withdrawing all pending requests that I be arrested and questioned because you have no reason to believe I have committed any violent crimes. Finally, I'd like you to phone up the great blue cop computer in the sky and say the magic words needed to withdraw whatever procedures you have started against me."

"What do we get in exchange, a Revlon make-up case and a trip to Puerto Rico for two?" Hanrahan queried disgustedly.

"A complete description of the deranged character who blew Aldo Speldon away. I am absolutely straight about helping you. I may have done a few things you guys don't dig since this," Williams added, tapping his right knee, "but I've never been into any kind of drugs near as bad as this radioactive stuff."

Hanrahan reached over and took a pull on Rivers' beer.

"Here's the rest of my plan," Williams went on, clasping long fingers behind his bullet-shaped head. "I'll tell you enough so you'll know I'm not bullshitting. Then we'll all mosey down to LAX real friendly-like, and I'll catch the first nonstop to Paris. One of you will come along and I'll explain the rest on the way, including a detailed physical description of the dude I saw running through the woods holding a long gun."

Williams paused, allowing himself a Cheshire cat smile. "If you want to send a police artist along, I'll see he gets a decent drawing, or, if you prefer, I can do the drawing myself. That's it. If you want to lock me up instead, I'll come quietly, but if you put this blackbird in a cage, your chances of getting him to sing about what happened in those trees Sunday night will be about as good as a Klan wizard walking untouched through Watts on a Saturday night wearing a sheet. You dig?"

"Okay," Hanrahan said casually, surprising Rivers with his easy acquiescence. "But there is something I want said on tape. I want you to state you weren't involved in any of the violence Sunday night. Winking at white powder is one thing, but I don't deal 180s. And dig this, Rembrandt, if it turns out you were involved in any of the killings, no cassette, or for that matter, no ocean, is going to stop us from tracking you down. Half the reason I'm willing to go along with your charade is that I know no brother as big as you is going to be hard to find, and extradition is easy enough for murder."

19

Rivers and Hanrahan got back to L.A. International at about 4:15. The airport security people arranged for them to stretch out in one of the VIP boarding lounges until they were called for the 6 a.m. flight. They dozed again on the plane but, even so, both were groggy when they parted in the parking lot at the Oakland Airport a few minutes past 7:00. Phil Orpac and an LAPD artist were to leave with Williams on a morning flight to France. It would be a number of hours yet before Orpac could be expected to radio the rest of the verbal description, and late in the day before they would receive the drawing transmitted from Paris.

When Rivers arrived at the morning meeting a few minutes before 8:00, he was delighted to see Mary Finnegan was already there with the donuts. He grabbed three to make up for having been short-changed earlier in the week and made the coffee while the others drifted in. Everyone was on time, and he briefly outlined the events of the previous night, quickly getting to the point.

"Williams described the killer as being a white male, probably in his middle or late 20s, wearing a dark sport jacket or suit jacket over a white shirt. He also wore dark slacks, maybe corduroys, and some sort of heavy outdoor boots. He was carrying what Williams thought was a rifle."

"What did he look like? We're not going to get far arresting young men wearing corduroy pants," Tamura said, sounding disappointed.

"Phil is getting a description on the plane and will send the sketch when he arrives. Williams claims to have an excellent visual memory, so with the help of the artist we hope to get something fairly accurate."

"Couldn't Williams' whole story be a hype? Was there even enough light for him to see?" Mary Finnegan asked.

"Remember, there are three spotlights on the top of the building and several more on the pole at the west end of the parking lot," Carl Burnett replied.

"How did Williams know the man he saw killed Speldon and Rathman, James?" Lorenzo Jones asked.

"He didn't, until he read the morning paper. He claims he heard four or five booms in close succession and then saw this guy with a gun running across the lighted area between the station and evergreens where he was waiting. He had just found Willie Thompson's body; even though Willie had been knifed, his first thought was that the man with the rifle had killed him, However, while the guy was stumbling and crashing around in the trees, trying to get to the road, he decided there was no way he could have been Thompson's killer."

"What else did Williams say?" Lorenzo Jones asked.

"He said the look on the man's face reminded him of the way he used to feel after a big game that he'd spent days waiting for and worrying about; and then suddenly it was over, he had done well, and his team had won."

"What do we do until we get the full description?" Tamura asked. "Most of our other leads have been at least ninety percent wishful thinking from the start."

"Let's just wait for the drawing," Rivers agreed. "Did you get anything from Bell?"

"If he was involved, he fooled me, but he gave me an earful just the same. I wrote a detailed version, but the gist is he claims Roger Warren and Lucy Speldon were intimate."

"The old triangle motive!" Jones leered as he stroked his chin in a knowing fashion.

"Are you sure?" Rivers demanded.

"I'm sure that's what Bell told me. Beyond that, I'm not psychic," Tamura shot back, annoyed.

"Looks like you've got Lucy Speldon to question," Rivers said.

"Warren too?" Tamura asked, hoping he felt too tired to handle it himself.

"Sure, why not? And while you're over there, see if you can rattle a vice-president named Douglas Heisman. Ask him where he was

154

Sunday night and whatever else you think might annoy him. I'm not after anything specific, but I'd like to know what you make of him."

Rivers paused and looked slowly from one familiar face to the next. Telegraphing his own feelings, he asked, "Are you guys awake?"

"Lieutenant Orpac asked me to keep checking out the tips from the public. Are you interested in a rundown on them now?" Lassiter stammered from where he sat a little behind Lorenzo.

"Thanks for reminding me, Lassiter. But first, what about... Strange, or whatever his name is?"

"It's strange," Lassiter started, then blushed when the others laughed. "I mean, it's odd," he continued doggedly. "He called again right after the morning meeting yesterday and whispered he was glad it was finally all over. Now that the right man had been taken care of, he said, there won't be any more killing. I took him to mean he had killed someone, but I checked and there were no murders reported in the Bay Area on Monday or early Tuesday morning. Also..."

"What did the University come up with?" Tamura asked.

"Not much," Lassiter replied, edging forward on his straight chair, obviously pleased to be the center of attention. "There are no Stranges currently enrolled at Berkeley. They're checking the other campuses. Yesterday though, when I asked him his name, it sounded as if he whispered 'Stain,' or maybe 'Strain.' I called the University back and they suggested supplying a list of every undergraduate and graduate student whose name starts with the letters ST. When I talked to Lieutenant Orpac, he had me call them again and ask that all students who have dropped out or graduated in the last three years be included."

"Fine," Rivers said quickly, fearing the eager young officer was about to progress to what he'd had for lunch the previous day. "Have there been many other calls?"

"A pile," Lassiter replied, holding his thumb and index finger about half an inch apart. "Speldon was basically a pretty popular man. We have suggestions from all over the world—Australia, Canada, Venezuela, Chile, and even South Africa—not to mention the letters that just wish us good luck."

"South Africa?" Jones sputtered. "Those honkies are so worried about black power they don't have time to worry about nuclear power. Come to think of it though, I can't imagine a better place for a nice, hot nuclear waste . . ."

"Cut the shit," Ben Hall interrupted. "No one around here is singing *We Are Marching to Pretoria*."

Rivers nodded his thanks to Ben. Jones had broken the strict departmental rule prohibiting racial comments, and it was a relief to have a fellow black officer call him on it.

"Now pay attention," Rivers said. "Phil's in Paris. Lorenzo and Mary, you'll have to help Lassiter. Go through the kook list carefully. Show anything interesting to Sara."

Whoa, Rivers thought, I must be tired to be calling Tamura by her first name again. He had to admit, though, she looked especially lovely this morning in a magenta leotard top and tight Levis. It was probably just due to sleep deprivation, but he'd had to resist the urge to make eye contact. All the more reason to wrap up the meeting fast and go straight to bed, he thought.

"Carl, please use this lull time to think everything through from the beginning," Rivers continued. "Does Williams' description give you any ideas?"

"Not really, James. This might be the exceptional case where we find the killer and then figure out the reason for the killings, but I'm not optimistic. In the end, I suspect we'll still have to do it the other way."

"Huh?" Mary Finnegan exclaimed from her seat next to Carl Burnett on the couch.

"If we can understand the why of the killings, it shouldn't be hard to figure out the who, but looking for the killer with nothing more than his physical description won't be easy," Burnett replied.

"Don't you think we're getting closer to both the killer and the reason?" Tamura asked, thinking to herself that Carl and Mary seemed to end up sitting next to each other on the couch rather regularly. "It must be wrapped up in the politics of Speldon's life somehow. Rathman really does seem to be a dead end. Oops! Sorry, I didn't mean that the way it came out," she added, giving

Lassiter an understanding grin.

"Sometimes I think that there are only fifteen people in Berkeley and the rest are produced with mirrors," Carl replied patiently. "There must be twenty thousand people in the East Bay who roughly fit."

"The fact that it's a youngish man is . . ." Tamura started to reply.

"Hell, we knew that from looking at the boot tracks Sunday night," Carl interrupted, starting to sound annoyed. "If we're honest, we have to admit it's taken us four days to establish nothing much. Sure, we've tentatively eliminated some suspects. So what? Unless we're going to pretend eliminating the innocent is the same as catching the guilty, we have to admit we know very little."

"You don't think we're even on the right track, Carl?" Mary Finnegan asked.

"If the track is right, then the train doesn't fit," Burnett replied, uncharacteristic annoyance still on the edge of his voice.

As if realizing he wasn't being very nice, he leaned forward from his seat on the low couch and snagged the last donut with a deftness that a praying mantis would envy. He took a delicate bite, taking care to tilt it so the lemon custard didn't drip on his lap. When he spoke again, it was in a relaxed tone that everyone knew meant they may as well settle in.

"The war between the states was about slavery, cotton, states' rights, and a dozen other big issues . . ." A duet of groans from Hall and Jones interrupted Burnett.

"Ironically, though," the technical sergeant continued unfazed, "it was a little thing that kept the war going so long. Both North and South were literally on the wrong track when it came to invading each other. You see, the two regions used tracks of a different width, so trains from one side couldn't go on the track of the other. The Union spent a bunch of time trying to modify their equipment to fit on Confederate track, but it never really worked. In the end, everyone had to walk and the war was fought at fifteen miles a day."

"So?" Tamura finally asked, guessing from several vacant smiles she wasn't the only one whose effort to follow Carl's history lesson had gotten derailed short of understanding.

"So my great-grandpappy chopped cotton for his great-grand-pappy for an extra year," Jones contributed helpfully.

"I mean, things will go a lot easier when we accept what's going on in this case rather than trying to get what's going on to fit our ideas of what we think ought to be going on. Or, to put it another way, suppose, just suppose, Sara, the killings had nothing to do with Speldon or his politics."

"I thought we agreed this just didn't add up to a random killing," Rivers said tiredly.

"Agreeing there must have been a reason isn't the same as saying the reason was Aldo Speldon or his politics," Carl replied. "We checked Rathman and have eliminated the people he knew because we can't find anything suspicious. And even granting that the Speldon murder dripped motives, we haven't come up with a half-likely suspect so far, unless this love triangle changes things. As far as I can see, we've attached ourselves to Speldon's life like barnacles to a boat bottom because we would rather be stuck than admit we don't know what to do next."

"Maybe you're right. I'll think about it after I sleep," Rivers said, stifling a yawn. "Tamura, wake me when the picture comes in. Is there anything else before I leave?" he added, not bothering to resist another yawn.

"I think my spending more time on the KILO angle is dumb," Ben Hall stated. "Incidentally, I followed up on the lists of names Dorsey and Ellen Friedman came up with. Black, white, yellow, and beige—all of the KILO employees seem to have genuinely liked Rathman. I also checked the possibility of jealous lovers, but couldn't find any. When we get the drawing, I'll show it around, but in the meantime . . ."

"Have you any suggestions, Ben?" Rivers asked.

"Yes, the drug connection. That's something I know a lot more about. If I can get with a couple of my buddies in Narcotics, maybe we can figure out who did in Willie Thompson—assuming, that is, that Oscar Williams is playing straight and didn't slide to Paris behind a moving pick. You know, that man scored a lot of points, despite the fact he never was a great pure shooter like Robertson,

West, or the Ice Man. He did a lot of it on guile. There haven't been many big men who could fake as well as Oscar Williams."

"Working on Willie Thompson's death is exactly what needs to be done," Tamura said.

Rivers nodded as he gathered his belongings.

"Ah, er, James," Lassiter said as bravely as he could. "Everyone has been too busy to follow up any of the other violence reports."

"I glanced at them. There's nothing that can't wait, is there?" Tamura asked.

"There is an I.D. on that wino stabbed in People's Park last month, and a Professor Storey called about the brakes going out on his car," Lassiter said.

"Are you guys hurting for bread so bad you're fixing cars on the side?" Rivers asked impatiently.

Tamura willed herself not to respond to Rivers' characteristic insensitivity. "Lassiter is right, James. I forgot to tell you. Storey's a philosophy professor at Cal who lives on a steep part of Cragmont, close to Grizzly Peak. Yesterday morning the brakes on his Triumph failed. Fortunately a colleague asked for a ride at the last minute and Storey turned uphill to pick him up. Had he turned downhill, as he normally does to drive to campus, he would surely have gone over a cliff about a hundred yards along."

"Aside from the obvious fact that anyone who drives an English car isn't very bright to start with, what's it to us?" Ben Hall asked.

"Storey had the car towed to his regular garage. The owner, who's worked on Triumphs for twenty years, claimed he'd never seen that sort of failure before," Tamura continued. "He checked it carefully and told Storey he thought the brake line had been cut."

"Has anyone looked into it?" Rivers asked.

"Things have been too crazy around here. I had the patrol officer on Storey's beat stop by the garage and take the defective line to the county. The lab promised a report by this afternoon," Tamura concluded.

20

Tamura was delighted by her solo assignment. Her joy in sleuthing was always muted when she had to follow Rivers' lead. Perhaps she should custom-order a T-shirt with "Japanese do it better alone" on the chest. It would surely get more attention from Rivers than a properly drawn memo, especially if she got a size too small.

Enough fantasy; time to formulate her approach to Lucy Speldon. *Do I directly confront her with Walter Bell's story or do I figure out some way to sneak up on it?*

Tamura interrupted her own thought by jerking the steering wheel sharply to the left, narrowly avoiding a middle-aged woman on a moped.

"Damn it," she said out loud as she realized the swerve had caused her to pass the correct spoke of the Marin Avenue traffic circle. She concentrated as she went around a second time, breathing easier only when she was safely heading north on The Arlington. She hadn't liked traffic circles since the time she got caught in the inside lane at the Arc de Triomphe at rush hour. Afraid to cut into a line of nose-to-tail Renaults and Citroëns, she had circled for half an hour. Finally, a white-gloved Parisian gendarme haughtily stopped at least a hundred cars and waved her to the side while the French motorists honked their derision. As embarrassing as it had been, she had been grateful for the official intercession, as she still had half a tank of gas.

Tamura bumped along The Arlington past enormous homes, monuments to those few years in the first third of the twentieth century, after natural-gas hookups made heat cheap and before the combination of New Deal reforms and the labor shortages of the Second World War resulted in live-in maids going the way of the carrier pigeon and the Dodo bird. Her thought was not on gracious living, however, but on how she was going to question Lucy Speldon. No lightbulb flashed on in her brain; perhaps she would have to wing it. Despite Walter Bell's damaging tale, she was sure there must be a sensible explanation for Lucy's lack of candor. No matter how hard she tried, Tamura had difficulty seeing Lucy Speldon in the role of a murderess. If James were in her shoes, she thought, he would likely deal with Lucy by coming on all hostile and accusatory. But what did that prove except that he hadn't recovered from being a lawyer? Or perhaps, to be fair, she should say hadn't *completely* recovered. For despite the occasional frosty moment, their relationship seemed to be thawing a little.

The permanently perched seagull looked benignly down on Tamura as if greeting an old acquaintance. She did her best to ignore it as she rang the bell. Her mission was hardly friendly and she was damned if she was going to let her resolve be softened by one of Lucy Speldon's fanciful creatures. Lucy had lied, meaning that even if she wasn't the killer, she was trying to shelter someone who might well be. I may be new to murder investigations, Tamura mused, but all those hours watching Jack Webb and Broderick Crawford weren't wasted. Where there was one lie, there were likely to be more.

The door popped open. Tamura couldn't suppress a little gasp of surprise as she forgot all her tough-guy resolutions. Lucy Speldon was dressed from head to toe in the color of an aspen tree in early spring—intense, bright green. Her hat was green. Her suit was green. Her shoes were green. Even the ceramic Job the Airedale pin on her lapel was green, although closer to the color of a midsummer sugar maple than to a spring aspen.

Lucy Speldon giggled at Tamura's incredulous look. "I just came from a memorial service for Aldo at Point Reyes. Black just didn't seem right. Official mourning gives me the creeps, and green was Aldo's favorite color."

"You do look lovely, Lucy," Tamura smiled, touching the older woman's green sleeve. "May I come in for a moment? I have a few more questions."

The look of girlish delight faded quickly from Lucy Speldon's face.

"Of course. I'm sorry I'm so discombobulated. I still feel as if I'm dealing with the world through three layers of gauze. Now, what brought you up the hill looking so resolute?"

"Your relationship with Roger Warren," Tamura said quietly.

The lines and wrinkles on Lucy Speldon's pixie face all turned down together. Even her body seemed to lose its bounce, and she looked her age.

"Oh my, you found me out. I had a nightmare Monday night after we talked. You had found out the truth and looked so disappointed. The worst of it was I could say nothing in my own defense. You treated me as a friend and I lied to you—or at least, didn't tell you the whole truth. Unfortunately, I don't have a better explanation today."

Tamura didn't say anything.

Lucy Speldon shook her gray curls as if to clear her head. "It was all so long ago and since I knew in my heart, or thought I did, that it was completely unconnected with Aldo's death, why make things harder for Roger? I knew how tacky it would appear if you found out some other way, but it was a question of loyalty and . . ." Lucy let the sentence trail off and reached for her lime green handkerchief. "There really aren't any decent excuses, are there?" she added after a good blow.

"How about the whole truth and nothing but the truth now?" Tamura said, allowing her over-broad imitation of Jack Webb to take the hard edge off the moment.

"You'll probably be disappointed. The whole thing was over almost before it began. You have to understand, the setting was so romantic and we were both a little lonely. Oh Sara, I do feel embarrassed."

"Why don't you just describe what happened," Tamura said, guiding her to the window seat.

"It was three years ago, the year the big energy conference was held in Europe. I love France, and when Aldo got an invitation to speak, I jumped at the chance to go along, even though we were mostly going our separate ways. When the conference ended, Aldo came home, but I decided to wander around on my own for a few weeks.

"I remember perfectly the day I met Roger. It was early fall,

162

warm and beautiful. I was sitting on a park bench in Grenoble. A large white duck came waddling by pretty fast, closely followed by a small Dachshund with the shortest legs I'd ever seen. A few seconds later, a fat, elderly woman with legs almost as short as her dog's came puffing along, shouting half in German, half in French, for someone to grab her Max. I got sucked in and joined the chase."

Lucy Speldon brightened just a bit as she continued. "I'm pretty nimble for my age, you know. I can still stand on my hands and touch my nose to the floor and all that. Anyway, I made a leap and caught the end of the dog's leash with my foot, pulling him off his paws. Even though I had him securely caught, he was still frantically trying to get at the duck. The end of the story is the best part. Max wrapped the leash around the legs of a man passing from the other direction. The man tried to pull free. The duck pecked at him. The old lady ran up. Beset from all sides, Max forgot his deportment and peed on the man's leg. Poor Roger," Lucy Speldon chuckled.

It took a few seconds for Tamura to be sure she had a firm grasp on the thread of the narrative. Then she asked, somewhat incredulously, "The man the dog peed on was Roger Warren?"

"Yes—such nice gray gabardine pants, too. You can imagine how embarrassed I was. I had met Roger a few times in formal, somewhat strained social circumstances. And there I was, the wife of his principal antagonist, holding the leash of a silly Dachshund that had just peed all over him. For a moment neither of us knew what to say. Then we just burst into laughter. Even the old woman, who by that time had her precious Max in her arms, laughed.

"After we rinsed Roger's pants as best we could with water from the fountain, he invited me to lunch. The long and short of it is that between the veal marsala and the crème caramel, we fell a little bit in love. You know, two lonely people in *la belle France*. Oh, I know, I'm old enough to be your mother and you probably think me a bit dotty to boot, but as you have surely heard, wine often tastes best when it's been in the bottle for a while."

"So you spent some time together," Tamura put in, steering the conversation back to the point.

"Yes, we had a wonderful week. But that's all, Sara; a precious interlude. When we left France, it was over. Maybe it would have ended anyway, but under the circumstances—oh, how can I explain?"

"You both had a lifetime of allegiances. They seemed almost weightless in a place where no one knew you, but at home they were too heavy to bear," Tamura assisted.

"It has something to do with integrity, too. A holiday in France was one thing, but here . . ."

"You never saw Roger Warren again?"

"Not even at a public function. How on earth did you find out about us?"

Tamura paused, wondering if she should reveal her source.

"Did Roger tell you?" Lucy asked, sounding a little disappointed.

"No, Lucy. Walter Bell saw the two of you go into a hotel in Grenoble," Tamura answered, deciding there was nothing to be gained by being close-mouthed.

"Goodness. And we thought we were being discreet." She sighed and ran her fingers through her curls. "Well, I'm not sorry it happened. I still feel a lot of affection for Roger and I'm absolutely sure he couldn't murder anyone in cold blood."

"You haven't even spoken to him in the three years since?"

Lucy shook her head. "After your first visit, I almost called him. But somehow I couldn't. Not telling you was bad enough. I just couldn't add collusion to deception."

Tamura nodded, stood, and said goodbye. She knew she had to fight her tendency to believe people. It stood to reason there wasn't a great future for a gullible detective. This time, however, she didn't bother to challenge her belief with every possible doubt. There was something fundamentally sincere about the way Lucy Speldon told her story.

21

By the time Rivers collapsed on his bed, it was almost 11 a.m. He felt like he had finished a triathlon. As exhausted as he was, however, he couldn't stop his over-amped brain. It replayed his encounter with Chief Bacon following the morning staff meeting as if it were a slow-motion video recorder. With the mini-drama flickering against the inside of his eyelids, it occurred to him how wonderful it would be if one could really apply filmmaking techniques to police work. Every time things went wrong or you thought of a better remark or strategy, you could simply stop and do it again — lights, camera, action, take two, and all that. No question about it, with a little editing, a working cop's arrest rate would soar. But of course, since technology had no respect for morality, the crooks would surely use the new techniques as well. Suppose both sides could do a second or third take. Would the result be exciting or boring? Hard to say, but, stuck as he was in a one-take world, the best he could manage was a mind's eye replay.

He froze the action, focusing on his meeting with Bacon. Filtered sunlight in a chocolate-brown room. Two tall men standing, facing each other on a Bokkara rug, burnished red-gold where the sun touched it. A study in contrasts. Roger Bacon in steel blue and pressed gray speaks to Lieutenant James Rivers, his rumpled, red-eyed underling. Bacon's quiet voice is nicely modulated. What does he say? Ah yes. Rivers is not to drive himself so hard. He should allow himself more rest. The Chief realizes the Lieutenant has been terribly short-handed, but everything will be easier soon because Captain Rafferty is cutting short his vacation to reinforce the troops.

Next the film shows the Lieutenant getting upset. His body tenses. He waves his hands. He talks loudly. What does he say? Something about this being his case and how unfair it is to give it to Rafferty when it's only been a few days since the murder.

165

Rivers is embarrassed watching himself. He wishes he could edit out all the repetitions: "this is my case," and "chickenshit." But the imaginary celluloid rolls on, unstoppable.

Unruffled, cool, and articulate, the police chief warms to his role as compassionate pedant. Indeed, as the camera focus becomes tighter, he begins to look older and wiser, a little like Spencer Tracy as Father Matthew Doonan in *The Devil at Four O'Clock*. He begins what amounts to a monologue, as the sulking lieutenant becomes silent. Rivers hears him say things about the value of teamwork versus individual competitiveness and how their best chance to catch the murderer is to pool their skills. Bacon talks about his belief that many problems Americans have working together harmoniously are caused by the school system which over-rewards individual achievement and doesn't sufficiently honor efficient and effective group working relationships.

Here, the production gets fancier. Both men fade from the picture, replaced by another scene entirely. In a flashback Rivers sees a boy aged seven or so, a flame-haired youth in short pants clutching a Captain Zoom lunch box. He recognizes the lunch box before he recognizes himself. He is shouting at his teacher that he, not a classmate, deserves to be appointed hall monitor. The teacher shakes her head and tells him he must share the honor with the other student. He begins to cry.

Rivers rolled over on his stomach to ease his aching back as the scene dissolved. Not much has changed, he thought, except I didn't cry on Bacon's thousand-dollar carpet. God, that day in second grade seems a long time ago. Miss Slaughter had been right, of course. It had been better sharing the job, and once after the last bell, he and Carol had even kissed shyly on the stairs.

Well, if Miss Slaughter had been wiser than he was all those years ago, he supposed there was just a chance Roger Bacon could be ahead of him now. Perhaps having Rafferty back wouldn't be so bad after all.

22

Tamura left her car in the nearly empty parking lot of the North Berkeley BART station. Although her proletarian soul rebelled at its unhappy combination of space-age design and third-rate technology, she felt that taking the semi-reliable transit system was better than piloting a car into the one-way jungle of asphalt, high-rises and three-dollar-an-hour parking garages the tourist bureau had the gall to call "The City." BART's cars looked almost as good as an expensive Italian automobile, and unfortunately they worked about as well. But what could you expect from equipment designed as if intended to fly to Mars, then built in Mexico to undercut the minimum wage? The Bay Area would be far better off with a decent trolley car. About the only good thing you could say about BART was that taking it was a foolproof excuse for being late.

Tamura randomly chose one of six or so leftover blue and white computer tickets from her wallet. It was part of her transit efficiency theory. Never buy a ticket for a large amount or you'll lose it. Never buy a ticket for the exact fare you need to get to your destination or the machine will confiscate it, and next time you'll miss your train while trying to coax a raggedy dollar bill into a slit in a stainless steel wall. Always get a ticket for more than you need so that when you leave the station you get your ticket back, and thus quickly enter the station next time.

Tamura stood on the platform watching for the electronic notice board to signal the arrival of the San Francisco–bound train. Instead, she was told about cheap socks at Sears, friendly tellers at Crocker Bank, and why she should watch the Channel 6 news. "Exciting new developments in the Speldon murder investigation," the little lights lied. She wished the media would exhibit some respect for the truth, but she had to concede that there probably wouldn't be many viewers if they said "police at a standstill." She shifted her gaze to a billboard covered with the face of a dissipated urban cowboy, filter cigarette hanging from pouting lips. She shook her head. Why did men equate tough with sexy? Making love with a vibrator would be more intimate than curling up with that much alienation.

A three-year-old urchin wearing striped overalls and an engineer's cap squealed past, interrupting Tamura's grumpy musings about the weirdness of the twentieth-century male ego. A disgusted-looking pregnant woman called half-heartedly after the tot.

"Jason, you come back here. You're going to make us miss the train. Jason, this is your last chance, and I mean it."

The boy peeked around the corner of a bench, caught Tamura's eye, and flashed her a wicked grin, as if to say he had heard that one before. Then, just as his mother was closing in for the catch, he faked right, spun left and disappeared behind the up escalator. The heavy woman, not to be outdone, moved quickly around the other side of the moving stairway and scooped him up by the overall straps before he reached the third step.

Just then the sleek gray bullet train purred to a stop. The doors sprung open. Tamura made herself comfortable in a soft seat, and the train whispered on. Italian cars are wonderful when they work, she thought, beginning to feel more cheerful.

Tamura emerged from the underworld to find herself in the glass and steel canyons of the financial district. Like most people born in Los Angeles, she had a secret appreciation for its vertical drama. And not only did she find hanging walls of colored glass exciting, she was exhilarated by the hustle of the canyon's inhabitants. Always a closet Vogue freak, Tamura paused a moment to appreciate the cut and color of the executive armor. She had long since come to terms with the fact that Basile suits and Bottega-Veneta bags weren't made for the salaries of provincial policewomen. But she wouldn't mind if someone wanted to give her a few silk threads and a hundred-dollar haircut.

From the foot of Nob Hill, the Warren Building rose in phallic black splendor, its fifty-six stories barely topped by the point of the Transamerica Pyramid. In an attempt to soften the aggressive power of the dark steel monolith, a well-meaning landscape architect had wrapped a tree-filled plaza around its base, complete with colorful Calderesque sculpture. It was about as effective as painting smiles on the front of 747s.

Douglas Heisman worked on the forty-sixth floor. His outer office looked like it had been cloned from the cover of Abitare Magazine. The woman at the Knoll desk in the center of the Kilim rug, looked so much like Deborah Harry that Tamura expected her to break out in a chorus of "Call Me." Instead, when the candy-apple lips parted, a high, whining voice inquired if she was Officer Tamura. Tamura, who had made an appointment, restrained herself from remarking on the brilliance of the deduction. No sense in being bitchy, she thought, as she watched Little Miss False Eye-lashes suck in her stomach and puff out her chest before opening the door to the inner sanctum.

Douglas Heisman appeared in the doorway. Still playing "celebrity look-alike," Tamura decided he resembled a Teutonic version of Luciano Pavarotti, minus the good humor. Unfortunately, his hard, colorless eyes and round, toad-like head better qualified him to play the villian in a Modesty Blaise adventure than Siegfried in "The Ring." Tamura, who wished she could shoot and kick half as well as Modesty, was glad to meet him in a neutral setting, complete with computer terminal and view of the Embarcadero.

Heisman installed Tamura in a deep leather chair in front of his desk. Then, moving around the wide teak surface, he settled his bulk into a swivel chair covered with faun glove leather. Finally he fixed his eyes on hers. There was something aggressive about the way he did it, as if he were spearing a fish.

"I'm happy to meet you, Officer Tamura, but forgive me if I say I'm not clear as to the purpose of this visit. As I'm sure you know, the real authority in this building resides a few floors up."

As Heisman finished his sentence, his gaze actually flashed toward the ceiling, as if to be sure it was still in place.

Tamura said nothing.

"Or have you come to me for background information on our exalted leader? If so, I'll have to ask you to leave. Even if I agreed with those who suspect Roger Warren's hand behind the violence, and mind you, I'm not saying that I do, it would be improper for me to say so," Heisman continued unctiously. He held his hands palms up in a gesture of supplication, but they were belied by his ice cube eyes.

"Are you implying that Roger Warren is responsible for Aldo Speldon and Frank Rathman being murdered at the same time you pretend to be a loyal employee?" Tamura demanded.

"If you continue to use that tone with me, young woman, I'll have to ask you to leave immediately," Heisman responded, his voice sharpening. "If you dare to even suggest I . . ."

"Save your indignation, Mr. Heisman. We know about your attempts to cast doubt on Roger Warren's leadership ability by making him appear senile," Tamura interrupted, wondering if she was exceeding her authority. "You have little to gain by adding hypocrisy to disloyalty."

Heisman's face flushed, the unpleasant pink color extending to the crown of his bald head. Tamura could see his heavy shoulder muscles tense under his expensive suit jacket as he willed himself not to respond.

Fine, two could play a waiting game. Tamura simply willed her mind quiet, remembering how her Buddhist grandmother could sit silently for hours with no apparent effort.

After a long minute, the stand-off was broken by Heisman. He forced his heavy lips into a conspiratorial smile. "Why are we starting off on this antagonistic footing? We whose cultural heritages are so similar. Why if the Germans and Japanese ever joined forces the world would surely be far more efficient and prosperous."

Tamura, who imagined the massive traffic tie up all the cars would cause, stifled a grimace before it could flaw what she hoped was her most inscrutable expression. "Historically, it wasn't a very successful alliance, was it, Mr. Heisman? And anyway, why would you want to make a deal with a cop? From what we hear, you have already found a bunch of people to help you frame Roger Warren. And that connects to why I'm here. If Warren was seriously suspected of killing Aldo Speldon, it would serve your purposes very nicely, wouldn't it?"

"Obviously, Miss Oriental nosy parker, you are very poorly

170

informed," Heisman replied in a hostile tone, which for the first time betrayed his Germanic roots. "But to instruct you so that you will no longer ignorantly accuse an innocent man, I assure you I was out of the country when the violence at the radio station occurred."

Tamura said nothing, staring back at Heisman as if she found him inherently unbelievable.

Again there was a long minute of silence. Again Heisman broke it, this time in a loud, threatening, heavily-accented voice. "If you dare to repeat any of your despicable accusations outside this room, I will sue your commie police department for so much it will need foreign aid from Cuba to pay the judgment."

"Better dead that red, eh, herr Kommissar?" Tamura replied, rising and moving toward the door. A glance back at Heisman showed the unnatural pink of his face deepening into an unpleasant shade of purple.

As she opened the door, Heisman's strangled voice hissed after her, "Repeat any of your Jap lies and I'll slap you with a libel suit so fast . . ."

"Slander, Mr. Heisman. If you're referring to the spoken word, slander is the legal cause of action," the blond receptionist amended in a no-nonsense voice as she stepped through the door just opened by Tamura. "But then, if I remember my law school tort lectures correctly, isn't truth an absolute defense to both libel and slander?"

"What are you saying? Who . . ." Heisman began, as he directed his attention to his new antagonist.

"Karen Simmons," she replied, pulling off her blond wig and shaking her head to loosen short, auburn hair. "I'm the assistant director of corporate security at the Western Reserve Agency. Mr. Roger Warren hired us . . ."

Heisman reacted as if slapped. He swore in German as he rose and moved aggressively around his desk. Tamura silently cursed the vanity which had caused her to leave her gun at home. Live and learn. This was the first time she felt endangered because she wore a skirt too tight for a waist clip.

Tamura found it hard to think clearly. What had seemed for a moment to be a game had turned serious. Heisman was approaching from her side of the desk, arms outstretched, clearly intending to assault her and probably Karen too.

Tamura took the offensive moving to hit Heisman in his soft midsection. She connected solidly. Heisman emitted a little grunt of pain but kept coming, his heavy hand catching her on the shoulder and tearing her white cotton blouse down the front. Instinctively, Tamura shielded her breasts with her left arm as she squirmed out of Heisman's grasp, falling to the floor.

Karen Simmons seemed frozen, making no move to avoid the angry man as he turned his attention to her. Then, when he was almost upon her, she executed a quick, balletic turn to the right. Heisman, slightly off-balance as a result of Tamura's renewed attack from the rear, tried to grab the slender young woman. Simmons stepped past his arm and kicked him sharply below the left knee cap.

Heisman went down with a howl, rolling onto his back with his knees clutched against his chest. He looked like the craven loser of a dogfight, offering his vulnerable parts to the victor.

Karen Simmons stuck her head out the office door. A moment later they were joined by four uniformed security guards. She turned to Tamura. "Do you want to charge him with assaulting an officer?"

"He's not worth it. I'd have to spend the rest of the afternoon at San Francisco police headquarters filling in forms."

Simmons nodded. The guards set about gathering up Heisman and his possessions.

As Tamura left what was obviously now Heisman's former office, she could hardly believe she hadn't just taken a detour through a comic book. A Nazi-type executive versus Superwoman in a wig. Myrna Loy would never have fallen for it.

In her slightly dazed state, Tamura was childishly pleased by her foresight in bringing along a cardigan sweater. She slipped it on over her torn blouse and buttoned it to the top. As she waited for an elevator to take her to fifty-six, Tamura tried to make sense of this latest turn of events.

Was any of what had just happened relevant to the Speldon/

Rathman investigation? Heisman, a legitimate bad guy, had been found out and fired. So what. The fact Heisman was guilty of corporate espionage didn't make him a murderer, Tamura reminded herself as she stepped out of the elevator.

Roger Warren was waiting in the reception area. He introduced himself, extended his hand, shook Tamura's politely, and gave it right back to her. A man secure enough to let go, she thought.

The top floor was a surprise. Instead of tight corridors leading to overposh executive offices, it was a bright, plant-filled meeting area. The walls were glass, creating the effect of a greatly enlarged observation tower such as one might find on a mountain top in an area where there was a high fire danger. A cement overhang and small trees and vines partially screened the sun. High above the city, there was no need for curtains.

"Passive solar design at two-thousand feet," Warren remarked, following Tamura's gaze. "We use this space for meetings. Any department head can reserve it and bring their people up. Our executive offices are scattered throughout the building. I don't want anyone, including me, getting delusions of divinity. But enough small talk. You're not here to discuss the tricks big corporations use to keep employees happy are you?"

Before Tamura could reply, Warren touched her arm gently. "Why don't we talk over here where we can see the view," he said, leading the way to a sitting area which looked east toward San Francisco Bay.

As they seated themselves he asked, "Are you hungry? Why don't I send down to the cafeteria for beer and sandwiches if you're up to it."

Tamura nodded. Now that she thought about it, she hadn't eaten all day.

The food seemed to arrive almost before Warren had replaced the phone. Almost as quickly, Tamura polished off a pastrami on sourdough rye, three pickles, most of a bottle of Anchor Steam beer and a brownie. Warren sat back and sipped a cup of tea. When she'd finished, he nodded, looking like a pleased father.

"Now, ask away," Warren said.

An hour later, riding home under the bay, Tamura marveled at the changes in her mood the afternoon had produced. From being mauled to lunching in the penthouse; a police officer's work was never done. But what had really happened that meant anything in the investigation? As with Lucy Speldon, she couldn't help being drawn to Roger Warren. Sure, he was arrogant, opinionated and, beneath his executive veneer, a tough old bastard, but every time he smiled, Tamura found herself grinning in return. She had to remind herself several times during their talk that history is loaded with attractive murderers.

As soon as she had mentioned Lucy Speldon and Grenoble, Warren had freely admitted the entire interlude, and seemed almost glad to discuss an affectionately treasured memory. When she asked him if he had seen Lucy again after Grenoble, he let his light blue eyes wander out over the city to the Bay, where two gigantic oil tankers were passing; one loaded heading in, and the other, riding higher in the water, going out.

Warren smiled and remarked softly, "No, just two ships passing . . ."

Tamura thought he looked wistful. She had wanted to respond, to explain that imagining Lucy as a huge ship set on an inexorable path was just plain nonsense. Anyone should be able to see she was more like a sailboat ready to turn with a fresh breeze. Tamura had restrained herself. It was one thing to eat a murder suspect's kosher dills and quite another to advise him on his love life.

Only now, looking out at the blackness of the transbay tunnel, Tamura realized that Roger Warren hadn't given her a satisfactory answer to her most basic question. Why hadn't he told Rivers about Lucy Speldon? Was he being chivalrous, or was he covering up?

23

Rivers reluctantly allowed the clamor of the telephone to drag him out of a dream. It was a shame. Once more he had been sitting on the big rock watching two women swim in the sun-warmed Guatemalan lake. But there was a difference from his earlier dream. The women were no longer twins—one light, the other dark. Indeed, they no longer resembled each other. One was Sophie Warren and the other Sara Tamura. Except for this transformation of the main characters, the dream was much the same as before. Sara and Sophie were treading water so that their breasts rose now and then from aqueous distortion to ripple the calm surface. And as before, both women were laughing up at him.

Disoriented after his long sleep, Rivers couldn't remember where he had left the phone. It was dark and he staggered out of bed toward the sound. Finally he snagged the cord, reeling it in hand over hand until he could grab the receiver, which had tumbled off its cradle.

"What time is it?" he croaked.

"At the tone, it will be exactly 6:13 p.m.," a light, musical voice replied.

"Funny, I just left you," Rivers said.

"What?" the voice asked, clearly confused.

"In the water. It's okay, I'm awake now."

"James, is everything okay? It sounded for a moment as if you were preoccupied," she added with an uncertain giggle. "I know I shouldn't call you at home, but I tried you so many times at your office that someone finally gave me your number."

"I'm glad they did. How are you?"

"The truth is, not so good. I can't seem to get out from under feeling miserable. I can't sleep and I just don't seem to be able to talk to anyone, except for you. I start to explain how horrible I feel to my friends but I get stuck and don't know what to say. Everyone wants to know why Aldo was killed or who did it, or when the police will arrest someone. Either that or they want to tell me their latest conspiracy theory. I spent a couple of hours singing sad songs to myself but now I feel manic. I've been pacing the house, chain-smoking cigarettes—which is pretty dumb, since I don't even know how to smoke."

"Why don't I come by?"

"Would you? You're kind of my last hope. There's my dad, but he's still a major part of my confusion."

"Sure, but can you practice inhaling for an hour? After I solve the problem of my missing pants, I need to check things at work."

"Sure, don't hurry. I feel better just knowing there'll be someone to talk to. I have food, so don't stop to eat."

"I'll see you a little before eight. You live on Benvenue, right?"

"Twenty-thirty-six, near the corner of Woolsey, on the west side, upstairs."

"Keep a light burning."

Rivers turned on his own light, did a few quick Yoga stretches and then tapped out his office number. The switch board put him through to his own office.

"We thought you might sleep for ten years, like Ichabod Crane," Carl Burnett drawled by way of saying hello.

"Rip Van Winkle, you mean. And I think it was more like twenty years—a fact which your parochial southern mind would doubtless have grasped long since if Washington Irving had come from South Carolina."

"Well, whoever did it, for however long, you can try and break the record if you want," Carl replied. "The plane was delayed by fog and it was the middle of the night, Paris time, when Phil arrived. He's at a hotel now, but has to wait until early morning over there to transmit the picture, which means it will be sometime between ten and twelve this evening before we get it. Everything else is quiet, but there is something you better prepare yourself for. Rafferty is on his way back."

"So the Chief managed to track him down," Rivers said casually, trying to eliminate any shade of disappointment from his voice.

"Rafferty called in. Apparently, newspapers carrying the Speldon story finally caught up with him on some Greek Island. James, this is not an ordinary case and it will be good to have Sean's wiley mind working alongside ours," Burnett said with emphasis as if trying to forestall argument.

"When will he be here?" Rivers replied, realizing that his last twinge of jealousy was gone and he, too, would welcome Rafferty's return.

"Late tomorrow night or Friday morning. He has to close up the house where he's staying and take a couple of boats before he can get to the airport in Athens. He left a message for you. It says to tell you that by the time this is over, you should at least know the words to 'Blue Moon.'"

"What's that supposed to mean?"

"Got me. I only know Sean claims it's one of the seven greatest songs ever written."

"Tamura might know what he means, or it could just be Rafferty's been out in the Greek sun too long."

"I'll ask her if she calls in. What are you up to?"

"I'll be at Sophie Warren's," Rivers answered, looking up the number in his pocket notebook. He gave it to Carl with a request that he pass it along to the switchboard.

Rivers pulled on his most faded jeans, the ones that were getting thin in the seat, and went downstairs to say hello to Julie and Mickey. When he came in they were in the kitchen eating dinner with Jeannie and her son Brian. Everyone gave him the silent treatment, animatedly carrying on a conversation about the adventures of Han Solo and Chewbacca as if he wasn't there. Rivers said nothing, tiptoeing to the sink with exaggerated steps. He filled a bowl with water and, still moving like a pussyfooting Orkan, began making the bleeping sounds of a rampaging R2D2 while flicking bits of water into their faces.

The studied effort not to see him gave way to shouts of "You silly Daddy," followed by a couple of minutes of good-natured rough-housing. Rivers momentarily forgot the tension of the investigation as he rolled on his back and let the three kids try to tickle him. Julie, as always, succeeded first when she pulled off his sandal and went to work on the sole of his foot. It was hard to resist prolonging the fun, but he had an appointment to keep. He reluctantly shook off his small tormentors and kissed them good night.

As Rivers steered Dartha along College Avenue, he began singing to himself. It was clear and pleasantly warm—perhaps 60 degrees. He felt good. Perhaps he would catch Speldon's killer and perhaps he wouldn't, but in the meantime, he could damn well relax. He thought briefly about Rafferty and his reference to "Blue Moon." He fiddled with the right end of the AM dial trying to find the obscure oldies station the Captain doted on. He couldn't get anything but rock and gospel, so he switched his attention to looking for street numbers on Benvenue.

Sophie's house was similar to his own—large, square, and brown-shingled, with one flat over the other. Rivers pressed the bell, and the door popped open almost instantly. He stepped inside and found himself on a square of carpet at the bottom of a tall staircase.

"You have to close it," Sophie said from where she stood a half dozen steps down from the top landing. "My little gizmo opens it from the top, but you have to close it yourself."

He did, and then started up the stairs. She was wearing a red silk kimono over black drawstring pants. For a moment he felt unsure—did they kiss, hug, or shake hands? What's appropriate, he wondered, when you come to visit a stranger with whom you somehow feel almost intimate?

Sophie solved the moment by reaching down and taking his hand. Like Jill guiding Jack, she led him up the last few steps and along a narrow hall into the large front room, where there was a fire in the hearth. It was a comfortable, uncluttered space, dominated by several large pillows covered in bright Indian cottons and an assortment of greenhouse-sized plants. Across the short end of the room, under the windows at the front of the house, a long work table was piled high with books, journals, and a stack of yellow pads. Rivers smiled when he saw she used the legal size too.

"Would you like some wine?" she asked, nodding toward a bottle of Fetzer red on a low table to the right of the fireplace.

"Sure," he said, folding his legs under him and sitting on the

178

surprisingly soft beige rug. He felt wonderful after his long sleep, as if everything was so right with the world that words were unnecessary.

Sophie filled the two plump pear-shaped glasses, lifting one to catch the fire as she passed it to Rivers. "To better days," she said and gently touched his glass with hers.

After a few minutes of companionable silence, she spoke again. "Um, James, I'm a little shy with new friends anyway, and your being a cop makes it worse. Now that you're here, I can't remember half the things I wanted to ask you. It's okay with me to sit here and beam at each other all night. Just the same, the brave part of me wants to tell you I have a hot tub in the back yard and I could probably find some Mendocino homegrown, if you wouldn't go all official or shocked."

"Lead the way, I'm in Homicide, not horticulture," Rivers said with a smile as he gathered his legs under him.

This time she took his hand with a tighter grip, and led him back down the hallway through the old-fashioned kitchen and out onto a recently added deck. He followed her down the flight of stairs to a brick patio, where the moon illuminated the bathing area.

Rivers bent over and unlatched the cover of the hot tub. Lifting the large circular wooden top involved a bit of peasant physics, and it took him a moment to find a grip that worked. Once he had it aloft, he faced another problem—where to lean it. He turned to ask and saw Sophie standing slim and pale in the moonlight, her clothes hanging on the edge of a trellis.

Rivers was so mesmerized by her deer-like beauty that he momentarily forgot his awkward burden. His back, however, was less impressed. Even this most serendipitous arrangement of female anatomy couldn't mask its urgent warning signals. Sophie chuckled as she grabbed one edge and helped him lean the lid against a picnic table.

Rivers pulled off his shirt, stepped out of his pants, and slid into the tub. The water held him like a hot, velvet glove; he shut his eyes and sighed.

"James," Sophie said finally, offering him a newly lit joint.

He opened his eyes. She was between him and the moon, her face in shadow.

"James, when will this whole thing be over?"

"I don't know. It's as if we've been making up demons and then chasing them. I've thought the whole thing through so many times that it has me dizzy. One of the men I work with even believes the crime that took place last Sunday evening and the one we're investigating are somehow different. Weird as it sounds, he has me half-convinced. Our best hope for a quick solution is a sketch drawn by someone we would like to believe saw the killer. I'm expecting it to come in later tonight. Assuming it's good, we may be in pretty fair shape. The next step is to show it to everyone who knew either Speldon or Rathman. Then we cross our fingers and hope that the wheel of fortune is ready to circle our way."

"So you think the picture might solve it?" Sophie asked, surrendering the joint.

"Maybe. But even if the witness is as reliable as we hope, he saw the killer at night in dim light and is translating his recollection to paper a few days later. We aren't going to get a photograph."

"Do you still believe my father was involved?" Sophie asked as she took back the joint and snuffed it out in an abalone shell next to the tub.

"From a political point of view, it doesn't even make demented sense for him to have killed Speldon. Of course, there are the personal involvements, too," Rivers continued. He didn't think this was an opportune moment to mention the relationship between her father and Lucy Speldon, but he felt bad about it. Letting Sophie continue to think her involvement with Aldo Speldon was the main reason the police suspected her father was a crummy thing to do but, in this situation, he had to act like a cop first and a friend second.

"So the brutal truth is you not only suspect my father, you suspect him because of me."

Rivers took his time replying. "A parent's urge to protect a child can have . . ."

"How do you qualify as an expert?" Sophie interrupted sharply.

"At what?"

"How a parent would feel? Did you read that stuff in the policeman's handbook?"

"I have two of my own. They're only in grade school but, if you remember, there's no age limit to occasional hard times."

Sophie paused and then said in a subdued voice, "Somehow I assumed you weren't married. I mean, I wouldn't have . . ."

"I'm not . . . or, I guess technically I am, but it's been four, no five, years since Linda and I have been together. Neither of us has bothered to get a divorce, but . . ."

"Where is she?"

"Running a restaurant in Costa Rica, of all places. We went to Central America to climb the volcanos and hang out on beaches for a sort of second honeymoon. It turned out to be a romantic adventure all right, but only for her. One siesta, when I was sitting under a palm tree writing her a poem, she fell in love with a Swiss guy who taught Spanish to Americans. She told me we were incompatible because I preferred thinking about making love in the moonlight to actually doing it after lunch."

"Pretty cruel."

"People usually are when they fall out of love. I felt awful, partly because it made me realize I'd ended several relationships badly and, in a weird karmic way, I deserved my fate. Anyway, Linda opened a natural foods restaurant in one of the beach towns so she could afford to stay. It's a typical gringo trail cafe — lots of yogurt, fruit smoothies, and herb tea. Believe it or not, she's doing great. The kids spend summers and a month over Christmas down there, but it makes sense to all of us for them to go to school here."

Rivers felt the water ripple against his chest. And then, almost as gently, Sophie was moving against him. Sitting on the tub bench, he tried to hold her, but it was awkward. Damn knees, he thought as he stood, lifting Sophie so they could embrace face to face. She put her hands under his buttocks and pressed her loins against his. He bent his knees slightly to allow his eager penis to enter her.

At the last instant, she twisted away. "James, I've got to see to it we don't have a population explosion."

Without further words, they climbed out of the tub and almost frantically tried to towel each other dry. Here a breast, there a knee — it was hit or miss at best.

Sophie turned and bounded up the stairs. Her pale behind flashed an invitation to follow, like a white-tailed doe in mating season. Rivers responded with all the subtlety of a buck. With her head start she beat him to the bedroom, where they collapsed panting, laughing, and hugging. After a moment, Sophie set about improving the atmosphere, flinging back drapes to let the nearly full moon in, pushing a button to release Nat King Cole from his plastic prison, and lighting a red candle on a bedside table.

While Sophie went to the bathroom, Rivers wiped himself completely dry on the bedspread, climbed between the plum-colored sheets, lay back, and shut his eyes. Even in Berkeley, sleeping with a suspect wasn't approved police practice. He supposed if things went wrong, he could be fired. But of all life's little problems, keeping his job didn't seem a high priority at the moment. Then, as if to quash any lingering doubts, Sophie was beside him, sliding her hand down his chest and along his stomach to where his rising erection waited.

"I want you," she murmured as she climbed astride and guided him to her wet, warm center.

After the fast, almost aggressive start, making love with Sophie was an odd experience, more poetic than sexual. Their eyes stayed open; Rivers felt mesmerized by the clarity of her light blue ones. Perhaps it was the candle, or maybe the moon, but he felt himself surrounded by a golden aura. If he had any doubts before, he knew now that this person hadn't killed. They moved lightly above and under and around one another, as if dancing with the moonbeams. Rivers was amazed by a sweetness he had never found in sex before. He felt the sweetness turn to joy and then finally to an exquisite, almost spiritual ecstasy. Even Sophie's climax wasn't the sort of earthbound, visceral eruption he was used to. At the same time he missed the healthy, animal-in-rut dimension of lovemaking, he was amazed at the numinous feeling which replaced it. Still holding his eyes on Sophie's, Rivers felt as if their bodies were literally rising from the bed. And as she moved ever so gently against him, his body tingled with pleasure, a feeling that was as intense as it was ephemeral. Finally, when he too let go and their bodies throbbed together, it truly seemed to him that they were two bells ringing together in an empty sky.

24

Tamura fingered the Identikit drawing which had finally come from Paris. The face staring back at her was the quintessential Berkeley citizen, circa 1965 to 1975. Longish hair, beard, white skin, driven look. It was all there: the sometimes intellectual, sometimes drugged, sometimes radical student hippie who had launched a score of demonstrations and in the process badly shaken the smug towers of academia. Although campus styles had mostly shifted from hairy radical chic to close-cropped complacency, the city was still home to many of those who had followed Mario Savio and the other would-be Dantons and Robespierres to the Sproul Plaza barricades. It wouldn't be an easy face to find in this town.

Tamura glanced toward the clock on Rivers' desk. Ralph's plump calico torso blocked her view. Leaning over to move the stuffed beast aside, she gave him a few fond pats. It was twenty-five minutes to ten, still early enough to locate James and show him the picture. Even if there wasn't much they could do with it until morning, this was a big moment and it deserved to be shared. She dialed the switchboard and found Rivers was at Sophie Warren's. Good, she could show the picture to the folk singer at the same time. There was another incentive to action. Botts ice cream store, home of the chocolate-dipped creme caramel on a cake cone, was only two short blocks from Sophie's. It wasn't as if she was a glutton, she thought, but if she happened to be in the neighborhood on business anyway, well, even ace investigators have to eat.

As Tamura left the police building, she was startled by the brilliance of the moon. Was it the full moon of the harvest? No, too late in the year; it must be the hunter's moon. Even the heavenly signs auger well, she thought, as she decided against the Nova, with its ever present danger of going bump in the night, and walked two blocks to University Avenue. She was just in time to climb aboard the 51 College which would drop her directly across from the half-dead rubber plant in Botts' front window.

As she made her way to a seat in the rear of the bus, she caught herself mentally checking the male faces against the sketch of the killer. It was easy to eliminate the two earnest sophomores supplying each other with three sentence solutions to the world's problems (we should get the Russians to fight the Chinese and then clean up the mid-East and Southeast Asia while they are occupied with each other). Likewise an octogenarian wearing a tie decorated with golden bears (I can't remember just what day today is, but my dear, let me tell you about the wonderful Big Game against Stanford in 1926) seemed an unlikely suspect. And she could safely rule out the two black hospital workers on their way in for the night shift at Alta Bates, as well as Dr. Mah, Mojo Man and herbalist, an eccentric who had established a secure place in the pecking order of Berkeley oddballs by always dressing in feathers. That left two men in their early 30s, both of whom looked vaguely like the man in the drawing. Both were clean-shaven and had shortish hair, but that was, of course, no reason to eliminate them. If you could afford bus fare, you could buy a razor blade.

The drawing, Tamura reflected, presented a familiar police problem: how to find the right grain of sand when presented with your average beach. But first things first. She was quickly off the bus, into the store, and soon, cone in hand, crossing College toward Benvenue. Here she slowed down so that by the time she reached two-o-three-six, the evidence of her dalliance would be safely tucked away next to her belly gun.

Tamura admired the tree-lined, brown-shingled graciousness of the pre-World War I houses. It must have been pleasant to live a middle class life around the turn of the century, she mused. There were the benefits of electricity and trains, you could get your appendix removed, but you weren't assaulted by TV, 747's and nuclear power plants. Then she realized with a start that she was thinking caucasian again. After all, it wasn't until 1909 that her grandparents arrived in Southern California, so poor they were delighted to get a dollar for laboring all day in the sun. As much as her life—especially her love life—could stand enrichment at the

184

moment, she decided she had better stick to the 1980s.

Tamura licked the fingers of her right hand while she knocked at two-o-three-six with her left. Like trying to swat a mosquito in the dark, licking never accomplished much. She reached gingerly into her purse and found her red bandana. It was Rivers, she remembered almost fondly, who had taught her the most essential item of any detective's equipment was a kerchief. "If you're going to spend a lifetime eating on the run, it makes sense to carry your own napkin—not to mention the convenient way it doubles as a bandage," he had remarked.

No answer. Better try the bell. Could Sophie be asleep? It was barely ten o'clock. Perhaps it would have been wiser to have called first.

Tamura was half-way down the steps when she heard the door click. She turned and blinked as the porch light went on. When her slightly myopic eyes finally focused, she saw a leggy woman with tousled blond hair, wearing nothing but a Mexican sarape, standing on the porch. She recognized Sophie Warren from her pictures. In ten years, her looks would very likely fade, eventually becoming hard-edged and angular, but now it was easy to understand why this pretty warbler was so popular.

"I'm Sara Tamura from the Berkeley police. I'm sorry to interrupt your evening, but . . ."

"That's okay, Sara, I suppose you've come to talk to James."

Despite herself, Tamura allowed her face to register surprise. How could James still be here when Sophie had obviously just come from bed?

It was Sophie Warren's turn to look confused. "Didn't you want James?"

Tamura recovered as best she could by pulling the drawing from her shoulder bag and handing it to Sophie. "We just received this sketch. It's supposed to be a good likeness of the person who killed Aldo Speldon and Frank Rathman. Does it mean anything to you?"

Sophie stepped back and gesutured Tamura to follow her inside under the ceiling light. While the singer studied the sketch, there was a movement above. Tamura looked up to see Rivers standing on the top step buttoning his shirt and looking sheepish. The ice cream suddenly felt like a lump of lead in the pit of her stomach.

"You selfish bastard . . ." Tamura exploded, "everybody else is working their tail off on this case while you're screwing yours off. It's so typical . . ." Tamura bit off the rest of the sentence as Sophie touched her on the arm.

Tamura blinked back a tear and looked into the other woman's eyes. They were filled with compassionate concern. Tamura wanted to say something, but couldn't find the words. Pretty dumb. Why the hell did she feel so angry and betrayed? She bit her lip in an effort not to cry. Giving up, she fumbled in her bag for the ever-handy bandana.

Rivers was too stunned by the energy of Tamura's attack to respond, leaving Sophie Warren the task of smoothing things over. She acquitted herself well.

First, she reached up the stair, took Rivers by the hand, squeezed it, and suggested he wait in the car. Then she turned to Tamura and said, "Tonight I'm a bit of a mess, so I don't have a lot of words. And I don't mean to be presumptuous and make things worse. But for what it's worth, let me just say I called James, invited him over, and I guess, to be truthful about it, I seduced him. I don't know what your feelings for him are, but it's obvious to me, even if it's not to you right now, that you do have some. I don't know what more to say except I was pretty needy. I couldn't seem to talk to any of my friends, and James somehow seemed like the person who could . . ."

"You don't have to . . ." Tamura tried to interrupt.

"I know, but I just want to say a few more words. Being with James was beautiful, but I'm in no shape to even think about deeper meanings until life gets back to normal, whatever that is. Now I just want to go to bed and sleep for two days. But when I'm more together, maybe you and I can have coffee? The only antidote I know for these crazy mix-ups is for everyone to care for each other."

Sophie's obvious sincerity calmed Tamura. "I'm the one who should apologize. All of us at the department have been under a load of pressure. I guess I just went a little crazy. I know you are going through a difficult time."

186

"Thanks," Sophie said simply, moving to hug Tamura.

"And I would like to have coffee sometime," Tamura said as she opened the front door to go.

Sophie nodded. "God knows I wish I could help you with your investigation, but I don't recognize the face at all," she added as she returned the sketch.

Rivers was leaning against a telephone pole by the street. He pulled himself erect as Tamura came down the walk. For a few moments, they stood looking at one another. Neither said anything.

"Can I run you home?" Rivers asked finally, half-expecting her to refuse.

"That would be nice," Tamura replied, keeping her voice carefully neutral.

Driving west on Ashby, Rivers mumbled something confused about feeling foolish and wanting to get a good look at the drawing, as if they were somehow connected. He asked Tamura if she would mind stopping by the department for a minute.

She nodded, but didn't reply, remembering even talky old Myrna Loy could keep her mouth shut when she had William Powell on the run.

Once at the office, they found Burnett, Hall, and Mary Finnegan huddled over the sketch. Rivers joined them, noticing immediately the rodent-like face looked, as if a large mouse was passing itself off as a human. The mouse-man had hair on his jaw, but it didn't extend far up his cheeks. The face itself was narrow, but the eyes were wide-set and bulging.

Tamura suggested that he looked both crazed and wild. Mary Finnegan mumbled her assent.

Just below the picture, there was a brief physical description. It read: "Caucasian, 5'11" to 6'1", slim—perhaps 160 lbs.—medium brown hair, possibly receding, eye color unknown, age approximately twenty-five to thirty-five years."

Rivers again hoped Oscar Williams was on the level. Trusting him was a calculated risk, one that could waste valuable time if he was feeding them a line of bullshit. But was there any choice? In this odd, slippery, blob of a case, Oscar's story was the first possible handle.

Rivers thoughts were interrupted by Carl Burnett calling a tired "see you in the morning," as he gathered up his coat and leather satchel and followed Ben Hall out the door.

"I guess the leg work really begins mañana," Mary Finnegan remarked matter-of-factly as she picked up her coat and looked to see if Tamura was leaving. Tamura hesitated, as if wanting to say something to Rivers. Then thinking better of it, she picked up several copies of the drawing and walked with Mary along the dim corridor.

Rivers leaned back in his chair and looked at the sketch for several minutes. He had secretly hoped the drawing would be of someone he recognized. It wasn't. The longer he looked at the rodent-like features, the more he drew a blank. He shut his eyes and tried imagining the mouse-man firing a shotgun from the muddy field outside KILO. It didn't work. The dream image of Sara and Sophie floating in clear warm water kept replacing the crazy, protruding eyes and thin beard.

Ah well, when it's a choice between beauty and the beast, you can't go wrong turning out the beast, Rivers chuckled as he leaned forward to pull the chain on his desk light. Just as he clicked it off, his eyes fell on the letterhead of the Alameda County crime lab. With a sigh, he pulled the chain again and settled down to read the memo. Mercifully, it was succinct. The brake lines on Professor Aaron Storey's car had almost surely been cut, probably with electrician's snips. The report concluded that for them to fail immediately and totally as they had, someone must also have pumped the brake pedal to push all the fluid out of the main cylinder.

A handwritten note appended to the typed report with a paper clip indicated Officer Rizzouli had spoken to Professor Storey by phone. "The Professor is hosting some sort of metaphysics conference and is too busy to visit with mere flatfoots, even ones who are trying to exercise their feeble little intellects to figure out who is trying to kill him." The note continued, "Bearing rejection with its usual fortitude and grace, the BPD persevered and sent a beat officer to Storey's home. She, Officer Lavina Blakely, that is, spoke to Storey's wife Adele, who didn't appear overly concerned. Adele

bar

188

Polen stated she was sure 'the accident' must have been a prank of some neighborhood kids gone haywire, but finally agreed to corral her husband the next day when his class schedule permitted and bring him down to headquarters to discuss the incident. The meeting is set for 5 p.m. In the meantime, despite the woeful lack of appreciation shown by the Storey's, a beat officer will nevertheless drive by their home on a regular schedule."

Rivers grunted. Only in Berkeley was every other cop a secret writer. There would be a department poetry group if they weren't careful.

Rivers reread both the memo and the note slowly. It was hard to conclude much about the incident except that Officer Rizzouli didn't like Professor Storey or his wife much. Even if they weren't appropriately grateul, it didn't mean they were wrong about what had happened. Indeed, Rivers found himself in tentative agreement. The whole idea that there was a murderer loose who killed by cutting brake lines seemed more than a bit improbable. He could see the headlines now, "Mad Car Murderer Severs Sirocco," or "Terror Stalks the Toronado." Well, it was too late to do anything more about it tonight anyway, and tomorrow they would probably find out the vicious killer was in reality Storey's teenage son who had worked on the car incompetently and would rather see Daddy tumble off a cliff then 'fess up and risk losing his allowance.

This time when Rivers tugged the bronze lamp chain, he resolutely kept his eyes off his desk. It was barely midnight when he came out of the building to find that clouds scudding in from the Pacific had blocked the moon and were dropping a light mist. As he started Dartha, he remembered Captain Rafferty humming the first bar of "Blue Moon." Something about the moon seeing a man standing alone without a dream. For the life of him, he couldn't see what the old song had to do with the murders. He shrugged. Another long sleep ahead and a morning run before he put his attention to finding the mouse-man. The prospect cheered him.

As Rivers pulled into his driveway, he saw a light in his upstairs flat. For a moment he was frightened, as all parents occasionally are when they leave their children in another's care. Were the kids sick, or hurt, or even dead? If he was a better father, he would be home to protect them. He forced himself to walk, not run, to the door. The rational part of his mind was telling the guilty parent in him not to jump to hysterical conclusions.

"Is that you, James?" Jeannie called as he opened the door.

Her tone reassured him, but still he asked, "Is everything okay?"

She came to the top of the stairs in a red terrycloth robe and gave him her best midnight smile. "Sure, the kids are all asleep up here. When my back was turned, they started watching one of those Creepy Creature horror movies on TV. Then yours refused to sleep up here by themselves and mine refused to sleep downstairs by himself, so here I am."

"Thanks, love. I wouldn't have made it through this week without you," he said, quickly forgetting his anxiety and giving Jeannie a routine kiss on the forehead on his way to the refrigerator.

Jeannie stood by the kitchen door. "James, I watched the last half of the horror movie too, the scariest part." She took a couple of steps forward and put her arms around him from behind just as he finally found the peanut butter and Calistoga Water.

"And I don't want to spend the night alone either," Jeannie added, squeezing him so tight he couldn't grab the cottage cheese and salsa.

"I figured something was up when I saw you looking like a 1940s fire engine."

"What do you mean, a 1940s fire engine? I wasn't even born until the summer of 1951," she said with real annoyance, letting go of him and turning toward the hall door.

He juggled the food to the kitchen table and followed her.

"Not you, the robe," he said to her back. "You're old enough to remember, it's the color fire engines used to be before some efficiency freak discovered yellow shows up better at night. Come on now, stop pouting."

"Unless things have changed more than I think they have, red is still the best color for seducing neighbors," Jeannie retorted, thawing a little.

"Ya hoo," Rivers replied good-naturedly. "But listen, I missed breakfast because of getting back from L.A., lunch because of sleeping, and supper because of, well, because of the investigation, and I've got to eat something."

As he talked, Rivers poured gobs of jalapeño salsa into the cottage cheese, stirring it with chopsticks. When the entire tub was bright red, he added garlic salt and freshly ground pepper and began eating it straight from the carton.

"You call that eating? Didn't you know the real reason Nixon was impeached was because he put ketchup on cottage cheese?"

"If he had just had the good sense to use hot sauce, he would still be in the White House. And speaking of hot sauce, fire engines and red robes, I would be greatly pleased if you would spend the night with me, even though there is no more hot-date brandy."

"I thought you'd never ask," Jeannie said with a giggle. "But just in case you did, I put a couple of logs in the fireplace and nipped next door and borrowed a few snorts."

"Hennessy?"

"Korbel."

"Sounds like where we left off Sunday night."

'You catch on fast."

25

Thursday morning, December 1. It was raining hard. The year seemed almost literally to be running out. All the officers concerned with the murder were in Rafferty's office by eight except Phil Orpac, who wouldn't be back from Europe until noon, and Tamura. No one said anything.

Rivers waited a few minutes before starting the meeting to give his assistant a chance to claim her straight-backed chair by the door. Mary Finnegan had faithfully brought the donuts, but they were out of Peet's coffee. Somewhat grumpily, Lorenzo Jones called down the hall and got someone to agree to bring along seven cups from the squad room's Mr. Coffee. Tamura didn't appear. Rivers finally started the meeting without her.

"As you know, it's time to hit the bricks, wet or not. Everyone connected with Speldon and Rathman will need to see the picture. Ben, you take care of the drug angle. Make sure everyone in Narcotics knows that getting a positive I.D. is top priority. I don't need to remind you we haven't got Willie Thompson's killer yet either, and we can't be absolutely sure the killings aren't connected.

"Lorenzo, you and Mary talk to every living soul at the Marina, including the people living illegally on the boats. There are some umbrellas in lost and found if you didn't bring yours. Tamura and I will deal with the Warrens as well as everyone else close to the victims. Phil can help when he gets in."

"What about releasing the picture to the media?" Burnett asked.

"Maybe later," Rivers responded. "There is no sense being inundated with tips until we've checked all the obvious people. Carl, if you have a couple of free hours, I'd appreciate it if you'd see those folks who caretake Roger Warren's house in Mill Valley and after that, Eileen what's-her-name — O'Hara, the woman Rathman lived with. Get some help from the Oakland people to show the drawing around Rathman's neighborhood."

"Sure, but James, at the risk of boring you to death with my same old song, what makes you confident we're showing the picture to the right people?"

"Who else do you suggest, Carl?"

"Damn it, James, if I knew, I'd tell you. Don't you realize we've been having this same circular conversation all week? It's as if we're looking for a raincoat. You keep ordering us to look in the hall closet. I keep telling you that if the coat was there, we would have found it by now. Then you ask me where we should look instead. I say I don't know. You shrug and suggest we go back and look in the hall closet. James, do you even get my point? Just because I can't tell you whether the next best place to look is the attic or the basement or the barn, it doesn't mean I'm wrong about the raincoat not being in the closet or . . ."

"Does anyone get a hit as to who the person in the drawing might be?" Tamura interrupted from where she stood just inside the door. "I mean, is he a musician, a carpenter, or a meter reader? Or, to put it another way, if we all agree he isn't in Carl's, or is it James', closet—I missed the first part because my alarm clock died—then where is he likely to be?"

Rivers looked up, surprised Tamura had slipped in so quietly. "Those are good questions. I don't disagree with Carl, but if we're going to de-emphasize the people close to Speldon and Rathman, where do we look?"

"So we guess this guy is a hippie or a sensitive artist type or a mutual fund salesman. So what?" Lorenzo said disgustedly. "Except for the wild look, there are a half a dozen white losers like him living on every block in the Flats. Come to that, even the look doesn't get you far. This town is the crazed honky capital of the universe."

"Sara, this is probably reaching," Mary Finnegan added thoughtfully, "but to me he doesn't look so much wild as terribly hurt. You know as if he'd lost his self-respect."

"This is supposed to be a criminal investigation. I don't think this psychological profile stuff does anything but waste time," Ben Hall interjected. "This dude looks like he's about to jump out of his skin for one simple reason—he just killed a couple of people. But remember, the killings were last Sunday. If we pass him this morning taking his dog for a leak in the rain, he'll probably look as grumpy as we do."

"Maybe, but the whole crime is so violently nuts, I wouldn't bet on it. When anyone goes that far over the line, it isn't easy to come back. What scares me is he might look just as crazy this morning as he does here," Finnegan replied, snapping the back of her forefinger on the face of the sketch to produce a sound curiously like a shot.

"Let's quit insulting each other just to put off getting wet," Rivers said after a pause.

When the others had pulled on their rain gear and gone out, Rivers went into his own room and spent a few minutes taking care of housekeeping details. One of these was to have Lassiter ask as many of the main figures in the case as possible to stop by the department. Why run all over the Bay Area in the rain if they could just as well come to him?

* * * * * *

Housekeeping done, Rivers plopped down in the chair next to Tamura's desk. He wanted to say something about the night before, but couldn't find words. He felt like he was back in ninth grade, trying to talk to Joy Roth after Algebra class. For a moment, when it looked as if Tamura was going to say something, he almost relaxed. She didn't. Could it be she was experiencing the same sort of shyness? Whatever was going on, their relationship had obviously changed from pointed remarks to pregnant silences.

Finally, giving up hope of any sort of personal communication, Rivers asked Tamura for a rundown of how Lucy Speldon and Roger Warren explained their European tryst.

Tamura was both grateful and disappointed their relationship seemed to be safely back on a business footing. She had an urge to wipe her sweaty palms on something, but instead made fists as she related her day, including considerable detail about the incident with Heisman, and her discussion with Warren. She concluded that despite compromising appearances, she didn't believe either Lucy

Speldon or Roger Warren was involved.

Rivers greeted her views skeptically. "If Warren and Speldon let their hair down for a few mad days in Europe, what's the guarantee they've kept it pinned up since?" he asked.

Tamura shrugged, forgetting her damp hands as she turned them palms up.

Rivers wasn't convinced. That Roger Warren and Lucy Speldon were both charming didn't get them off the hook as far as he was concerned. Just the same, for reasons he didn't want to examine, Rivers decided not to start an argument with Tamura. Instead, he nodded and returned to his desk.

Almost immediately the switchboard buzzed. An overseas operator with a French accent asked Rivers if he would accept a collect call from Oscar Williams. *"Mais oui,"* he replied. Switching to his best tough cop accent, he continued. "What is this, man? European vacations aren't enough for you? Now you want free phone calls, too? How's the weather, anyway?"

"You got to be jiving. With all the sweet young things lolly-gagging around, who's got time to notice? But listen my man, before I completely disappear under a pile of panting *jeune filles,* I thought I'd check in. I'm into keeping my part of our arrangement, because this black turkey has finally found the perfect barnyard and has absolutely no interest in being put into your coop."

"The sketch looks great, but it's still morning here and we just got the hunt organized. It will be a while yet before we know anything. In the meantime, the taxpayers are getting pretty stingy with their dimes. Have you got something to tell me?"

"I hear you. I'm mostly calling 'cause I got this hot flash. The more I think about the drawing, the more I'm not sure it gives the whole feeling about the dude."

"What do you mean?"

"Take a look. It's just a face, no background. The rest of the paper is white 'cause I didn't know how to fill it in."

"You mean all mouse, no house?"

"That's it. It's hard to say from a face—or sometimes even from an outfit—who a person is. I mean, these days, every other dentist wears blue jeans; I know dealers who dress like undertakers, which

195

they often are, of course. Still, there are lots of times you can sense where a person fits. You know, jocks look alike and hang out together; Jesus freaks smell too clean; your average doctor acts like a grown-up Boy Scout, and so on."

"Enough bullshit."

"So, okay. Last night I took a walk—I mean a promenade—to sort of get my *pieds* on the turf. I got a room near a place called the *Jardin de Luxembourg*—that's Luxemburg Gardens in English, you know. It's near a school they call the *Sorbonne*. The point is, every place I looked in the coffee shops and student bars they got around here, I see this dude. *C'est* wierd if *vous* catches *moi* drift."

"How do you translate that into Berkeley, *si vous me comprenez?*" Rivers replied, reaching back to grab a little of his high school French. He was starting to feel excited. Tamura had asked if anyone could guess how the owner of the face in the sketch fitted into society and Carl Burnett had repeatedly questioned where they should be looking. Here was Oscar Williams, about to supply an answer to both questions.

"I got you. There's a place on the north side of the U.C. Campus—the Cafe Depresso, a buddy of mine calls it."

"The one that looks like a New York subway station sans graffiti?"

"That's it. I can sort of see our mouse hunched over, drinking some kind of wicked Italian coffee a poor ghetto child like me can't even pronounce; looking as if he knew Sylvester the cat was waiting just outside the door. That's all. If I tell you more, I'll be lying."

"Where can we get hold of you to identify this guy when we get him?"

"Write me care of the Louvre."

"Don't shit me, Oscar."

"Seriously, Lieutenant, I'll be around. As your nasty D.A. friend pointed out, there aren't a lot of places for a black giraffe to hide. But you tell that dude to get some sort of official immunity papers together and lay them on Lincoln if you want this beast loping across any U.S. border voluntarily. Hey, I got to go. You should see what just sashayed past. Be easy, man."

Rivers put the phone down with a smile. A coffee shop near the campus, huh? It was worth a try. Lorenzo and Mary could show the picture around the obvious ones as soon as they finished with the Marina.

A few minutes later the front desk buzzed to say that the waiting room was filling up with important looking citizens. Rivers told Amanda Gonzales to wait five minutes before sending them up. In the meantime, he glanced at the list of names Lassiter had gotten from the University in an effort to identify the mystery confessor. There were pages of names beginning with the letters "ST," but only a few sounded much like Strange; these were circled with red ballpoint. Rivers reached for the phone to buzz Lassiter to ask why the University hadn't included a printout of all the addresses.

As he did so, it rang. Conveniently, it was Lassiter. There had been another call from Strange. This time they had it on tape. The call had been similar to the others, with the man again apologizing profusely. As before, he spoke in a muffled whisper, but this time Lassiter was sure the name he gave was Strain, or Strane. Rivers glanced at the list and saw that it contained three of the former, but only one ending in "e." Lassiter said he would call the campus immediately to ask that they concentrate on those four names, two of which had no addresses. The lack of address meant they were no longer registered, which meant checking to see if the Alumni Office knew where they were.

Rivers spoke to the people in the waiting room in small groups. He showed the sketch to Walter Bell, to several groups of local environmental activists, to present and former employees of KILO and so on. Everyone seemed to be genuinely disappointed when they drew a blank on the face.

Roger Warren, looking subdued in a dark grey suit, was ushered in alone shortly before noon. Rivers was surprised when Warren apologized for being rude on Tuesday night and thanked Rivers for putting in a good word with his daughter.

"Did Sophie call?" Rivers asked.

"Yes, last evening, fairly late. She said she knew in her heart I hadn't had any part in killing Aldo. Then she asked if we could meet for lunch. She said something about your giving her a helping hand with growing up. I have no idea what you said, but I'm grateful. If I can ever help you, let me know."

"I haven't crossed you off my list of suspects," Rivers replied, realizing to his annoyance that he was smiling.

"In your situation, I wouldn't either, especially since Ms. Tamura found out about my friendship with Lucy Speldon," Warren said, as he studied the sketch Rivers had handed him.

"But that doesn't change anything. I wasn't involved and I'm certain Lucy wasn't either," Warren continued. "No matter how sticky it seems now, I'm sure you'll agree eventually. I have no idea who this distasteful-looking fellow is, but I guess he's higher up on your list than I am."

Charles Pierce was the last to come in. "What about lunch, Sherlock?" he said, as he poked his head around the office door.

"Can you eat and look at a portrait too?" Rivers responded.

"I was going to suggest Siam Cuisine, but if you want, we can take a can of sardines to the museum instead," Pierce replied.

"Not the right background. I need something a bit more current. How about one of the cafes by the campus?"

"Sure you're not confusing art with a mid-life refresher course in co-eds?"

"Women students, Charles. Co-eds have been defunct for twenty years. But your point is well taken. Normally I'd just as soon flirt as eat, but this is work. I got a tip from an ex-forward who fancies himself such a good artist he can see backgrounds that aren't there. Come on, I'll drive and explain on the way."

"Let's walk. It's only ten blocks and the rain's stopped."

The two men came out the front door under the Hall of Justice sign and turned left. At Allston they walked uphill past the prison-like high school, and then by one of Berkeley's nicest buildings, the Italian Revival post office. They ignored a "do not walk" sign as they dodged across Shattuck Avenue. Safely on the curb, they continued past Trumpet Vine Court, locally famous as the home of Vivoli's ice cream parlor, and then across Oxford Street to the University of California campus. They followed narrow paths through redwood glades, and over rolling lawns. Everything was green, lush and peaceful as it had been since the Vietnam protests. It was hard for Rivers to believe the United States' first and largest student insurrection had been incubated in this sylvan setting.

The two men crossed a six-step bridge over Strawberry Creek before skirting Zellerbach Theater, the campus performing arts center. When the elegant and expensive hall had been built in the 60s, a rebellious student generation renamed it King Hall, after the heroic black preacher. For several years, not even the campus tour guides dared call it anything else. But the collective memory of the undergraduate community is short, and the administration had only to repeat Zellerbach often enough, and before long, all but a few balding grad students called the hall by the name of the million-aire toilet paper king who paid for it. Come to think of it though, now that Martin Luther King Jr. had been dead long enough to be viewed as respectable, the University administration would almost surely hold a ceremony and rename some old building after him. And to double the irony, probably most everyone on campus would keep calling it by its former name.

Rivers and Pierce entered Sproul Plaza itself, where one fall day in 1964, the first student sit-in caused Chet Huntley to announce a "Revolution on the Campus." The two men had been students at the law school a few hundred yards further up the hill when the Alameda County Sheriff had dragged the eight-hundred or so students out of Sproul Hall and off to the county jail at Santa Rita. And even though neither had been arrested, maced, or hit with a baton, they had been deeply moved. Like wars, depressions and the other catastrophic events which have always separated parents from their children, the student movement specially marked and defined their generation.

Rivers and Pierce detoured to the right to avoid a gathering of socialist feminists carrying signs and marching in a large circle near the student union. They then turned back to the left to avoid a smaller crowd of Jews for Jesus overflowing the Sproul Hall steps.

"Where are we going?" Pierce asked.

"The Med."

"The Mediterraneum Caffe? I haven't been there for close to fifteen years. I bet those same beatniks who thought Jack Kerouac was alive and living under a bridge at Big Sur are still nursing their espresso in the corner."

"Probably, although I suspect they must worship some other anti-hero living under a different bridge by now."

"Is this part of the investigation, Sherlock? Am I really going to play Watson for a moment?"

"My tipster says the Med is the right sort of gallery to view the portrait which interests us."

They crossed Bancroft and walked slowly along the east side of Telegraph Avenue, boxed between gaggles of nineteen-year-olds. On their right was a row of bedraggled-looking street vendors who Rivers had heard could make five hundred dollars on a good day. To their left, the inevitable row of campus-area storefronts filled with Indian imports, discount falafels, and "Nuclear War Cures Cancer" bumper stickers.

"If you think about it, James, the Med is about the only place on this street that hasn't changed since we were in school," Pierce said as they approached Channing Way.

"I do think about it," Rivers replied. "Telegraph used to be a real street with the record shops, bookstores and cafes mixed in with barbers, lockshops, and a five-and-dime. Now it's all tourist drek and Grey Line buses."

"Which just goes to show that when you try to remake the world, you're as likely as anyone else to end up with day-glo T-shirts."

"Maybe we ought to shop for a little Geritol? We're starting to sound as if we're a hundred and ten."

They got their food at the window at the back of the cafe. Rivers had spaghetti, three-bean salad, french bread and a glass of the cheap red, because it was that kind of place. Pierce shrugged and ordered a hamburger. They took their trays up the narrow stairs to the half loft and claimed a tiny graffiti-scarred table. When they finished eating, Rivers showed Pierce the sketch and explained about Oscar Williams' intuition.

"Williams has a good eye. The guy in his sketch would be right at home here," Pierce said as he looked around.

"What about an anti-nuclear rally?"

"He wouldn't be typical."

"No?"

"It's hard to generalize, but there is a sort of common denominator for each age group. Our little old ladies do tend to wear running shoes and Einstein haircuts, not polyester pantsuits or designer clothes. The folks in their forties tend to dress in L.L. Bean shirts and hiking boots pretty much the way they did when they went to hear Joan Baez in 1968. Younger men don't look like this guy."

"How's that?"

"Don't act dumb, James. Eco-freak kids are into running shoes, T-shirts covered with smiling dolphins, and clean jeans, with a copy of *Ecotopia* in the back pocket. They're so serious, they think 'Nuke the Whales' is high sarcasm."

"So?"

"So, it's hard to tell from this, but your boy looks like a run-of-the-mill, nicotine-stained Dostoyevsky freak to me. We don't get many of them."

26

That Thursday morning, Tamura felt like the rabbit in *Alice in Wonderland,* late for a very important date; a date with a killer who might kill again if she didn't hurry. As she left the morning meeting, she tried to visualize where the encounter would occur and who the killer would be. She couldn't. Beyond the strong premonition that it wouldn't be long before the mystery was resolved, she could see nothing. Curiously, this feeling of being on the brink of discovery overflowed into her personal life. It was a bit unsettling.

A hurried visit to the Speldon home proved fruitless as far as identifying the drawing was concerned. Nevertheless, Tamura wasn't allowed to leave empty-handed. After being introduced to her son and daughter, Lucy insisted Tamura take a saran-wrapped plate of cookies. They were made of yogurt and gingerbread, shaped like dogs, and came complete with raisin collars.

Next, Tamura headed impatiently for KILO. On her hurried drive from the East Bay ridgeline to the bay shore, she rolled through more stop signs than she usually did in a year. Despite her rush, when she finally arrived at the KILO entrance, she turned instead into a small parking area on the other side of the access road facing the Marina. She felt jangled and needed a moment alone in the fresh air. Looking out toward Angel Island, Tamura allowed herself to become distracted by a rainbow-hued spinnaker unfurling like an angry jellyfish. She became so hypnotized by the small boat with the big sail battling the breeze that for a moment she almost forgot why she was there.

Finally, as the boat two-stepped over the white caps, Tamura turned and headed across the parking lot toward KILO. She felt cleaner and clearer.

As Tamura poked her head over the landing to the second floor, she was greeted by a slow drawl. "If it's my man Dorsey you're hunting, you're on the wrong trail."

Tamura looked up to see Jango sprawled on the couch in the secretarial office.

"Can you point me in the right direction?" she asked.

"He's over at the new studio," the sleepy-faced deejay replied. "I'm just resting my eyes up here 'til he gets back, 'cause I'm suffering a severe bread shortage and I need my man to toss me a few crumbs before the fifteenth."

"When will he be back?" Tamura asked, trying to rein in her impatience.

"Whenever he gets the new computerized record-playing machine put right. It screwed up again and he's having to pay real live deejays to fill in. You can bet he isn't pleased. Those turkey oldies-but-goodies we play on AM don't bring in enough to buy a roll of Charmin. In a way though, it's kind of reassuring when computers have enough taste to lie down and quit rather than play Kate Smith singing 'Moonlight Over Vermont.' That shit is down-right embarrassing."

Tamura's wandering mind snapped to attention. She demanded and got the address of the new studio from Jango and ran down the stairs. An adrenalin rush carried her easily over the two football fields or so of asphalt back to her car.

27

By the time Rivers returned from lunch, the sun was chasing the last scattered clouds out of a blue sky and the temperature was dropping. Only three more weeks until Christmas, he heard someone say. A holiday break would certainly be nice. Maybe he would take Jeannie and all three kids cross-country-skiing at Yosemite for a few days. With all the recent rain, there would be plenty of snow in the mountains. For a moment he let his mind free to imagine the sun glistening on the snow crust. Then, almost fiercely, he interrupted his daydream. There could be no vacation while he was playing hide-and-seek with a killer.

Rivers leaned back in his chair, put his feet on the desk, and shut his eyes. For no reason that made any particular sense, he remembered an incident which had occurred a few weeks before. He had been helping his son Mickey with a particularly nettlesome arithmetic problem and had come up with the wrong answer. This was all the opening Mickey needed to launch into a long lecture on how hard school was these days. He concluded it with the serious assertion, "It's back to basics, Dad."

A catchy cliché, Rivers thought. Now if he could only figure out what was basic to this amorphous, ill-defined invesigation. Maybe if he reviewed all the evidence one more time. Okay, but where to start? What was the most basic question? Perhaps if he could just ask it, the identity of the killer would be forthcoming.

How about this: Why the hell had a half-crazed looking refugee from a coffee house used a big shotgun to kill Aldo Speldon and Frank Rathman from ambush a little past 9:00 on the Sunday after Thanksgving in the rain at a second rate radio station? Or: If the killer had wanted to kill just one of the two men, why hadn't he done it at some other location? Which led to the question: Which of the two victims was the target?

Rivers shook his head. Getting back to basics was at least as hard as untangling a ball of yarn.

Not only did they not know who the murderer was, but after four days of hard work, they still weren't sure who he was trying to kill. And if they hadn't figured that out, what were they sure of? Precious little. They had Oscar Williams' drawing and they had the odd, unprofessional, gratuitously violent way the killing itself was accomplished. Assume for a moment, Rivers thought, the killer hadn't been after the obvious target, that somehow Frank Rathman had been the intended victim. Where did that get you? Not far. Rathman's life appeared to be particularly barren of suspects.

Okay, let's try another question. Were they somehow dealing with another example of the random sort of violence psychologists get paid too much to blame on the increasing alienation of modern life? They hadn't ignored that possibility. But, considering the relatively remote location of KILO and the fact the killer had crossed through trees and a muddy field in the rain, it seemed likely he intended to kill the people behind the window. And Tamura's idea that they might be dealing with a deranged personality out to kill a media celebrity for notoriety didn't stand up to scrutiny either. Even assuming Speldon was famous enough to fill the bill, the whole point of that sort of killing was that the killer got to be hauled off on-camera.

So, where did that leave them? Back to square one. There must be another question to ask, otherwise it meant resifting the same old facts and suspects, hoping this time some connection between killer and victim would surface.

Rivers reprimanded himself for again drifting into conjecture. Stick to what you know, he told himself. Stick to basics. What else could he say about the investigation with certainty? Well, there was the obvious thing that had bothered them all from the beginning. The killer had shot at silhouettes, and given the opaque nature of the glass, he could never have identified his victims. So, the next question became, could he have killed the wrong men?

Rivers felt the glimmer of a possibility. He leaned forward and disconnected the phone wire from the back of the instrument.

Assume the killer did mess up. How could he have gotten so

murderously confused? Rivers reached for a pad of yellow legal paper and wrote:

Possibilities For a Fuck-Up
    1. *The people on the KILO program before Rathman and Speldon were the targets and the killer was late.*
    2. *The people on the following program were the targets and the killer was early.*
    3. *Somehow, either the guest or the host on "The Talkies" had been changed at the last moment without the killer knowing it.*
    4. *The killer was at the wrong place altogether.*
    5. *Some other possibility I haven't thought of.*

Numbers one and two had long since been checked out. The program immediately before Rathman's talk show was a replay of a two-hour live concert first broadcast a few weeks before. The one following was "The Sunday Supplement," KILO's standard late evening show hosted by a woman deejay, Robyn Samuels. As it happened, the engineer who played the concert tape had gone home when the show ended at 8:30 and Samuels hadn't appeared until a few minutes before ten. There was no reason to suppose either was the intended target.

So much for the first two possibilities, but what of the rest? Had either Rathman or Speldon been last minute substitutions? No. Eight-thirty was Rathman's regular time slot and Speldon's appearance had been promoted for weeks. So, eliminate that one and go on to number four.

Well, what about it? Was there a chance the killer had somehow ended up at the wrong place? It hardly seemed likely, as KILO AM/FM was written on the outside of the building in large hot pink letters, not to mention the several prominent parking lot signs.

Oh my God, could that be it? Rivers thought excitedly. Could the answer to the question no one asked have only two letters? That was what Rafferty meant about "Blue Moon"! It hadn't made sense to anyone because they had insisted on thinking of KILO as the home of hot, wild music. Only Sean, who listened to oldies but goodies, thought of KILO as an AM station. 'Blue Moon,' hot damn! Rivers almost shouted. Maybe Carl's master/slave fable was right on all along. When they considered the possibility the killer might not have been after Speldon, they had gotten no further than considering Rathman as the other possible target. They hadn't ever thought the killer might have gotten mixed up and been at the wrong plantation altogether.

"Lieutenant," Lassiter almost shouted as he banged open Rivers' door without knocking. "Officer Tamura is on the phone, she's been trying to get you on your direct line but it rang so many times she guessed you'd unplugged it so she called the switchboard."

That woman might make a detective yet, Rivers thought as he leaned forward, snapped the plastic wire into the back of the black box and picked up the receiver.

"James, I have something," Tamura said excitedly.

"Me, too. If you were half nuts to start with, it wouldn't be too hard to assume that a program you heard on KILO AM was being broadcast from the same studio as KILO FM. After all, we've over-looked the AM band altogether for four days and we get paid to do this."

"That's it, James, but I'm ahead of you," Tamura interrupted. "Pay attention because unless I'm way off base, we don't have much time before the killing is likely to start again. KILO AM is a tiny operation which broadcasts out of a half-finished part of KILO's new radio station down the street from Juan's Place. You know, the Mexican restaurant on the corner — just down from Fantasy Films. The main KILO operation is set to move in the spring, but for now ninety percent of KILO is at the Marina where it's always been. Here's the point. KILO AM airs their public affairs program on Sunday evenings because it's relatively dead time. To save money, they don't do call-ins, only interviews taped ahead."

"What was on at 8:30 and 9:00 last Sunday?"

"A discussion between some KILO public affairs person and a Cal professor about the decline and perversion of western mysticism by the Neo Nazi movement."

"That doesn't sound too helpful."

"That's what I thought until I found out who the guest was."

207

"Well?"

"Aaron Storey."

"The 'look Mom, no brakes,' professor?"

"The same."

"Sara, by God, I think you've got it. Hold on while I get Lassiter to track down Storey."

"It's no use, James, I tried to call him at home and at his office. There's no answer. I think you'd better have patrol stake out his house while we try the campus. Storey has a class this afternoon and then he's supposed to come see us at five. He won't be able to if the killer finds him first."

"I'll meet you at the administrative office for his department. Where is it?"

"Philosophy is in South Hall. It's that old building across from the Campanile. Since he's the department head, his office must be there as well."

"Boots and saddles, my friend, I'll see you soon."

Rivers moved quickly toward the door. Lassiter tried to block his path, saying something about more news. Rivers pushed past. Halfway down the corridor he turned and saw Lassiter hesitating, as if he didn't know whether to give chase or revert to his scarecrow imitation.

"Tell me on the way," Rivers yelled.

As Rivers loped down the back stairs, he could hear Lassiter pounding along the corridor above. By the time the rookie officer burst into the sunshine, Rivers had started Dartha and backed her out. He leaned across the wide front seat and unlatched the passenger door. Lassiter accurately timed his leap as Rivers changed gears. With hardly a hesitation, they were off down Grant Street.

As Rivers maneuvered the elderly Dodge through traffic, Lassiter tried to tell his story. But when Rivers downshifted and swerved to pass a Saab Turbo, Lassiter ended up with both hands on the dash, teeth clenched. He had barely recovered enough to try again when the driver of a white truck bearing the slogan "Life Extension Through Cryogenic Suspension" leaned angrily on his horn as Rivers cut him off to swing left up Durant. When they got caught behind a covey of bikers at the Dana Street light, Lassiter finally got past the third word.

"What I've been trying to say," he almost shouted, as if by increasing his volume he could somehow ward off interruption, "is that one of the patrol people just called in a positive I.D. on the sketch. Several people recognized it in the cafes and that bookstore on the north side of campus. Nobody seems to know the man's last name, but his first name is Jeffrey. The guy who works in the bookstore says he's sure he's some sort of graduate student, maybe in religion, because he's always goes straight for the theology . . ."

"Philosophy—not religion—philosophy," Rivers said quietly, his words drowned out by three Harley hogs accelerating in unison. "Everything is falling into place fast now. Let's just hope we can keep up."

The park-like campus of the University of California is almost entirely closed to cars, with a few exceptions—such as the Chancellor, several emeritus deans, and the freshman daughter of one of the traffic booth guards. They don't gain a great deal, however, as the few narrow roads, regularly dead end in cul de sacs.

Knowing this, Rivers didn't try to drive onto the campus at either of the main gates. Instead, he swung the car left at Bowditch, a block south of the campus, and continued across Bancroft into a delivery driveway that runs between a partially underground parking garage with a tennis court roof and Kroeber Hall, the anthropology building. The narrow roadway appeared to end at a cement wall about a hundred feet ahead. But instead of stopping, Rivers downshifted and turned hard left. When no crash came, Lassiter opened his eyes and realized that, thanks to an optical illusion, he was still alive and bumping along a little service path between the wall and rear of the garage. Stopping on a paved apron next to the women's gym, Rivers stepped on the emergency brake and was out and running before the disoriented Lassiter figured out how to open Dartha's door.

Rivers easily vaulted a three-foot fence and ran across the playing field behind the gym, dodging a women's field hockey game as he went. When a large red-headed woman menacingly raised her hockey stick, he faked left and dodged fast to the right, giving her ample behind a sharp pat as he passed. Most of the other women booed, but a long-legged Chinese girl smiled and winked. As Rivers scrambled over the fence on the field's north side, he looked back to see that Lassiter, with his tight uniform and ten pounds of equipment hanging from his belt, had wisely dared neither fence nor stick-wielding women, and was running the long way around.

Rivers continued across a stone bridge over Strawberry Creek, through a walled courtyard between two mock tudor buildings, up weathered granite stairs, and finally into an open square. Directly north, he saw the great grey Campanile, the phallic bell tower that had symbolized Cal to generations of horny adolescents.

Rivers paused, trying to remember which of the ivy-covered buildings surrounding the common was South Hall. Just as he was about to ask, he saw Tamura push out the front door of a mid-Victorian brick monstrosity. "James," she said a little breathlessly as they met at the bottom of the steps, "Storey's teaching a class in Room 312 Dwinelle. That's just north of Sather Gate. The class is over at 3:00 and then he's supposed to come back here for a departmental meeting at 3:30."

"If that clock is right, it's not much more than five minutes to 3:00 now," Rivers replied, nodding at the bell tower as Lassiter came clattering up, his uniform and gun drawing not altogether friendly stares from several passing students.

"We've got to hurry," Tamura said urgently. "The woman in the department office, a Mrs. Foster, told me I was the second person to ask for Storey in the past half-hour. The other was a former graduate student named Jeffrey . . ."

"Don't tell me. Jeffrey Strange—the man who's been confessing all week. Did you show her the sketch?"

"Yes, but it's Strain, not Strange. She recognized him and then told me the scary part. Strain is carrying a long athletic bag."

"What do we do?" Lassiter said, his voice squeaking.

"You get down to the campus police office in Sproul Hall. Sara, tell him what to say when he gets there, and then follow me down to 312 Dwinelle. I'm off."

Rivers ran down the hill, dodging knots of book-toting students. He was feeling increasingly frustrated by the premonition that no matter how fast he moved his legs, he was never going to catch up with Strain. It was as if he was back in the old nightmare he sometimes had about catching a plane. In it he dashed around a strange airport, trying to find the right gate a few minutes before the plane was to depart, only to be impeded or diverted when he neared his destination. It was a tormenting dream in which he never caught the plane. Instead, he seemed doomed to keep running endlessly past a parade of initials—TWA, PSA, AA, KLM, UA until he finally awoke in a sweat.

* * * * * * * * *

"Can you find Sproul Hall?" Tamura asked Lassiter, forcing herself to talk slowly.

"Yes, yes. I know where it is. But what do I tell them when I get there?" he replied excitedly.

"Keep it simple. We suspect an ex-grad student named Strain is trying to kill Professor Aaron Storey right now. Show them the drawing. Tell them we're pretty sure Strain is carrying a shotgun in one of those long athletic bags and that we're almost certain he is mentally disturbed and is the killer of Aldo Speldon and Frank Rathman. James and I will be at 312 Dwinelle Hall, where Storey is finishing his class. Have them get people over there PDQ. Then call headquarters and talk to Sergeant Hall, or Lieutenant Orpac if he's back. If neither is there, get through directly to Chief Bacon. Get some of our people to the campus police building, pronto. We'll holler when we need help. In the meantime, no one, including you, should be dashing about trying to be a campus hero."

"Got it," Lassiter said. He ran off, leaving Tamura alone in the shadow of the tower. She glanced up at the clock before she began running down the hill, conscious of the unpleasant lump made by her waist holster and wishing she had worn a bra to contain her bouncing breasts.

Rivers was into Dwinelle Hall and bounding up the stairs less than a minute after leaving the Campanile. Even with the delay caused by a couple of wrong turns and a pause to ask directions from a woman in a wheelchair, he arrived outside Room 312 a full two minutes before the hour. He was giving himself a mental pat on the back when he realized something was very wrong. Room 312 was empty.

Rivers pushed into the center of a group of students a few feet down the hall. "Where's Professor Storey's class?" he demanded, too frustrated to be polite.

"He just left," a short nineteenish-looking woman with frizzy blond hair, braces, and plump thighs answered. "I was telling him my theory about Saint Augustine being a sexually repressed hypocrite when this guy—one of the T.A.'s I think—burst in. He was very upset and started rapping. He kept calling Professor Story a mother . . . you know, a mother . . ."

"Fucker," a thin young man with pimples chimed in, his high loud voice dripping condescension. "It was really very infantile. He called Professor Storey a motherfucker over and over, as if you can communicate using obscenities."

"Professor Storey tried to quiet the guy down." The frizzy blond continued. "He was saying 'my dear Strain, get a hold of yourself,' but Strain just got wilder. Finally, when Strain grabbed him, Storey said 'class dismissed' and went off with him."

"Where did they go?" Rivers demanded.

"Toward the back stairs," a tall black woman said, inclining her head to the right. "I suppose . . ."

Rivers never heard the young woman's assumption. He was running along the corridor. Just before he reached the stairs, he darted into an empty office for a quick look out the window. It was easy to spot the two men he was looking for heading uphill across a small circle of grass. The younger man hugged a long purple and red sausage bag under his left arm while he gripped the older man's sportcoat sleeve with his right hand.

Just as Rivers was about to turn away, he spotted a familiar face among the passing students. Sara Tamura was walking towards the two men on a rapidly converging path. She was less than fifty feet further up the hill.

Rivers tore out of the office. He knew that no matter how fast he went, there was little chance he could get into a position to effectively help Tamura. The thought that he was not going to make it kept racing through his head as he plunged down the stairs roughly shouldering students aside.

He was right. Just as he got to the door, he heard a shot, and then, as he bounded into the sunlight, two more. Rivers hesitated, helplessly blinded by the glare. Finally, he was able to pick out a body sprawled like an abandoned doll on the circle of grass; a Raggedy-Ann whose long black hair tumbled wildly across the green. He ran toward her.

"James, get down for God's sake. I'm okay," Tamura yelled.

Rivers dived for the pavement in mid-stride, like an Olympic volley baller saving an opponent's spike. Two more shots cracked. He didn't know if they were aimed at Tamura or him.

Rivers reached for his gun, determined to fire back, despite the passing students. Finally, he focused on his target. By this time, Strain was a hundred feet further upslope, half pushing, half dragging Storey back in the direction of the Campanile.

Rivers raised his gun.

"No, James. No!" Tamura yelled frantically.

For a moment Rivers seemed caught by his determination to strike back. Then he shook his head as if breaking a trance and slipped his police special back into its holster. It would have been crazy to fire with so many people close by, even if he was a good shot, which was far from the case.

Tamura sat up. Someone handed her an old fashioned white handkerchief. She pressed it against her upper arm, watching as it slowly turned crimson.

"I would have had him if that idiot Professor hadn't screamed when I pulled my gun. He must have thought I was with Strain— part of the Japanese red army, or . . ."

"Are you okay?" Rivers asked anxiously, gently moving the handkerchief to see how badly she was hit.

"It's only a scratch, as they say in the movies," Tamura responded. "Let's get moving before Strain really hurts someone."

Rivers helped her up and they started after them. Before they'd covered 20 feet, several campus police officers blocked their way. It took valuable seconds to convince them they shouldn't arrest Rivers for shooting Tamura. Unbelievably, even with their identities established and blood dripping from Tamura's arm, the younger of the two campus cops tried to question the right of the Berkeley City Police to be on campus.

Rivers, who by now was sure he was permanently residing in a nightmare, lost his cool. "Listen, son, I don't give a fuck whether you help me, follow me, or report me to your supervisor in triplicate, but if you don't get out of my way right now, I'm going to shoot you in the leg," he snapped.

"It's okay, Lieutenant, we'll follow your lead," the other of the two said quickly. "Tommy here caught three people stealing books from the ASUC store this morning and he thinks he's ready for TV."

Rivers smiled his thanks and turned toward Tamura. Sweat streaked her unusually pale face. He grabbed her good arm just as she started to totter and helped her find a seat on the wall in front of Wheeler Auditorium.

"Go ahead, James. I'll be along as soon as I can."

Rivers squeezed her shoulder, nodded at the campus police and sprinted up the hill. He followed the same wide esplanade he had run down barely ten minutes before. Back and forth—run, run, run. Just as in his airport dream, Rivers felt a depressing sense of impending doom.

Strain must be headed back to South Hall, Rivers thought. He would almost surely go to ground in the building where he felt most at home.

As Rivers ran into the open area between South Hall and the Campanile steps, everything seemed peaceful, almost idyllic. Several students were reading on the sunny steps and others strolled through the square, textbooks tucked securely under firm young arms. Everything looked clean and new after the rain, and Rivers fantasized for a moment that some great projectionist in the sky had changed the movie from "Bloody Friday" to "Samantha Goes to College."

Rivers considered asking one of the seated students if they had seen Storey and Strain. Rejecting the idea, he continued toward South Hall. Here ten or so marble steps hung from the brick facade like a napkin from a coal miner's collar, resulting in the main entrance being on the second floor.

Just inside the door, Rivers found several people crowded around a frail grey-haired man sprawled against the wood-paneled wall. He was dressed in a vaguely English, slightly old-fashioned professor's suit and was identified as Professor Albert Hanger. When Rivers showed his identification, everyone began to speak at once. Amid the babble, he was able to pick out a phrase here and there.

"It was incredible . . ."

"Did you see Strain's pistol?"

"That was no two-iron in his bag either."

Finally Rivers put his hand out like a traffic cop and shouted, "Everyone quiet!"

They all stopped in mid-sentence. Academics must be used to being shut up, Rivers thought, a little surprised by his own power.

He turned to a plump, middle-aged woman in a blue wool dress who he guessed accurately was Mrs. Foster, the departmental secretary Tamura had spoken to earlier.

"Tell me where Strain and Professor Storey are now. The rest can wait."

"Well, we were here in a group, talking," she replied in a no-nonsense voice. "I was explaining what that beautiful young Japanese detective said, when suddenly Jeffrey Strain came in, half-dragging Professor Storey. Professor Hanger here tried to reason with Strain, but he knocked him . . ."

"Excuse me. Where are they now?" Rivers said, forcing himself to be polite.

"I only know Jeffrey dragged Professor Storey up the stairs there and clubbed him with the back of a gun when he tried to resist," she answered, nodding toward the wide wooden stairway a few feet along the hall.

"I followed them part way up," contributed a young blondish man who looked so neat Rivers judged him to be a junior faculty member without tenure.

"They went left along the corridor on the next floor. Storey's office is the last one, at the southeast corner. The little room Jeffrey shared when he was a teaching assistant — before Professor Storey rejected his thesis — is next door."

215

Rivers started up the wooden staircase, his feet slipping into the small indentations made by generations of aspiring scholars. He wasn't past the tenth step when he heard the booming of a shot-gun—two bursts in quick succession.

People began screaming outside.

Rivers turned and made for the front door. Too late, too late, the unwanted mantra again beating in his head as he pushed his way into the sunlight,

For the second time in fifteen minutes Rivers had to blink away the glare as he searched for bodies. He saw several students running in the direction of the Campanile and a few others crouched in front of the building. No one appeared to be hurt. Finally he spotted Tamura. She was with the two campus cops, standing in the doorway of a building labeled Moses Hall. The bloodstained hand-kerchief was still tied around her left arm. She was holding her automatic in her right hand.

Tamura quite clearly didn't know what to do.

Rivers thought her quandary reasonable. What was their next move anyway? One choice would be to pretend their job was done and turn the whole affair over to the hostage squad. To the unin-formed, it would probably look as if the Violent Crimes unit had efficiently done their job by bringing the killer to bay. The truth, Rivers knew, was very different. If he hadn't been so slow-witted all week, if any of them had been a little quicker to understand, even a few minutes faster, Strain would be in custody and Storey would be safe.

There was another truth, more pertinent now than recrimina-tions: the officer in charge of the hostage squad wasn't bright. He remembered someone saying just last week that although it was a lie that George Disney couldn't walk and talk at the same time, he always tripped over compound sentences. But even if Disney were the ablest man on the force, there was no time to wait for him to arrive. Assuming Storey was still alive, it was likely to be a tempo-rary state of affairs unless something was done fast. Which brought him back to the same question that was obviously bothering Tamura—what to do.

"Put down that gun, throw it out on the grass. I don't want to hurt you. I don't want to hurt anyone else," an eerie, high-pitched

216

voice screeched out, sounding like a child who fears he is badly hurt. Forgetting her momentary confusion, Tamura looked at Rivers inquiringly. He made a tossing motion and Tamura threw her gun out onto the lawn where Strain could see it.

Rivers edged another step away from the protection of the doorway. The voice had come from above and to his right. He craned his neck and tried to spot Strain, but a large external chimney and a ledge blocked his view. He took another step. Now he could see that the window at the southeast corner of the building one floor above him was smashed. He could see little else.

"I'd like to talk to you, Jeffrey Strain. Let's sit down and talk this over. Maybe we can make sense of it. I'm Lieutenant Rivers from the Berkeley Police and I'm sure there must be . . ."

"No, no. It's too late. He wouldn't talk to me. He never had the time. You have to believe me. I tried to talk to him. Everyone knows I tried, but he just kept on saying, 'my dear Strain, my dear Strain, can't you see I'm busy and I have no time today?'"

"Maybe we can talk now if you will just put down that gun," Rivers shouted back.

"He rejected me. After all my work, after years of effort, he just kicked me out, fired me from the department forever. I had to do something, but what could I do? He had all the power and I had none."

So that was it, Rivers thought. A frustrated graduate student made to feel worthless, striking back crazily. When you thought about it, it was surprising it didn't happen more often. Top schools such as Cal could produce incredible psychological pressures, burdens which faculty and administration were often ill-equipped to handle or, in some cases, even to acknowledge. Mental and physical breakdowns, even suicides, were the sad but fairly standard baggage that came with graduate education. They were violent acts directed inward, the student blaming himself for failure. Murder, the ultimate expression of aggressive, outward-directed violence, was almost unheard-of on campus, where, although it was acceptable to attack or even destroy with words, weapons were viewed as the last resort of the ignorant.

Rivers had an idea. He again hand-signaled to Tamura, this time working his thumb and fingers back and forth like the bill of a quacking duck.

Tamura cocked her head to the right, obviously not understanding. Rivers tried again, this time pointing at Tamura with one hand and mock-quacking with the other. Still no comprehension. He couldn't delay any longer. He had to respond to Strain.

"Violence never solves this sort of problem, does it, Sara?" As he talked, he continued to work the fingers of his left hand back and forth in what he was convinced was a brilliant imitation of a gabby fowl.

Tamura nodded and immediately joined the conversation. As she did, Rivers stepped back into the lobby. Several people tried to speak, but again he raised his hand. They stopped.

"Are you willing to take a risk?" he said to the well-dressed blond man.

The young man, an Assistant Professor named Sandworth, looked quickly at Professor Hanger who was still sitting against the wall. He cleared his throat and said, "Yes, of course."

"Put this on and stand outside the door about four paces," Rivers instructed, taking off his brown corduroy sport coat and holding it out.

Sandworth hesitated.

"Crap or get off the pot," Rivers demanded impatiently.

Sandworth's ruddy face turned pale, as if he had been slapped. He grabbed the proffered jacket.

"Go far enough so Strain can glimpse you past the chimney, but not so far he can get a clear shot," Rivers said calmly as if he was giving directions to the interstate. "If he looks down, he'll see a tall man with light hair. Hopefully that will convince him I'm still there. Mumble a few words now and then to sustain the illusion, but say as little as possible. Officer Tamura, the young Asian woman in the doorway of Moses Hall, will take the lead."

With the efficient aid of Mrs. Foster, Sandworth replaced his expensive Ivy League tweed with Rivers' off-the-sale-rack corduroy. He looked determined now, relishing his role as a man of action.

Rivers touched Sandworth on the arm as he prepared to go out. "No heroics. Don't go more than four steps. If you hear shots, duck back quick."

28

Tamura was at a loss as to how to keep Strain talking. She understood what Rivers had in mind, but she felt weak and dizzy and wasn't sure she could stand up long enough to play her part. She had to resist the almost uncontrollable urge to look at her arm to be sure it was still there. When she gave in she became nauseous. In addition, Tamura felt herself to be in a hopelessly disadvantageous position, closed in as she was by the stone archway of Moses Hall. Strain was almost directly above her to the left, but the low arch prevented her from seeing him. Ironically, during her student years, she had been twice trapped in this very building. First when she had rashly joined hundreds of other students during a sit-in to protest the invasion of Cambodia, and again the next year, in Professor Duarte's lectures on logical positivism, each of which seemed to last two weeks.

Along with her memories of half-forgotten academic tyrannies Tamura felt a wave of honest empathy for the scared young man behind the broken window. Even when she was a student, Storey had been notorious as a dictatorial son-of-a-bitch. On impulse, she stepped out from the arch, exposing herself to the young man above.

"He pushed you too far, didn't he, Jeffrey?" Tamura said, tensing herself to jump for cover if he shot and somehow missed.

It seemed an eternity before Strain replied.

"He wouldn't even read the re-draft of my dissertation. I spent months making every single change he asked for and then he wouldn't even read it. He never intended to let me pass. Never, never, never. Seven years I'd been working on my Ph.D. Seven years. And all I get is 'my dear Strain, I'm too busy just now, don't you see?'" As Strain quoted Storey, his voice became prissy and cold; indeed, so icy that Tamura decided she'd better interrupt him before he talked himself into killing Storey immediately—assuming, of course, he hadn't already done so.

"Couldn't you appeal his decision or something?" Tamura asked, feeling stronger and less dizzy now that she was out of the arch and into the sun. It had been her own university experience that an appeal would do little good. The academic establishment, she had learned the hard way, professed an enormous amount of respect for "due process" except when it was applied to themselves. Just the same, her immediate job wasn't to express her cynicism about graduate school fairness but to keep Jeffrey Strain from imposing his own summary justice.

Strain began to laugh hysterically. "He *is* the department head. Don't you see? Once the bastard rejected me, I had no place else to go. And half the reason he rejected me was because I ridiculed one of his pet theories about God being dead. All along my family thought I was crazy to spend half my life working on a degree I probably couldn't even use to get a job. They wanted me to be a 'real' doctor. I should have listened. I mean, how could I go home and face my dad? All those years, all that money, and I didn't even get the degree. Now I can't ever be anything. I'm a goddamn murderer. Dear God, what am I going to do?"

Again, Tamura was frightened. This time not by Strain's madness but by his lucidity. Once more, she tried to change the direction of the conversation.

"I never finished my Masters thesis in anthropology," she replied. "I had ten years to complete it and my time ran out this fall. All I feel is relief. Letting go of being an academic isn't the end of the world, Jeffrey. There are lots of other things you can do with your life."

Even as she spoke, Tamura knew she wasn't convincing. Even if Strain put down his gun right now, he had to know he would be put in a steel cage for the foreseeable future, if he wasn't executed. Maybe she should bring the inevitability of jail into the open, but damn it, too much candor might push Strain over the edge. She glanced surreptitiously at the Campanile clock. How much more time would James need?

29

With Sandworth on the porch, Rivers ran up the worn wooden stairs, pistol in his right hand. When he reached the corner where the stairwell opened into the second-floor hall, he paused and peeked. The wood-paneled corridor was empty.

Rivers' first thought was to run the seventy-five feet or so to the southeast corner of the building and burst through the door, gun drawn. He didn't consider it long. The city of Berkeley didn't pay him enough to be a Kamikaze. The hallway simply left him too exposed. If Strain caught him there, he would have no chance.

There was no window in the stairwell and Rivers couldn't hear what was going on outside. Did he have time? Was Tamura succeeding in keeping Strain by the window, or was he even now about to try to escape down the hall? Even assuming he had a few minutes, how the hell could he use them to get at Strain?

Then it came to him. The fussy old building itself might provide a way to get close to Strain relatively danger-free. Rivers darted across the hall through the open door of a large reception room to the tall schoolhouse-type windows. With effort, he lifted the left-hand sash. His hunch was correct. The overhanging ledge some enthusiastic Victorian architect had tacked onto the front of the building ran all the way around.

Three cheers for an age when doing it right meant decorating the back, Rivers thought as he lowered his feet onto the ten-inch ledge, balancing his stomach on the windowsill. Worried the stone might be rotten and give way, he trusted his weight to it gingerly. It was solid.

It was easy to slide spider-like along the outside of the building, holding onto one or another of the stone flourishes that embellished the brick wall. Rivers was about thirty-five feet above the ground but didn't look down. He knew from his experience in the mountains that acknowledging the existence of a substantial drop only increases the precariousness of a perch.

There were two places ahead that looked difficult: where the ledge crossed chimney columns which stood out from the side of the building. At each, Rivers would have to traverse almost ten feet of sheer wall, with neither geegaw nor curlicue to reassure his inquiring fingers. He hesitated at the first chimney, his fear of falling making his feet leaden. Then he thought about the alternative of going down the corridor.

Rivers moved quickly ahead, arms outspread. Holding onto the bricks was easier than he anticipated; a century of weather had eroded the mortar enough to provide purchase. Even so, when he had the second chimney behind him, Rivers allowed himself a small sigh of relief.

Four minutes from the time he left the entry hall, Rivers reached his destination—the last window at the southwest corner of the building. He was closing in on his quarry, but he couldn't ignore the refresher course in relativity he had been receiving all week. No matter how fast he moved, it would be judged too slow if Strain pulled the trigger before he got to him.

Rivers tried to raise the heavy window. It was either locked or stuck. He reached into his back pocket with his left hand and found his red bandana. He wrapped it around his fist as best he could with one hand and tapped an oblong pane. Nothing happened. Rivers tapped again, a little harder. Still no result. He gave the window a frustrated smack. It shattered, making a noise which to his ears was loud enough to rouse the dead.

Rivers slid along the ledge a couple of feet so he was no longer directly in front of the window and drew his gun. He watched the door to the office inside intently. It didn't open. He counted to thirty, slowly. Still nothing. He moved back in front of the window, reached through the broken pane and turned the brass latch. As he slid the window up, someone spoke.

The sound nearly knocked Rivers off the ledge. He teetered for a moment and then grabbed a gargoyle as he realized the speaker was on the ground below.

Rivers didn't look down. Instead, he slid a shaky leg over the sill and wiped his brow on his sleeve. If I live to write my novel, he thought, I'll have to change the title from *The Sleeping Policeman* to *A Cowardly Cop Matriculates*.

Phil Orpac and Mary Finnegan stood directly below. Each wore a flak jacket and a crash helmet. Rivers remembered Orpac had been a non-commissioned officer in Vietnam and admired the way he stood, legs wide, automatic rifle cradled nonchalantly in the crook of his right arm. Finnegan, on the other hand, awkwardly held a tear gas gun, barrel up, as if it were an overgrown pea shooter in danger of losing its load to gravity. He knew how she felt.

Thirty or so feet behind Orpac and Finnegan, Rivers saw a small army of campus and city police, eighteen or twenty in all. He had been so intent on keeping himself on the ledge, he hadn't heard them arrive. They stood in a cluster, quietly, with the exception of several who were running a rope to keep people away from the building.

Would they have enough sense to stay quiet and out of sight? Storey, and perhaps others, would surely die if Strain saw a bunch of uniforms. Rivers suddenly realized he was stalling, worrying about things he couldn't control to avoid facing up to the frightening task only he could accomplish. He swung his outside leg into the office.

Mary Finnegan's coughing stopped him. She pointed toward a campus cop who was running toward the building with a long pole. Orpac took off his flak jacket and wrapped it around the end. He balanced his helmet on top and raised the pole. By hanging over the sill, Rivers was just able to grab the protective clothing. He slipped into them, feeling like a six-year-old who has been handed his teddy bear on a stormy night.

Rivers gave the officers below a thumbs-up sign.

Mary Finnegan blew him a kiss.

30

Tamura could think of nothing else to say. She looked forlornly at the young professor in front of South Hall, wishing it was James inside the tacky brown jacket. Her dizziness returned. She wanted badly to sit down.

Ten, fifteen, then twenty seconds ticked by, each seemingly slower than the one before. It was as if she were on stage and had forgotten her lines. Aha! Perhaps that was the way to do it, she thought, remembering a similar problem she often had in the improvisational theater class she took one evening a week.

Ruth Zaporah, the guru of "Action Theatre," taught an improvisational technique in which actors made up the play as they went along. To fill the inevitable blank moments, Ruth asked her students to pay attention to their own body processes. If a knee hurt, make shaking it out part of the performance. If a song, even a silly one, ran through your head, sing it. And so on.

Tamura started with her throbbing arm.

"Jeffrey, did you mean to hurt me?" Tamura asked, sounding tentative even to herself. "My arm hurts a lot, my clothes are covered with blood, I think I might pass out and I don't even know if you're going to shoot at me again."

There was no response.

"Jeffrey, I know you're there, I just saw you move. Tell me what you're thinking." This time Tamura's voice was more demanding, sounding as if she really wanted to know.

"I'm sorry. I really am. I won't hurt you again. If I could have talked to you before this happened, maybe . . . I didn't mean to hurt Mr. Speldon either, you know. I even went to an anti-nuclear rally at Livermore once. I just wanted to get back at Professor Storey, to hurt him worse than he hurt me."

"It's no fun to hurt a person who's exposed and helpless, is it?"

"It all came out wrong," Strain replied in a voice so low that Tamura had to step toward South Hall a few paces to hear. "When I dreamed about hurting him, it was easy, but then it all went wrong. It's not my fault the others got killed. He's the one who started it and he's the one who will have to pay."

31

Rivers found himself in a high-ceilinged, richly paneled senior faculty office. It was the sort of room a grateful society had routinely bestowed upon its educated elite before Ph.D.s became an expensive cliché, and hostile taxpayers reduced even the most eminent to a metal cubicle on the fourth floor of a cinder-block box. He moved quickly across the room and passed into a smaller but equally opulent reception room. He tried the door to the hall. It was locked. Then he noticed the little brass knob beneath the handle. It turned easily and he opened the door a crack.

The office door directly across the hall announced in pretentious gold lettering: Aaron Storey, Department Chairman. Rivers was surprised to see it open a few inches. He couldn't see into the room but could hear a muffled voice, probably Tamura's. Strain was quiet.

Here he was, finally up against the moment he'd been chasing all week. Generations of philosophy students had passed through that door discussing life and death, heaven and hell, but cops don't concern themselves with deeper meanings. His job was simple. He had only to grip his gun, kick open the door, and enter the room. If he lived, they'd give him a medal. If he died, someone would wrap his body in a plastic bag and mop the floor.

Rivers moved into the hallway, concentrating on the door. Here goes, he thought, Harpo Marx at the O.K. Corral.

As Rivers took his third step, he collided with someone coming along the hall. Instinctively, he raised his gun and tightened his trigger finger. He was menacing a small, elderly man wearing crepe sole shoes and carrying a rubber-tipped cane. It was the old professor who had been sprawled in the entryway.

The would-be heroes glared at each other. While he had been playing Spiderman on the outside of the building, the professor, who looked remarkably like the world's oldest lizard, had obviously been creeping down the hall.

"I'll take care of this, young fellow, if you will be so kind as to remove your pistol from my chin and stand aside," the old man whispered fiercely.

"Jesus Christ," Rivers muttered, wondering how to simultaneously get rid of his frail ally and get at the man behind the door.

"Don't blaspheme," the fearless octogenarian said with authority as he turned and rapped on the pebbled glass of Storey's door with the ivory handle of his cane. It made a surprisingly loud noise.

Despite himself, Rivers flinched as the door swung open another inch or two. All was quiet.

"Jeffrey Strain, this is Professor Hanger. I want to talk to you this minute. I'm an old man, as you know, and I can't stand up for too long, so I'm going to risk being impolite and march right in. You will have to speak to me or shoot me. That's your free choice, of course, but one way or the other, I must sit down."

"Get away, sir, get away! I have no quarrel with you. If you were still Chairman, this never would have happened," the voice from within responded, sounding desperate and confused.

"You're absolutely right, young man. I don't like Aaron much either," Professor Hanger replied, as he tapped his cane across the threshold. "When I announced my retirement and he wanted my job, he was all flattery and attention. After he got it, he never had a moment for a civilized word. It was always, 'My dear fellow, I don't have time to talk just now. Perhaps later on,' or some other nonsense."

The old man was in the outer office now, walking like a wingless bird into a high wind. Rivers, a foot taller and fifty pounds heavier, was close behind.

Strain stood just to the right of the window in the main room, shotgun in hand. He was partially shielded by a three-drawer metal file cabinet. Storey sat on a chair about six feet to the left of the window, facing Strain. His hands were behind him, apparently tied to the chair. Dried blood streaked the right side of his face.

Strain swung the shotgun barrel away from the window, pointing it at the old man. Hanger continued to hobble forward, appearing not to see the empty black holes that marked the business end of the twelve-gauge. Rivers, who noticed them right away, fought his urge to shrink behind the professor's frail body.

Hanger kept his left hand on his cane and extended his right. He was less than five feet from Strain, and for a moment all was quiet.

"It's over, isn't it, son? You tried to kill a pompous ass but killed two good men instead. I'm sure you're wise enough to see the lesson in that. If you haven't understood yet and wish to go on playing God, please hurry and kill me too so I can avoid the embarrassment of wetting my pants. I'm eighty and my bladder can't take this tension."

Sweat stood out on Strain's cheeks where his beard stopped. He didn't move. Then his grip on the shotgun seemed to loosen.

Professor Hanger took another step forward, extending his right arm to grip the gun's barrels. Strain gave a little moan and pushed it toward him.

It was like trying to hand a two-by-four to a toddler; Hanger was simply too frail to accept the burden with his one free hand. Rivers leaned forward to help.

As he did so, Storey's bombastic voice rang out, "Get the crazy bastard, get . . ."

Strain's eyes, which had begun to look dull and glazed, snapped wide. He snatched the gun back before Rivers could grip it.

Rivers pushed roughly past the old man, raising his gun. God damn, he thought, I'm going to die because that asshole couldn't keep his mouth shut for another two seconds.

The shotgun exploded, a man screamed, and a pistol barked almost simultaneously. Half an instant later, another shot sounded.

For a long moment there was silence. Then armed men and women filled the room.

32

Tamura sat on a black naugahyde chair in a narrow hospital waiting room. It smelled of dead cigarettes and the sort of disinfectant used in gas station bathrooms. She was alone. She started to stand, but then, realizing she had no place to go, checked her impulse and crossed her legs instead. She was conscious of her dry mouth and speeding heart. Her bandaged arm, forgotten in the aftermath of the excitement, throbbed in its sling.

Finally a thirtyish black woman in a white lab coat entered and introduced herself as Dr. Lewis. Tamura stood.

"We lost him," the doctor said assertively, in the same tone a waitress might use to announce that there's no more duck. "The shock was more than an eighty-year-old heart could handle," she added more kindly.

"What about the others?" Tamura asked.

"Well, as you know, there was never any hope for Strain. After he fired the shotgun he apparently put his pistol in his mouth and . . ."

"Professor Storey," Tamura began.

"His right arm is a bit pulpy where we dug out several pellets, but he's not seriously hurt. In fact, he's pretty lively already. When he came out of the anesthetic, I introduced myself. He looked up at me and said, 'My dear woman, I'm sure you mean well, but I'd like to see a real doctor.'"

"It would be funny if it weren't so sad," Tamura replied. "So many people dead, and that insensitive bastard will probably never realize how much he was the cause of it all."

"I just patch them up, I don't judge them," the young doctor said, touching Tamura on her good arm.

Tamura wanted to reply, but found she was too tired to think. Doctor Lewis nodded and walked with her to the top of the stairs.

Tamura made her way through the lobby and out the front door. Clouds covered the moon, but the plaza in front of the hospital was brightly lit. She saw a light-haired man wearing faded jeans and a down vest leaning against a battered Dodge. He didn't look a bit like Nick Charles, but she was glad he was there.

Rivers smiled up at her. "Need a lift, partner?"

Ralph Warner and Toni Ihara live and work in Berkeley, California. They have co-authored several previous books, including *Ups and Downs: A Journal of Wilderness Loves and Lovers, The Treasure of Lost Dragon Castle,* and the *Living Together Kit.* They want it clearly understood that any similarity between themselves and James Rivers and Sara Tamura is purely intentional.

The Treasure of
Lost Dragon Castle
& other stories

Ralph Warner & Toni Ihara

$3.50

Four lighthearted mystery stories for kids aged 6 to 12. Meet private eye Albert Muldoon, his assistant Renfro, and Clem, the great detective dog, as they find the Treasure of Lost Dragon Castle and solve the kidnapping of one of the world's greatest race horses, Aunt Matilda.

"Muldoon is a great goofy goon."

Damon Ray Geddins
Class Clown — 6th Grade
Buckhalter Elementary School

To order send $3.50 (in California add $.23 sales tax) plus $.50 postage and handling to:

NOLO Press
950 Parker St.
Berkeley, CA 94710

8400